HOME

MADE

BANNERS

HOME
MADE
BANNERS

By Ralph Allen

LONGMANS, GREEN AND CO.
Toronto — London — New York

Longmans, Green & Co.
215 Victoria Street, Toronto 1

Longmans, Green and Co. Ltd.
of Paternoster Row
43 Albert Drive, London, S.W. 19
Nicol Road, Bombay
17 Chittaranjan Avenue, Calcutta
36A Mount Road, Madras

Longmans, Green and Co. Inc.
55 Fifth Avenue, New York 3

First Edition, December, 1946

Printed and Bound in Canada

HOME

MADE

BANNERS

CHAPTER

1

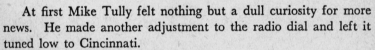

At first Mike Tully felt nothing but a dull curiosity for more news. He made another adjustment to the radio dial and left it tuned low to Cincinnati.

"The Germans characterized their thrust into Poland as a counter-attack with a pursuit."

It still didn't mean as much as it should. Mike fumbled at the dial again, clutching at the night air of the world outside for some voice, some phrase or some clashing of cymbals that would draw him closer to what had happened and wring some notice of it from the part of him that ruled his feelings.

He slacked his shoulders into the plump curve of his easy chair, dropped his head back against the top of the curve, and studied the room with absent concentration. He inspected the maroon plush of the chesterfield and the blue plush of the other easy chair that matched the one he was sitting in. He counted the books in the book-case and tried to remember the title of each one from the shape and color of its cover. He stared for a long time at the watercolor landscape above the chesterfield and noticed for the first time that there was a man standing at the foot of the cliff looking out toward the sea. He remembered shopping with

Tina for the frame of the picture and wondered whether a wider frame wouldn't have been better. He tried to remember where each piece of furniture in the room had been bought, and then he tried to remember what he had eaten for dinner on each of the last three days.

Then, abruptly, he brought his mind back to what he had heard on the radio, trying to shock or trap his mind away from its negativeness, trying to make it take some imprint from the news. In the same instant, he thought of his brother.

"I guess Joe will be going right away," Mike told himself, and tried to picture Joe in uniform, marching down a road somewhere with a rifle slung across his shoulder. A little current of excitement ran through him, and he tried to picture himself in the same setting. The excitement became stronger, and he surrendered to it with sensual enjoyment, pressing the back of his head against the back of his easy chair and closing his eyes and then cupping a hand over the high bridge of his nose to shut out the light. The vision took new shapes, and its population grew; now Mike and Joe were in the dream together. A thread of melancholy ran through it and a singing note of bravado. There were partings and reunions and parades and battles and sad, clean deaths. Mike felt better now, more wholesome and perceiving.

He allowed his hand to drop away from the upper part of his face and his eyes blinked open, squinting into the light. He looked at his wrist watch. It was after three o'clock. He snapped off the radio in the middle of a low waltz tune, turned off the lights and groped his way into the bedroom. He undressed in the dark and slid his body over against Tina's, waiting for the naked warmth of his thigh to stir her to wakefulness. She turned on her pillow and touched his face with her hand. "Hello", she said sleepily.

"I was listening to the radio," he said. "It's started."

"When?"

"They just announced it a while ago."

For a while the only sound was their slow breathing and the distant ticking of an alarm clock.

"Mike," Tina said.

"Uhhuh."

"Mike, you haven't got any fancy ideas, have you?"

"Maybe they won't be interested in my ideas. Maybe they'll just holler, 'Hey you!' and that'll be that."

"But if they don't. You know where you belong most, don't you?"

"Sure, Honey," he said. "What made you think different?" And then he added: "When they try to get me over there, there's at least two guys that'll go out of circulation. Me and the guy that's chasing me."

"Is the baby all right?" Tina asked him after a while.

"I didn't look, but he's been quiet."

Mike yawned and went to sleep.

CHAPTER

2

By the due processes of society, biology and the Saskatchewan Department of Education, Michael Tully had grown up to be what public opinion in his village considered a "good, average, sensible boy", which is to say that he was not quite as good, as average or as sensible as public opinion was willing to concede.

At the age of nine and a half he learned to roll cigarettes of dried leaves, corn silk or Orange Pekoe tea, and acquired a capacity to smoke them without getting sick. At the age of ten he was introduced verbally to the facts of life by a boy named Herb, and at the age of eleven he confirmed them, after a pallid and anticlimatic fashion, with the help of a girl named Elsie. At the age of twelve he worked at his first real job, sweeping out his father's drug store in the mornings and delivering prescriptions and magazines for an hour a day after school. When he was thirteen, he attended his first dance, a country hoe-down in honor of the impending wedding of a distant cousin, but by the time he had summoned enough courage to consider asking anyone to dance with him, it was time to go home. When he was fourteen he ran away from home in company with three other boys and a Ford touring car that belonged to the father of one of them, and returned after three days, hungry, broke, penitent and without any explanation that seemed rational even to himself. When he was fifteen he tasted liquor for the first time, stealing half a bottle of Scotch from beside the rear wheel of a car that was parked outside the village dance hall, drinking most of it, and subsiding with great promptitude into a stupor from which he was awakened some hours later by his own manly retches and a still small voice that bade him go and sin no more. When he was sixteen he fell tentatively in love with a girl two years older, and retained his self-respect only by the accident of discovering, the day after the girl eloped with a bank clerk, that there was a word in the dictionary called "misogynist". When he was seventeen he earned sixty dollars stooking wheat at four dollars a day and put most of the money into his first pair of tube skates, an outfielder's glove bearing the autograph of Hack Wilson, and a pearl-gray suit with eleven-inch pant cuffs and a double-breasted vest. When he was eighteen he played in a three-thousand-dollar baseball tournament in which the great though tarnished alumnus of the Chicago White Sox, Hap Felsch, participated as a member of an opposing barn-storming team, and all factors being weighed and assessed in the light of the standards that prevailed in those times and parts, this was the greatest experience of his early life.

Throughout these adventures, he found time to display a decent interest in the probity and physical welfare of his younger brother, Joe. He allowed Joe to follow him around a good deal more than might have seemed warranted by the five-year spread in their ages and by the younger boy's tendency to get lost, fall into unapproved portions of the river, throw up on as little as a pint of green choke-cherries, lose fist fights to smaller boys, and behave in other indiscreet and humiliating ways. The irretrievable, if degrading, truth was that Mike loved his kid brother far more even than he had loved the girl who ran away with the bank clerk.

From a succession of highly Christian and ruthlessly uninter-
esting ladies he learned, more or less in that sequence, that things
which are equal to the same thing are equal to each other, that
a straight line is the shortest distance between two points, that all
Gaul is divided into three parts, that A plus B squared is not the
same as A squared plus B squared, that "Amat" means "he loves"
in Latin, that "Ma tante est dans le jardin," means "my aunt is in
the garden" in French, that the constitution of Canada is founded
on the British North America Act, that H2SO4 is the chemical
symbol for sulphuric acid, that matter is composed of atoms and
molecules, that Hamlet said "To be or not to be", and that the
causes of the Industrial Revolution were the advent of machinery
and the restlessness of the people, preferably with a neat ruled
line under each.

He had what his teachers called a good head and digested
these and other intelligences regarded as essential to his advance-
ment in life as easily and casually as he digested his food. His
physical development proceeded more according to caprice than
to any discernible plan; from the ages of ten to thirteen he hardly
seemed to grow at all and it was widely held that he would be
small for his age, but at fourteen his body began reaching hungrily
for manhood and didn't stop until it had given him the disciplined
size of a light-heavyweight boxer. His body grew tall but not
spectacularly so, and under the stimulus of baseball and swimming
in the summer, threshing in the fall and hockey in the winter, his
arms and shoulders thickened and hardened. Under the hot dry
winds that blew across the prairie from June to October, his skin
took on a kind of protective camouflage; even in the winter it was
dry and tough and tawny, like prairie grass in August. His eyes
were the color of well-tanned birch bark, intelligent and of a good
size. His nose barely escaped being ludicrous and barely missed
being heroic. It swaggered off a tall bony bridge in a lean deep
curve, but the line beneath it was clean and straight, as though

some public-spirited aesthete had perceived the nose's intention to end in a hook and defeated it with a sharp chisel.

Until they tired of it, his male schoolmates called him Chief Eagle Beak, mainly on account of the nose and partly because of his general texture, which was lean and brown and close-grained. But no one mistook it for coincidence that when Mike was walking behind them, the girls of the village giggled louder, pushed each other off the sidewalk with greater animation, pulled the chewing gum away from their teeth with more delicacy and verve and made it crack louder, and generally steeped themselves in the more ladylike forms of sophistication to a greater extent than when he was not. Eagle beak or not, he was more attractive to women than most maturing males.

Except that he was partial to baseball, hockey, fishing and swimming, no one knew much about his tastes and inclinations, not even himself. With some censorship but little guidance, he wallowed indiscriminately through the meagre treasures of the small local public library, from Jeffrey Farnol to Ethel M. Dell. From the age of eleven he was an avid reader of the Saturday Evening Post. In Florian Slappey, Tish and Tugboat Annie and the soldiers of Leonard H. Nason and the prize-fighters of Charles Francis Coe, he found companions who were more real to him than the people he met in books, and through them he first heard the call of distant places and felt the urgent tug of what he was persuaded to consider life. For a while he thought he would like to be a writer. The last school teacher he had in the village, believing she saw some special vision in him, gave him what encouragement she could, but nothing came of it. When he finished high school he went to Winnipeg with the object of taking a degree in pharmacy and eventually returning to a partnership in his father's drug store.

With allowances for little squirming adjustments which he made himself from time to time, almost without being conscious of making them, his early career from this point on was controlled largely by accidents. The years of poverty were clutching ruthlessly at the prairie; when there was no drought there was rust, and when there was no rust there were grasshoppers. He had seen the harsh cycle begin and it was in its fifth year already when he began his second term at college and his father wrote: ". . . . The farmers are scraping up enough to feed the chickens and plowing the rest under, such as it is. And as usual, no crops, no money. If you want to come back and work in the store, there'll always be a place for you, though not much pay. Maybe you could get a part-time job there and carry on at the University, but from what I hear things are almost as bad in the city. Do what you think is best, son, and remember I can always raise fifty bucks even if it's to bail you out of jail."

The whole stupendous accident that was the nineteen-thirties fell for him, thereafter, into a series of smaller accidents, each with some small influence on what he did and became, but none strong enough in itself to lift him clear of the dead current of the times. He rode the rods for one summer, drifting without prospects or any motivation that he could define from the timber forests of British Columbia to the mines of Northern Ontario. One day, jumping off a moving freight car outside the Toronto yards, he sprained his ankle. A motorist picked him up, limping into the city after dark, and told him about a lunch-counter owner who could use a dish washer. The job paid eight dollars a week and two meals a day. It was the first full-time job Mike ever had.

He had been there almost a year and had won a promotion to counter man at ten dollars a week when he got talking to a customer about baseball and mentioned that he had once played ball against Hap Felsch. "Risberg too. Old Nigger Donaldson pitched in our town once. He was real old then, but still good enough."

The customer looked at him with interest. "Played any ball lately?"

"Last time was two years ago. Got a few sandlot games in Winnipeg when I was going to school."

"I run an amateur team for a bakery," the customer said. "Why don't you come out to practise some night and take a few cuts? Might do yourself some good if it turned out we could use you."

It turned out they could, and Mike went on a delivery run at eighty-five dollars a month.

One day his horse ran away and Mike flagged down a passing motorist and pulled the horse to a halt by leaping on its neck from the running board of the car. The horse was a very old horse and was more than willing to accept an excuse to discontinue its senile romp, but the chase happened to end near a school inter-section in nice time to catch the early home editions of the afternoon papers. The bread company, acting on the advice of an alert public relations counsel, kept the story alive for the morning papers by giving Mike a new job. His title was assistant secretary to the general manager and at first his duties were few and embarrassingly nebulous. But he tried hard, wore clean white shirts, learned something about the business, and within a year was not only earning his thirty-two dollars a week but had been raised to thirty-five. He moved into a good boarding house, joined a circulating library, took up golf and abandoned baseball and otherwise exercised the prerogatives of modest success.

His marriage was the first important happening in his life that he willed completely himself and brought to fruition without the immediate help or coercion of circumstances. Even his meeting with Tina Rhodes was the first meeting he had ever had with anyone that was wholly of his own design. He saw her first at a company dance, the long liquid lines of her show-girl's body disguised but not concealed under a dress of black lace and her handsome though curiously asymmetrical face sheathed in an arch of hair the color of a wet Irish setter. It was not until a much later inventory that he was able to trace this hint of lopsidedness in her face to her eyebrows, one of which was a perfect curve and the other almost straight. These, together with two small, paper-thin lines on each side of her wide red mouth, abetted, if they did not create, an indefinable expression in which a subdued and genteel ribaldry seemed to be playing a scoreless draw against a sense of almost aggressive propriety. Later still, Mike said: "You look as if somebody had just pinched your backside and you're not sure whether you ought to giggle or slap his face."

"Oh," she said, "so you've noticed my leer too."

Nevertheless, she was beautiful enough that Mike had to fight a year to get her. But when she married him, she gave herself to her marriage as unreservedly as women who have been much sought after will sometimes do. Mike entered on the project with something close to reverence. Their three-room duplex flat was his first home and she, with a few unimportant and fleeting exceptions, was his first woman; and between them, the home and the woman, they were like a clean furrow, driving back through the uneasy years of his aloneness, turning over the dead ground of his life and showing him the fresh loam beneath, clean and pungent and rewarding. Even after their second year of marriage and their third quarrel, Tina sometimes whispered, as her head lay in the warm cup of his shoulder at night: "Maybe this is that perfect marriage they've been talking about." Mike would answer comfortably: "If it isn't, it will do till the next one."

Their child was distinctly an accident, although after it was on the way Tina made no effort to interfere with its coming. Mike asked for a raise in pay and got it and they agreed they could handle the baby and that it would probably be fun to have around after they got used to the diapers.

*   *   *   *

During Tina's pregnancy her father took to dropping in on them two or three evenings a week, drinking a bottle of beer if there was any in the house, and talking with Mike about what he called the general situation. Mike hadn't known him very well before; the old man was a widower, living with an older daughter and her husband on a small pension and his small savings. Tina's father was a small man, with the unenvenomed irascibility that small men often have. He seemed perpetually angry, in an affable kind of way, and in his fading but alert blue eyes distaste for the world and all its works seemed always to be in a state of gentle strife with some secret jocularity.

Pop advertised himself as a socialist. He opened up to his son-in-law eagerly and the younger man responded shyly but gratefully, acknowledging and slaking for the first time in his life the thirst for serious talk. By the end of Pop's third visit they were on terms of name-calling intimacy. Mike was calling the old man a Communist, and the old man was calling Mike a Tory.

"Suppose I am, suppose I am," Mike said. "At least they don't put you in jail for that."

"No, but they let you ride the rods for that. They let you work for eight dollars a week as a scullery maid for that. And don't forget there are still lots of men your age holed up on railway sidings all the way from here to Vancouver, and the lucky ones are still getting eight dollars a week scrubbing grease. Or did you forget?"

"I'll tell you something, Pop," Mike flared, "I didn't forget. You know who my first vote went for? My only vote as far as that goes. Tim Buck. Yes, Tim Buck. Red as your flannel britches."

"You'd never know it to hear you talk now."

"No, you wouldn't," Mike agreed. "And I don't think it's just because I'm better off either. I can see now all I was doing was lashing out like a blind man."

"Well, what about the other blind men?" the old man demanded bitterly. "What are they supposed to do? Fold their arms and read Bennett's last speech or King's last speech in Braille?"

"Look, Pop, I guess you're partly right. A hundred percent right up to a point. We ought to do more. We ought to feed everybody and make more jobs. But when you say it's a Tory depression or a Grit depression, you know you're talking right through the middle of your hat. Just because we got grasshoppers and rust and no rain out West and a lot of harebrains down here sank their shirts in the market, and a lot of other things all over the world that nobody seems to understand, you want to tear the whole country apart."

"Jesus!" the old man snorted, "a man can be a bloody fool on forty dollars a week and a nine-tube radio."

"Don't swear in front of my wife!" Mike shouted.

"It isn't swearing and it's in front of my daughter!" the old man shouted back. "She knows a lot worse words than that and if she hasn't used them on you yet, she's a bloody fool too."

Tina, knitting in a corner of the room, waited, her moving hands fingering the silence like a ripening melon. Then, with a sure instinct, she plucked it. "Beer, Mr. Trotsky?" she smiled, nodding at her father. "Beer, Mr. Bennett?" she said to Mike.

Mike grinned. "Just like marrying into a circus," he said.

"I knew I shoulda beat more sense into that girl," Pop muttered contentedly.

It went on like that all fall and winter. If the talk wasn't Olympian either in tone or content, there was zest in it at least, and the younger man found his mind growing under it, clumsily, raggedly and without much direction, but with a hungry vigor. He began to read newspapers. He still turned to the sports pages first, but when the reports of the World Series and the Stanley Cup playoffs weren't monopolizing his attention he read about rearmament, the Nazis, the Fascists, unemployment and a little about the wars in Spain and China.

Pop talked endlessly about Spain, on which he had accumulated a large store of information and conviction.

"The trouble with you Pop," Mike said in exasperation one night, "is that you always want to spoil a good argument by dragging in facts."

But the old man pursued him relentlessly.

"Why get so excited, Pop?" Mike said. "What's a private Dogan war between a lot of Spiks got to do with us anyway?"

The old man held his head.

"Don't say it, Pop!" Mike cut in hastily. "I know what you said about the war you have to fight always starting some place else. But what would happen if every time a war started anywhere the whole world had to get its feet wet too? A couple of four-bit republics in South America start squabbling over the price of llama skins and pretty soon I'm going around on one leg. The hell with that."

Pop continued desperately: "But this isn't tailor's-dummy stuff. They're not fighting about trade or some other country's land or some diplomat's wounded dignity. This is a war started by rich people against poor people, because the poor people voted to give themselves enough to eat in a legal election and the rich people wouldn't stand for it. Forget about words like Fascist and Communist and you still can't tell me what's right about that. And you still can't tell me it's none of your business, because it bloody well is."

"I can see that you could be right," Mike soothed. "But Pop, we've got to give these things a chance. Back home my brother Joe and I used to go down to the river after school and talk to a guy named Charlie Brown. Charlie was the first veteran of the war I ever knew real well. It cost him a leg and made a bum of him, but he was a nice bum and he talked to Joe and me as though we were grown up. Charlie used to say it's only in his generation people started to realize no war can be any good. After every war people would get an awful scunner against that particular individual war, mainly because they didn't like picking up the check and counting the dead. Charlie used to say that only a few cranks and conchies seemed to recognize that every war—whether or not it hurt them and their friends personally— was part of an institution that was bad in itself."

"Whose side would your Charlie Brown be on in this discussion?" Pop asked.

"That's not the point," Mike said. "The point is that I don't think we ought to get too discouraged or rambunctious simply because people are only beginning to act on an idea they've just begun to really see. Maybe if we give the idea a chance and don't go off at half cock every time a little trouble starts—"

"Well!" Pop broke in with exaggerated weariness. "In that case you haven't got a thing to worry about. The one thing you can say for sure is that nobody has gone off at half cock. We're still selling scrap iron to the Japs. Arcand can get a police escort in Montreal, the same as Kuhn in New York and Mosley in London. Right now every dog track and football stadium from John O'Groat's to Land's End is sagging at the seams with people, or they were a few hours ago. From the rockbound shores of Maine to the sunny coast of California, every single Yankee with forty-two cents to his name is getting ready to go out and see Clark Gable. Pretty soon it will be nine o'clock, and Foster Hewitt will pat his tonsils into place and for the next hour and a half every man woman and child in Canada that isn't sick or deaf will be holding their breath to see if Apps gets his twentieth goal. Or is it Drillon and his thirtieth goal? My memory's not what it used to be."

"What's wrong with that?" Mike said aggressively. "It's not such a bad life, is it? What do you want us to do—spend our spare time at prayer meetings or on soap boxes or parading under home-made banners?"

"No," Pop said, "just try to get some kind of a balance."

Neither of them said anything for a while, and then the old man announced with unexpected amiability: "You sure think funny, boy, but I'm glad to see you're thinking."

The baby was born in March of 1939. They named him Joe, after Mike's brother, and Mike insisted there was a resemblance.

The baby absorbed their world all through the hot, moist summer, and amid the soggy excitements of learning about bottle formulas and Pablum, the sounds of the approaching war hadn't much more meaning for Mike than the offstage noises in a recondite play. By the end of July he was repeating the stock pleasantries about beating the draft authorities to the north woods, and almost believing he meant them. But when war was declared, the shock of the news itself was considerably less than the shock of realizing he didn't really know how he felt about it.

CHAPTER
3

At first the war did not reach into the fibre of Canada, but hovered above the country and a little outside it, feeling out the natural points of contact, slowly and awkwardly superimposing itself on the lives of the people without making fundamental changes in them. The nation listened solemnly to the solemn voice of the King and angrily counted its first fatalities from the passenger list of the torpedoed liner Athenia. It dedicated its soul to the war and flexed its muscles for the war, and then there was a pause. The country's purpose would never be purer, nor its unity firmer, nor would it ever feel so helpless and frustrated. With a standing army barely larger than a brigade, a rowboat navy and an air force just emerging from the status of a doubtful experiment, Ottawa nervously fingered its pince-nez and wondered, half aloud, where to start. Within the first week, the Prime Minister found it necessary to announce that Canada was not yet at war with Germany and that the decision to go to war or not to go would be made by parliament. A few newspapers and public men suggested that the most valuable thing Canada could do would be to remain officially neutral until she was prepared to send trained troops abroad;

even though this interim neutrality would be transparently counterfeit, it would still give the nation certain legal advantages in maintaining a channel of trade between France and Britain and the sympathetic non-belligerents of the West.

At the end of the first week parliament voted unanimously for war.

Watching Toronto feel its way through a hot and confusing September, Mike sometimes got the impression that he was looking at a very old newsreel, a blurred hodgepodge of random scenes, without continuity or focus. The flags came out on the buildings, and now and then a band swung up Queen Street from the University Avenue Armories, blaring brassily for gangway in the thick traffic. Sometimes a few new soldiers would march through the streets pumping their arms chin high like sticks of wood whose function and handling were new to them. Even the brokers' clerks on Bay Street tucked their brief cases under their arms like swagger sticks and walked with quick, jerky strides, as though they were images being shown too fast through a projection machine. Recruiting posters blossomed on the billboards and recruits took foot drill on the lake shore in their civilian clothing. The veterans of the other war began wearing their Legion buttons and their faded service ribbons, and in the crowded beer parlors they tended to herd together, like old grads on the eve of a homecoming game. But these things, the bands, the marchers and the rest of the physical going to war, were not yet the centre of life; life in Toronto, as in the other cities of Canada, was still like a movie montage, and the hesitant and uncertain processes of the war were only on the fringes of the montage. The rush-hour street cars continued to poke irritably through the narrow land canal of Yonge Street, no more crowded and no less crowded than usual. A couple of bored carpenters removed the flags and booths from the German government exhibit at the Canadian National

Exhibition, but otherwise the Exhibition remained a peopled, Popsicled, noisy duplicate of the year before.

Tina's father came out to sit with the baby one night while Mike and Tina went to see the evening grandstand show. Pushing their way through the midway afterward, they met a friend of Mike's from the bakery, an amiable little Jew who worked in the accounting department.

"Sammy Krugman, my wife," Mike said.

The other man nodded quickly and said with weighty casualness: "Well, I won't be seeing you for a while, Mike."

"Going somewhere, Sammy?" Mike asked.

"Army," Krugman said. "Best doggone outfit in it too." He named a local regiment with a long tradition of service in several wars. "Figure I might as well sign up tomorrow and get it over with."

"That's great, Sammy," Mike said. The warmth in his voice was fringed with wistfulness and envy, neither of which was lost on Tina. Involuntarily she tightened the possessive grip of her fingers on his arm.

"Yep," Krugman said happily, "I figure if a guy with a schnozz like mine won't fight those birds, nobody will. Boy, Mike! Imagine me in those pants!"

They pushed off in opposite directions through the crowd, and as though by tacit agreement, neither Mike nor Tina said anything about the man who was on his way to war.

The next afternoon, just before closing time, Mike saw Krugman again in a corridor of the bakery's main office building.

"When's the shooting start, Sammy?" he asked.

Krugman stopped and looked at him for a moment, holding his eyes narrow beneath their lids, as though pinioning something there he wished no one to see.

"Oh, I been thinking it over and I decided what's the hurry.

From what I read somebody is going to get hurt before this thing is over."

"That's about the way I've got it doped out, Sammy," Mike said.

Krugman went on as though he hadn't heard. "I went down to the barracks this morning. They wouldn't take me."

Mike flushed and started to say something, but Sammy was still talking. He was talking faster now, slurring all accent out of his voice, burying all feeling under a rush of words.

"It's only because of my height. They're not taking anybody less than five foot eight. This fellow at the barracks was real nice about it. A major I think he was. Had a crown on his shoulder. As nice a fellow as you'd want to meet. The way he said, there are so many fellows coming in wanting to join, a regiment like his can afford to pick and choose. He says they been turning guys away by the dozen. Not all of them just because—just because they're short guys, either. He said the colonel laid down a rule that nobody less than five foot eight gets in even if he's wearing the V.C. The way they figure, we're so shy of equipment it'll be a long time before they get training seriously, and this major said they made up their mind they might as well try to look good on parade in the meantime."

Now it was Mike who evaded the other man's eyes. "Well, I wouldn't worry about it, Sammy," he said, "I guess before long they'll be grabbing us all."

"Sure," Krugman said. "This major said there was half a dozen other regiments that would take me like a shot."

"Well, be seeing you, Sammy," Mike mumbled and started to walk away.

Krugman was at his side again before he reached the door leading to his office.

"This major took my name," Krugman said. "He said I should come back in a few months, but if I was in a hurry I wouldn't have any trouble getting into any other outfit in town. He was a real good guy. By the way, Mike"—he finished in an elaborately offhand tone—"I'd just as soon you didn't say anything around the office. A guy takes enough ribbing around here. About being so sawed-off, I mean."

"Sure, Sammy."

*   *   *   *

That night there was a letter from Mike's brother, the first in several weeks.

"Well," Mike said before he opened it, "I guess Joe's gone and done it."

But the letter only told about Joe's new job in the drug department of a big store in Regina. Near the end, Joe wrote:

"I see where there's not only no talk about conscription, but they're refusing to take volunteers from some of the skilled trades. I guess I don't qualify there, but there can't be a big rush anyway. I think I'll wait a while and join the air force. Saw Dad and Mother a couple of week-ends ago. The old town has changed a lot, but they're both well. Mother worried stiff about us, of course, but I told her as long as she'd keep making Saskatoon pie like she does I'd keep showing up to eat it. Honestly, Mike, what do you think about this business? I think you've got to give the English a lot of credit for standing up to Hitler the way they did, but sometimes I wonder what Poland has got to do with the price of wheat or you and me. And I think that stuff about Hitler wanting Canada is plain crazy. I guess that's a pretty hard-boiled way to feel about it. Don't suppose my ideas would matter much anyway, even if they weren't cockeyed. In the meantime you can tell Tina my size in socks is nine, but she doesn't have to start knitting yet.

"P.S.: I've got a new girl.

"P.P.S.: This time it's different, and I do mean different."

Mike tossed the letter across to Tina.

"Poor Joe," he said, "I guess he's having a lot of trouble making up his mind."

Tina was silent, absorbed in the letter. Then she put it down and rose quickly and walked across the room to him. "Poor Mike," she said, putting her hand against his cheek. "Poor everybody, I guess."

"What are you jabbering about now?" he grumbled. "I'm not—" He let the sentence drop unfinished, and when Tina walked back to the chesterfield, he rose and turned up the radio, letting the expert discords of a boogie woogie band fill the room.

"Looks like I might have a new job pretty soon," he shouted above the rhythmic commotion. "The old man's secretary's taking a commission in the 48th. If I get his spot, it will be worth eighty bucks a week."

"Mike, that's marvellous!" Tina yelled. "We'll be rich!"

"Well, don't count on it yet. But I always said you'd be wearing diamonds some day."

*   *   *   *

The boss called him in at the end of the week. Mike immersed himself gratefully in the new job, throwing himself into its labyrinth of new detail with fierce pleasure. He worked three or four nights a week and came home late to drop into bed half exhausted. Tina, watching with wise and wary eyes, made no comment but: "You know, Mike, work seems to agree with you. You were getting pretty crabby last fall."

"No time to be crabby these days," Mike grinned.

But as the winter broke up, his routine slackened, and with it the preoccupation with his job. A restlessness came over him; at home he would start to read three or four magazine stories in an evening and finish none of them. He began drinking more than he had ever drunk before. He and Tina had two or three large quarrels over small things.

One night he sat in a beer parlor until well after dinner time, and as he walked to his street car stop, feeling the blunted exhilaration of the beer, he met, in rapid succession, two acquaintances in uniform.

"Guess you'll be going over to join the First Division one of these days," he said to the first man after they had exchanged a few minor reminiscences. "Sure wish I was going with you."

Before they were out, the words seemed shoddy and cheap to him, and he tried to bury them under a flood of other words, quickly and almost furtively, as a dog buries its own excrement. Then he muttered, "So long," and turned abruptly away and walked down an empty street, holding himself with the marionette erectness of a man who is neither altogether drunk nor altogether sober.

He tried to pretend he didn't see the second soldier, but the man stopped him. Mike babbled desperately about the bakery, about his new job, about the shows he had been seeing, but the soldier still said what Mike had been trying to prevent him from saying. The soldier looked mysteriously up and down the street, waited for a street car to pass, and said importantly: "Don't be surprised if you don't see me again for a few years."

Mike looked at the collar of the soldier's battle dress, but could bring his eyes no higher. Then he was saying quietly and clearly, with a clipped astringent edge on every syllable: "Well, good-bye. Good-bye, you smug little bastard. I hope you'll pardon me for not carrying you down to the train on my shoulders, but I've got other things to do."

The soldier's jaw dropped open stupidly. "Mike!" he said. "What's wrong?"

"Go take a jump at yourself!" Mike snarled. He tried to find the soldier the next day to apologize and attempt an explanation, but he was grateful when they told him at his unit's headquarters that the soldier was not available. "God! What a heel I turned out to be," he told himself morosely. "I'd better quit drinking if that's what it does to me."

He did quit, for the rest of the spring. In Toronto it was a pleasant spring, this blitzkrieg spring, the Churchill spring, the Dunkirk spring. The news was bad, but there was a settling catharsis to it, and without knowing why, Mike felt more easy and matured than he had ever felt before. The war was taking shape, ominously and even desperately, casting long solid shadows into the years ahead, so far that no one dared to guess where it might end. For the first time, Mike really began to see the tragedy of it, and the size of it, and to see at once the smallness and inevitability of whatever part he might play in it. He read about the bombing of Rotterdam and the flight of the refugees in France and the stand of the British Expeditionary Force on the Channel beaches. He heard Churchill speak on the radio. He talked to soldiers waiting to go over to reinforce the small Canadian force already standing guard on the coast of England, and he found that he could talk to them without either secret shame or secret envy. Unbidden and almost unrecognized, a sedative sensing of his own unimportance came over him; in honest humility he watched his friends go away to the war and he did not find it necessary to ask himself each time if they were better men than he or worse.

He began making blood donations to the Red Cross. He grew a little garden at the back of their duplex flat and lost himself in his home again as he had done in the first months after the coming of the baby. He began buying war bonds, and he felt a thrill of pride as he and Tina rode past the waterfront late one night on the way home from visiting Tina's sister and saw the glow of the war factories red against the night sky. One weekend he made a trip to Detroit on business, and an executive took him around the business offices of the machine supply firm he was visiting, introducing him as "Mr. Tully, from Toronto." Mike felt the same possessive thrill when one man asked him in a confidential tone: "Say, what about this Churchill? Quite a guy, what?" and another said, almost apologetically: "Great job you people are doing up there."

Before he left, Mike was making ostentatiously modest little speeches. . . . "Yes, it's going to be tough, I guess. But we're in it to the finish". . . . "Yes, taxes are getting pretty hard to handle, but I'm not worried much about that. I figure I'll be on the business end of a gun before long." When he returned, he told Tina: "You know, we're making them sit up and take notice down there. They've even quit asking if British Columbia is in Ottawa, and I actually met several people who know we aren't a colony."

"Too bad we don't know it ourselves," Tina said with unexpected feeling. "Maybe we wouldn't keep getting dragged into these things."

Summer came, hot and anxious, loud with the distant sounds of the Battle of Britain. Mike's father wrote him that a schoolboy chum of his had been killed flying a Spitfire over the south coast of England. "He shouldn't have been there so soon, but he saw it coming in thirty-seven and beat his way across on a cattle boat." Late in October a delivery man came back to work in the bakery, wearing a black patch over one eye and with a withered fleshless claw where his right arm should have been. The man was cheerful, but apart; he guarded his apartness as a chaste lover guards his love, stubbornly and quietly, neither parading it nor explaining it. "Nobody knows what it's like if they haven't been there," he said once to Mike. "It's no use trying to know." Mike looked at him sharply, almost belligerently, but the man's eyes were far away; there was no snobbishness or reproach in them, but only an inwardness, and Mike thought he understood.

The old restlessness came back to him, nagging and merciless, more merciless than ever because this time he knew, for certain, whereof it came. Tina saw it too, but denied it acknowledgment. She recognized it too well already.

One Saturday afternoon, she said casually: "Herb Gillis is joining the army."

"Good for him," Mike said.

Tina paused a minute. "They say he and his wife have been having terrible fights. I don't blame him for going."

Mike was on his feet before her, his face close to hers, taut and livid, his tawny eyes frantic with anger and disgust.

"God damn you women!" he shouted. "God damn you bitches! You can't see past your own filthy sinks. You can't see that honest men are dying for your snivelling chattering little hen runs, your miserable back fence gossip, your prattling little bridge clubs. You can't see that a man goes away because he's got to go. That's not good enough!" he shouted. "Louse up his name, louse up his family, louse up the whole God damn world, but keep your own miserable little corner of it just the way it was!"

Tina's face had tightened with terror.

"Stop!" she sobbed, "Mike, for God's sake, stop!"

The door slammed and Mike was striding down the street, his hat jammed savagely over his forehead, the cold pale air of the autumn afternoon billowing through his unbuttoned coat.

For a long time he was conscious of no thought but a bitter resolve to reject all thought. Hours later, late at night, he looked up from a wet brown table filled with half empty beer glasses and heard a man in a white coat say wheedlingly: "Come on boys, give us a break. It's ten minutes past closing now."

A man named Bill was saying: "Aw right, aw right. We'll all go up to Maggie's."

"Who's Maggie?" Mike asked thickly.

"You'll love Maggie," a man named Pete was saying. "Come on Mike, home was never like this."

"Sure," Mike said, remembering dimly, "sure. People die at home. Let's go."

*　　　　*　　　　*　　　　*

You got a nice place here, Maggie. That's what I like too, not too many people around, just a few people you know. No, I never knew Bill and Pete before tonight but you can tell they don't make them any better. That's what I like about Bill too, a real sense of humor. That's good whisky, Maggie. You think we could have another? Hey, Pete, why don't you lay off that belly wash and have a man's drink?

Mike fell asleep twice. The second time he awoke in a faded, mouse-colored easy chair, with a stiff neck and a head that was still too blurred to accommodate a hangover. *Hey Maggie you got dust in your furniture. I can feel the dust in my nose. Or maybe that's just my mouth. Hey Maggie! I better have a drink.*

The whisky warmed him and cleared his head a little and he sat forward on the edge of his chair, moving his head back and forth until the stiffness began to go out of his neck. Pete and Bill and another man he hadn't seen before were across the room under a window rolling dice. A pair of dingy lace curtains were drawn across the window, but an anaemic ray of sunlight showed through the gap in the curtains, boxing out a mottled rectangle of sunbeams in the sour, dusty semi-gloom.

"Hey, what day is it?"

"Sunday."

"Any idea what time?"

"What do you care? Three o'clock."

A girl came and stood in Mike's line of vision as he looked down over his whisky glass at the worn dusty carpet of the room. His eyes met the hem of her yellow skirt where it flared obliquely across her bare knees. Her knees and the rounded legs below them were white in the pallid light from the window, white and curiously unclean. Mike stared at them and his eyes travelled up past the girl's loose breasts and past her white neck. Her face did not surprise him. It was the kind of face he expected to see before he looked for it, white like her legs, with a red mouth parted over white teeth and dark hair swept off her forehead.

The girl walked over and stood beside his chair.

"Where did you come from?" he said.

"I've been here a long time. I hoped you'd wake up."

Mike said nothing. Bill and Pete and the other man stopped rolling dice under the window and went to the other corner of the room. The third man sat down before an oak piano and picked out a few chords, and the three men began singing.

"I'm cold," the girl said to Mike. "Look."

She took his hand and pressed it against the back of her knee, into the bare, taut hollow of flesh. Mike smelled strong perfume and powder, but the strongest smell in his nostrils was still the sour dust from the carpet and the chair.

He drew his hand away, and said with a drunk's sad amiability: "You better peddle it somewhere else."

The girl smiled, "I don't peddle it. I give it away when I give it."

"I'm a misogynist," Mike said looking up at her in owlish triumph, proud of retrieving the word that had defended him years before, in another romantic crisis. "That means a woman hater," he explained. "Sorry."

"You'd sure have to be a good hater to hate what I could give you."

Mike stood up and finished his drink in a long thirsty gulp. At the last, he drew a deep breath and the fumes of the whisky cut harshly into his nostrils and the back of his throat, but again the stale dust-smell of the room was there when the whisky fumes had gone.

"Gotta sing," he mumbled and walked to the piano.

"That's lousy!" he announced loudly. "What you need is a good baritone."

The man at the piano stopped playing. "You said it friend," he agreed.

"Yeah, come on," Pete encouraged him.

"Come on, Mike."

The man at the piano thumped a few preliminary bars and Mike bawled along non-committally, a chord behind, until he caught the melody. Then he blared out the words, drowning the voices of the others:

> "The ole gray mare she ain't what she useta be,
> "Ain't what she useta be,
> "Ain't what she useta be,
> "The ole gray mare she——"

The man at the piano banged to a discordant halt and hammered the keys for silence.

"Smarten up," he jeered. "Hey Bill, tell your friend to smarten up."

"You got the tune all right, but you're out of date on the words," Bill said.

"O. K." Mike answered good-naturedly, "let's hear it. I'll pick it up the second time around."

He tilted his head at the exaggerated angle of a connoisseur and listened:

> "There are no bums in the Jarvis Street mission,
> "In the Jarvis Street mission,
> "In the Jarvis Street mission,
> "There are no bums in the Jarvis Street mission,
> "They're all in the army now."

Mike said in a queer, tight voice: "Sing it again."

They sang it slower this time, Bill and Pete taking the melody and the man at the piano vamping in at the end:

"There are no bums in the Jarvis Street mission,
"In the Jarvis Street mission,
"In the Jarvis Street mission,
"There are no bums in the Jarvis Street mission,
"They're all in the army now (the army no---oow.)"

Mike stood swaying beside the piano, blinking stupidly at the keyboard. He felt the words racing inside his head, and all at once he felt a shame and a yearning and a dinginess and he knew that in a minute he would either have to fight or cry. It was as though the words of the song, and the girl in the yellow dress, and the staleness of the room had each distilled itself and their three essences had been blended into a powerful drug from which some almost forgotten part of him was crying for escape. He mumbled: "I've gotta go to the can," and groped his way through a doorway into an unlighted hall. When he reached the end of the hallway, he looked back and saw with relief that no one was watching him. He turned the Yale lock on the door leading into the street, closed the door softly after him and hurried down the street.

It was dark again when he turned the key in the door of the apartment. His head had been sluiced clear, by hours of walking in the diluted late-afternoon sunlight and in the chill of dusk. He knocked on the door of the bedroom before he entered it, but he sensed the room's emptiness before he switched on the light. He stood for a few moments looking blankly around the room and then went out again. He walked into the living room. Pop was sitting on the end of the chesterfield with a reading light turned low beside him. The old man looked up.

"Hello, Pop," Mike said, and dropped into a chair where he could watch the old man's face.

Pop said: "I got a little jug of Scotch with me. Like a small one?"

"No thanks, I don't need it."

"Thought you might," Pop said. "You look pretty good though. I used to come back with my eyes the color of hemorrhaging oysters."

"Pop," Mike asked, "where's Tina? I'm going to bring her home."

"I think she's ready to come," Pop said.

"Is she at Mary's? Mike pulled himself to his feet.

"Sit down a minute," Pop suggested amiably.

"Pop," Mike said, "you don't need to say anything. I think I've got it figured out."

"Don't worry," Pop said, "there are certain occasions when I know enough to mind my own business. I'm not going to throw a speech at you. I don't give a damn what you said to my kid or she said to you."

"Well?"

"But I think you both ought to know what made you say it." Pop waited a minute and then continued: "I won't apologize for knowing about it. It's a long time since Tina had a mother to talk to. I been listening to her troubles since she was nine and I couldn't run out now."

"I'd want you to listen," Mike said, "even if it was worse. And I guess it was pretty bad."

"No," Pop said, "the only bad thing would be if instead of getting you two straightened out it left you more mixed up than ever."

Mike said: "I guess Tina knows as well as I do what we were talking about. It didn't have anything to do with Herb Gillis. Tina's afraid I'm going into the army and I thought she took a mean unfair way to say it. And I blew up. I wasn't mad for Herb Gillis' sake. The part about him might have been true, for all I know. I was mad for my own sake."

Mike's voice was fierce and low: "But Jesus, Pop, it's tough enough wrestling with this thing without your own wife throwing rabbit punches at you. It's tough enough seeing the other guys go away and reading about the ones that won't come back, and about the beating we're taking, and still staying home yourself writing memos about the price of flour. Oh, I'm not worried about anybody shoving a white feather at me. But I hoped Tina would see that a man gets almost sick thinking about what he ought to do, and even if she's his wife a woman has no right to make it any tougher than it is."

"I think Tina knows," Pop said, "but no woman ever born will fight fair when she's fighting to keep a man. Even if she hurts herself and hurts the man too, it just isn't in her to fight fair under those conditions."

Mike said: "I guess it isn't only women that are afraid to be fair these days. I just heard some men singing a rotten little song about the army. Not a dirty song. A rotten song, sung by three drunks to explain to themselves why they haven't got guts enough to join the army either. Just hearing it sobered me up. It made me realize that the mean little angles aren't confined to our house. If Tina plays her mean little angle to keep me home, or if I play a mean little angle to keep drawing my eighty bucks a week, what's the difference? There are plenty of others doing the same thing, and I guess half them don't even know they're doing it."

Pop's eyes were alarmed and hurt. "Don't talk that way son," he said, "it's not that bad. Don't get down on people. People are good, if they get half a chance to be."

"Pop," Mike said despairingly, "why don't we have conscription?"

Pop looked at him sadly. "You ever heard of Quebec?" He didn't wait for the answer. "Sure you have. Well, they had their way the last time, and I guess they'll have it again."

"I don't want to talk about Quebec, Pop," Mike was almost pleading. "I want to talk about me. Why won't somebody say:

'Look, Tully, it's your turn.' Or else say, 'Take it easy, Tully, we don't need you yet.' My God, Pop," he cried, "don't they see what they're doing? Don't they know there are married men, men with kids, who aren't sure they've got the right to leave their wives and kids, no matter how much they believe in the war? It's all right for the politicians to sit up there in Ottawa with a pencil and paper and figure out how many men they need and how fast they're going to get them by calling for volunteers. That's easy. But they haven't got the right to force the kind of decision they're forcing onto people like me. No, and not just people like me. Single men too. People like my young brother Joe. A kid that never had a decent job before, and wants to get married; and they say to him: 'Leave your job, kid, leave your girl, join the army, it's your duty. Of course somebody else will get your job while you're away,' they say, 'maybe get your girl too. But what's the difference? The other fellow will handle the job as well as you can. After a while he'll probably look pretty much the same to the girl as you did. After all, he's almost exactly the same kind of person as you are. Same age, same weight, same physical category, same background. The only difference is his conscience doesn't work the same. But what do you care about that?' the politicians say to my brother Joe. 'You've done your duty'."

Pop's expression was remote and gentle. "Yes," he said, "it's a cruel thing. It's a bad way to raise an army and it's a cruel way. It's cruel on every kind of people, on the women and the men. It's always cruel on a woman to take her husband or sweetheart away from her, but it's twice, ten times, as cruel when you tell her the man doesn't have to go if he doesn't want to. I wonder the women are as game as they are. Some of the women let their men go because they know it's no use trying to keep them. Some of them even let them go because, in their women's way, they understand it's right and honest to let them go, and that when a war is being fought in Poland or Spain or France or

wherever it's being fought, that's the place where a man has got
to start defending the place he lives. But most of them don't see it
either of these ways, wholly. They see a little bit of everything;
a little bit of what makes their man go away; and a little bit
of what makes the man down the street stay home; they see a
little bit of the goodness of the war their man is going away to
fight, and a little bit of its stupidity and not improbable
futility; they see some of the bigness of what makes him go away
and some of the littleness too; and they see some of the bigness and
littleness of what makes the man down the street stay home; and
they take all these things and try to make them balance, so that the
outcome will make them proud and confident and sure of their
man and the thing he's doing. But it's not easy to make it balance.
It takes a good game woman to make it balance, and the wonder
is so many of them succeed."

Mike said: "It wouldn't be that way if we had conscription.
It would still be hard, but every time a man went away, some
woman wouldn't have to start figuring out whether she'd finished
second to a brass band. She'd know it had to be that way, no
matter what either of them wanted."

"It's cruel on the men too," Pop said. "Not just on the ones
that go either. Once your country is at war, it's not right or
sensible to expect every man in it to make his own individual and
private declaration of war. That's asking too much of human
nature." Pop hesitated and then went on, in the slow flat accent
of half-remembered pain. "Last time I didn't go. I was nearly
forty but I was healthy; I could have gone. But I didn't and I
never forgave myself. Not to this day. My brother went. He never
forgave himself either, for going. We had the same thing then.
The government said it worked and I guess it did work. We had
a hell of an army. There was none better for its size, and it was
as big as anybody had a right to expect from a country as big as
this one. The Government stayed in office until just before the

end, and then we had conscription for a while, but it was too late to mean anything much. Maybe we'll get it sooner this time," Pop said, "but in the meantime we'll do all right. We'll have a big, good army and a big, good navy and a big, good air force, and there'll be enough volunteers to keep them filled. And every man who's old enough or young enough and fit enough will still have to dredge his own answer out of his own soul. When the answers are all added up, it won't be anything we'll have to be ashamed to let the rest of the world see," Pop said. "We'll make it work again, because we're either the best people in the world, or the biggest God damn fools, and sometimes I don't think there's much difference."

Mike said earnestly: "Pop, do you think I ought to go? Now, I mean."

"I couldn't tell you," Pop said. "Nobody could, not even Tina, and I hope she'll have enough sense not to try any more."

Mike said: "All that about it being unfair is right. But if a man decided he was really needed, he couldn't let that count, could he Pop? He'd still have to go. Suppose he decided we were losing. He couldn't wait for them to start doing it the right way. If we lost, nothing would ever matter to him again except that he sat back and watched it happen and didn't do what he could to prevent it. Sometimes when I get thinking about us losing, I think about the Frenchmen and Dutchmen and Belgians who sat back and let it happen to them. I guess they can blame the politicians and the soldiers the way we could if it happened to us, but no matter how logical blaming the politicians and soldiers would be, a man still couldn't get past himself. Not as long as he lived. That's a long time."

"Too long," Pop said. "I found it out for myself, in a kind of way."

Mike stood up. Some of the intensity had gone out of his lean brown face; it was steady and rested.

"Thanks for coming, Pop," he said. "I'm going to get Tina now."

*   *   *   *

It was another year before Mike enlisted. Neither he nor Tina said much about it, either then or in the interim. The government began drafting young single men into the reserve army and then asking them to volunteer for active service overseas. Reserve army draftees who refused to join the active army remained in uniform but they could not be sent out of Canada; they trained in the same camps and drew the same pay, but the political power of French Quebec shielded them from the necessity of going to war. Mike made a calculation and decided that his age, his married status and his son would give him at least three years' exemption from even the home-service draft. Perhaps the war would be over by then, he told himself, but the thought gave him no satisfaction. It only left him with a stranded, hemmed-in feeling, a feeling of keeping vigil for something that he was not sure he would recognize when it came.

One night, sitting on the chesterfield, Tina made a remark to him and looked across the room when he failed to answer. His book was hanging loosely between his fingers, resting on the floor, and his eyes were half closed, gazing cloudily at the ceiling.

She walked over and put her arms around him. "Mike," she whispered, "it's time you were wearing those fancy pants. I can't wait to see how you'll look."

He started to say something, but then he stopped and drew her down to him and dropped his head against her high, soft breasts. For a long time neither of them said a word.

CHAPTER

4

He stood at the entrance of the hut, holding the door inward against his leg so that it blocked off the cold sweep of the wind from the parade square and still left a wedge of daylight through which he could see. The wind brought water to his eyes and he drew his head back a little and brushed them dry with the glazed, new-smelling sleeve of his overalls. He felt the wind biting at his feet through their thin canvas shoes, and kicked his toes against the boards of the vestibule.

The men outside were neither moving nor completely static. They were a half-numbed swarm, heaving sluggishly within their boundaries but always keeping their boundaries, taking slow aimless little steps, stamping the stiff new soles of their boots against the frozen earth and slapping their arms cross-wise against their sides, but careful to make no larger movement, each man wary lest the swarm dissolve around him and move away. If the swarm flowed away from a man, he followed it, and when it flowed back he followed it back, jealous of his oneness with the swarm, jealous of his sameness and anonymity. And yet the men were not the same, and except for these numbed but watchful minutes before the day's first parade, they did not try to be. The day, as all days did, would bring out their differentness and some of them would exult in it. But it was still too early to be different now, and they took sanctuary in the swarm.

One man was wearing his wedge cap on the wrong side of his head and at the top of another's hiked-up pants a white size label showed below the gap at the rear of his blouse. Mike thought of calling to these two through the doorway but decided against it. The corporal was standing in front of the men now, on the edge of the concrete square, and the formless heaving of the swarm had stopped.

"Cigarettes out!" the corporal shouted in a voice that was meant to be crisp with authority, but only succeeded in sounding like a petulant whine. "Now remember," he shouted, "when marker is called, you will stand properly at ease. At the order, 'On Parade!' you will come to attention and fall in on the marker. And size yourselves. Tallest on the flanks, shortest in the middle. You've been doing it three days now, and it's time you knew where you fit. All right."

He watched them march away, then closed the door and felt in the dark vestibule for the long handle of the push broom. He snapped off the electric light switch on the wall at the end of the room, and looked down along the corridor between the empty beds. One of the three pot-bellied stoves spaced along the corridor showed a cherry-red navel against the black bulge of its midriff, and a thin plume of steam hung above the syrup pail on its top. But the rest of the room seemed lifeless and un-utterably gloomy in the grey light from its naked windows. He switched on the electricity again and began to sweep under the beds, banging the handle of the broom noisily against their iron frames.

The damp air became pungent with dust. He leaned the broom against a bedstead, walked halfway down the hut and turned off into the washroom. He filled a tin basin with water from a brass

tap, took it back into the hut and emptied it on the grimy wooden
floor in scooped-out handfuls.

Before he picked up the broom again he thumbed over a sheaf
of mimeographed orders tacked to a notice board at one end of
the room. Near the bottom of the first sheet he read a paragraph
headed "Special Parade:" *"All Reserve Army personnel of No.
87 Basic Training Centre will parade at* 1030 *hours in the drill
hall, Friday, November 28th,* 1941." A few sheets further down
he found and read a long list of names under the notation that
the following personnel had been taken on strength of Number 87
Basic Training Centre for all purposes, including rations, pay and
discipline, w.e.f. 26-11-41. He searched the list until he found:
"B1838388 Pte. Tully, M. H." He looked at the name for a while,
and then went over the other names in the same part of the list,
trying to see how many of them he could identify with the faces
that went with them.

Abel, Allen, Archibald. He remembered hearing them all at
roll call and hearing a startled "Sir!" acknowledge each, but the
names meant nothing more. Barton. That was the fat kid who had
so much trouble getting a suit of battle dress to fit him. Beamish,
Belson, Bowlder, Brown J., Brown S. L., Bryson and Carling.
He remembered the last two. Both draftees, but the night they
reported they went straight to the corporal's cubicle and asked
to be signed for active service, before anybody even suggested it.
Crasey. A rich man's son and proud of it, already talking
about getting out of there in a hurry and taking an officer's
training course. Crowther, Daniels, Davis, Denman, Dennis, Dolson,
Drayton. Drayton: the sick-looking one who was always doing
the wrong thing on parade and was suspected of crying himself
to sleep at night. Evatt. The big gambler, roll you for your shirt
and probably win it. Forsee. The one who slept in the bunk above
his own and never said anything. Francis, Fryer, Gerbchuk. Gerbchuk: the Hunky, loud but good-natured, never so happy as when

somebody was ribbing him about his deses and doses. Grimstead,
Gray, Grayson, Herman. Herman: the squarehead, but such an
earnest timid guy that nobody mentioned it. Hollis, Hulton, Inman,
Isaacs. Isaccs: the Hebe, lonely and shy. Judson. The one who
said he had ulcers and hinted darkly that the God damn M.O.'s
would find it out some day, to their sorrow.

Kennebec. There was a character. Knew everything about
everything. Knew more about politics than the politicians, knew
more about history than the fellow who wrote the book, knew more
about the army than the sergeant. Seemed to have his stuff
pretty straight at that. Used to be a school-teacher of some kind.
Claimed he fought in Spain and knew all there was to know
about army law and the infantry. Probably a Red. Not much
future for him with this gang. He was so damn superior they were
beginning to hate his guts already.

King, Kyle, Lawton, Lister. Lister: The big operator. Could
outdrink and out-whore any four men in the hut to hear him tell
it, and he told it often. Mason, McFadden, Miczawicz.

Nolan. The Yank. Six foot three and skinny to match. Said
he came up to win the war personally because that's what his
country would have to do sooner or later anyway, just like they
did last time. But nobody minded him. He had a good grin and
used it in the right places.

O'Reilly, Orton, Osmanson. Osmanson: The one who said
he couldn't stomach the cooking and lived on cup cakes, chocolate bars and milk from the Y.M.C.A. canteen. Prince, Pringle,
Provencher. Provencher: the Frenchman. When they tried to
needle him about Quebec, he pointed to his arm and said: "Look,
I got Canada badges. I am active. Pardon me, but go talk to somebody that has not got Canada badges. I see lots here without
them."

Robertson, Rogers, Seznyk. Must be another Hunk. Simpson,
Summers, Sumner. Sumner: The one who said they could wait

till hell froze over before they'd get him to go active. He knew
what it was like. Taft, Tasker, Tomlinson, Tully. Tully: The best
marcher in the platoon, the best stand at easer, the best stander at
attention, the best left wheeler. Tully: the hut orderly!

"Wow!" he said aloud, "I better get moving."

He grabbed his broom and began poking furiously under the
beds. But his high resolve soon withered. He put the broom aside
and began absently straightening a pile of blankets and a badly
rolled paillasse on the upper bunk of one of the beds. He looked
behind the bed for the name on the yellow tubular kit bag lying
on its side in front of a pair of boots. Carling. Oh well, Carling
must be a pretty good guy at that. First reserve man in the hut
to go active. . . . .

Strange business, having two different armies in the same hut,
one pledged to fight and the other pledged to do nothing at all
but march around a parade ground, learn a little bit about
weapons and map reading and gas and then go away to some
other camp to learn the same things all over again. Strange the
way the people who ran the camp seemed to be trying to make
you feel it was all the same thing and at the same time trying to
remind you that it was not the same thing at all. The way the
bunks were arranged, for instance. An Active man below and
a Reserve man above and then on the next tier, an R man below
and an A man above, all the way down the hut, forty-five A men
and forty-five R men spaced and mingled in an exact geometric
pattern. Kennebec, the man who knew everything, claimed this
studied arrangement was based on the theory that each set of
bunk-mates would become inseparable and that when the two
months' basic training period ended, the R man would go active
in order to remain with the A man. Kennebec said the reasoning
was ridiculous, like almost all the army's reasoning, and so far he
seemed to be right. There was no hostility between the R men
and the A men, not even anything that could be called coolness.

But it was pretty obvious that two R men and two A men had more in common than one R man and one A man, and during the ten-minute breaks in the training syllabus, the two kinds tended to split into two groups. If a man with a brass Maple Leaf on his hat and no Canada badges on his shoulders happened to stroll over from the R group to bum a light from somebody in the A group, it was all right though. Nobody snooted him or made cracks, and if he had a story to tell or a new observation to make about the platoon sergeant, nobody looked to see if he had his "Canada's" up before he got his laugh. Nevertheless, it didn't happen very often.

In some ways, you'd think the people who ran the camp weren't being very smart, if what they really wanted was the one-big-happy-family stuff. That piece in Part One Orders about the special parade for R men. The R men were always being fallen out and marched to the drill hall or to the warm lecture hut for special talks and exhortations while the A men kept slogging across the frozen parade square with the full corporal bawling orders at a mile a minute and the lance-jack strutting along behind the column and yapping at its heels like a tyrannical terrier. And Kennebec was right about the A men doing fatigues for the whole hut. Right now there were eight A men in the kitchen, a couple more on the coal pile, two others on the rations truck and himself on hut orderly. That was fourteen men a day, forty-two for three days. It would be interesting to see if they started giving fatigues to the R men after they finished the A roster. Kennebec said they wouldn't. Kennebec said the way they ran all these camps, they made everything as nice as they could for the R men at first, on the assumption that if they made it nice enough, the R men would go active just to oblige the N.C.O.'s and officers. That was the way these camps were judged by Ottawa, Kennebec said—not on how much the soldiers knew when they went on to their advanced training centres, but on how many of them had volunteered to go overseas. Kennebec said the camps were run by a lot of feeble old buzzards who weren't young enough to do any fighting themselves or smart enough to hold a chair job that called for any brains. The only chance they had for promotion was to taffy or bully a lot of punks who didn't know what the war was all about into going over and getting their guts spilled all across Europe. But then, Kennebec was probably crazy. When you asked him why he was a volunteer if that's the way he felt about it, he said: "That's different. I know what I'm doing. I don't need any lard-assed brass hat to tell me what to do."

Sometimes, to hear him talk about Chamberlain and Baldwin and even King, you'd almost wonder whose side Kennebec was on. But he didn't have to be here. He must be thirty-three or four at least, and when he put on his rimless glasses at night, his pinched, angry, condescending face made him look closer to forty. Probably if you got down to cases, there wouldn't be more than a dozen one hundred percent, honest-to-God volunteers in the whole hut. Even the A men, most of them, had been drafted into the reserve army before they volunteered, or at least had been on the verge of being drafted. Not that that mattered, of course. Still, Kennebec could have sat it out for the duration if he'd wanted to. So could Nolan, the Yank, most likely. And so, for another two or three years anyway, could B1838388 Pte. Tully, M. H.

"Boy, am I a hell of a guy," Mike said. "Took me two years two months and seventeen days to start pushing a broom, and now I'm a hero." He grinned sardonically and picked up the broom again.

*　　　*　　　*　　　*

At the end of the first week, Mike wrote Tina that he thought he was going to like it better than he had expected to. But before he finished the letter he sat frowning for half an hour at the Y.M.C.A.

monogram at the top of the first sheet and wondering what there was to like.

Not the full corporal padding out of his cubicle at the end of the room every morning at six o'clock to throw a sudden glare of electric light into your eyes and bawl with sleepy irony: "Come on you lucky, lucky lads! Come on you lucky lads!" Not the lance-jack flopping down the bare corridor between the beds in his unlaced fatigue boots, jarring and rocking the iron bedsteads with the heel of his palm until your sheer helpless resentment sent you stumbling to the washroom to sluice yourself awake with big sloppy handfuls of cold water. Not the smells of the hut in the morning, the decaying smell of a too-hot stove banked too high with too-soft coal, the laundry smell of damp new woollen socks, the astringent smell of cheap soap and disinfectant, the serge smell of new battle dress, the metal smell of steel helmets, the sweet lacquer smell of shoe polish, the rubber smell of ground sheets, the wool smell of blankets, the leather smell of new shoes, the canvas smell of webbing, the deadwood smell of a gritty pine floor, the steam smell of hot water; not, most of all, the animal smell of ninety bodies, all in chemical harmony, all fed according to the same diet sheets, all with precisely the same matter in their bowels, the same formula in their sweat and the same organic rubble in their breath.

Not the breakfast parades and the impatient, helpless fidgeting in the cold early-winter darkness until the corporal was satisfied the needs of the drill book were not jeopardized by the needs of nourishment. Not the hasty, unsavoring gulping of the greasy food and the ritualistic filing past the slop barrels filled with the obscene effluvium of your meal. Not the furious shining of shoes and polishing of cap badges and the fussing with your blankets and your kit until they were exactly like the blankets and the kit on the bed next door and whatever accidental personality or distinction had been retained by your little corner of this

·

narrow little world had been expelled and outlawed to the last shameful crease and the last monstrous fold. Not the endless peering by authoritative strangers into the brown kit box beside your bed, and their cries of outrage when they found that the button brush was on the right of the shoe brush instead of on its left or, worse still, that you had hidden a picture of your wife behind the tin of Silvo.

Not the morning inspections, where you stood like a prize Percheron at a country fair, frozen to attention and staring straight to your front, while a retinue of sergeants, orderly officers, platoon commanders and company commanders yanked at your cap, prodded at the neck of your tunic, pointed their swagger sticks at your gaitered hocks, and then, with a delicate blend of scorn and Christian patience, passed on to the next entry, obviously fearing the worst.

Itemizing it, there wasn't really anything that you had a right to like. Still, after a week, you felt it taking root in you, away back in some part of you whose functioning you did not fully understand, and perhaps would never understand. And the enveloping finality of it seemed to fill some old forgotten need. The need for a deity perhaps; perhaps the need to submerge yourself in what was stronger than yourself; perhaps the need to run with the herd in the rutting randy times of challenge and adventure.

Anyway, it was done. It was done and it could not be undone—neither the parades, nor the smells, nor the food, nor the corporal, nor the wrenching little moments of regret. It was like being on a train at night listening to the wheels click against the rails. The days went by, each one making the same brief metallic impact as the day before, and whether you found the impacts pleasing or discordant, you surrendered to their lulling sameness and inevitability. You could not get off the train and no one could put you off. You could not change the sound of it, any more than you could change the destination. There was no use even thinking about it, and that was the most comfortable thing of all.

"Man! That must be quite a story!" He looked up under the black corner of the upper bunk and saw Nolan's wide good-natured grin framed in the meshing of the spring. He shifted his legs across the bed and Nolan carefully folded his thin length into a sitting position, thrusting his head and shoulders outside the bunk to avoid the upper part of the bed-frame.

"This will probably sound screwy," Mike said, "but I was starting to tell my wife it isn't going to be so bad. But I can see I'd have a hell of a time proving it."

"I guess anybody would," Nolan said. "The way I reckon, there's a little bit of worm in the best of us. That's why we can put up with the army without liking any part of it. Everywhere you go, people are pushing you around, but in the army there's nothing you can do about it, and after you get to know about that, it's a kind of luxury. For a while anyway."

"Well, I hope it stands up," Mike said.

"Probably won't," Nolan said confidently. "Chances are in a month or two we'll hate it about as hard as any sensible person ought to hate this kind of a life."

Nolan unfolded himself again and made to walk away. "You better finish that letter. But if I was you I wouldn't say anything to any woman about liking the army, or even about the possibility of liking it. Tell her it's driving you nuts. That's what they expect. Makes 'em feel better. They'll treat you better too, when you get back."

"What's your rush?" Mike said. Nolan sat down again.

"What are you doing up here anyway?" Mike asked.

Nolan grinned. "I reckon I just came up for the ride. Had a year of college and my father died. Had a job for a year, but it wasn't much. This looked like as good a go as anything."

"You're kidding," Mike said.

"No."

"Maybe not me, but yourself anyway."

"We—el," Nolan admitted, "you could be about twenty per-cent right. I know this country pretty well. Used to come up here fishin' when I was a kid. At my uncle's. He had a place north of Peterborough. I like Canada. So maybe you're right to this extent: I wouldn't join just anybody's army."

"But what do you think about the war?" Mike asked. "You must figure it's a good war."

"I guess so," Nolan said. "I'm not so sure you people were very smart to get mixed up in it. That's a big ocean, no matter what anybody says. Oh, I know you're fighting for a lot of hi-falutin' stuff like democracy and the rights of man and the spiritual values of the universe. I'm not trying to be funny when I say that either. Only the last war it was the same things we fought for and we didn't get them. Maybe we'll get them this time, but a lot of people in my country don't think the odds are good enough to make it worth trying."

"But suppose Germany wins?" Mike said.

"That would be bad," Nolan conceded. "Mind you it isn't so easy down our way to get it straightened out. We haven't got all our politicians saying the same things and all the radios saying the same things and all our newspapers saying the same things. Most of us are on the same side as you, but there's still a lot of big people saying this is only another mess England has got herself into and wants us to bail her out of, and a lot of other big people saying it's hopeless to make anything out of Europe but a wallow anyway. Me, I always come back to thinking about the Jews. No matter what they say about Chamberlain and Hoare and Baldwin, and all of it might be right for all I know, I keep coming back to that poor old kike running down the street somewhere with a mob throwing rocks at him and his house burning down behind him and not a friend in the world but a few other poor old kikes. And I know the Germans are bad, and since I haven't got anything better to do anyway, I'm willing to fight them."

"But you still don't want your country to fight them?" Mike asked.

Nolan thought about it for a minute. "I'd just as leave we didn't," he said. "I'd just as leave we kept out of it. We didn't get an awful lot of men over there the last time, but we saw enough of what made Europe work to get our belly full. Maybe if we could kind of sit up in the bleachers just throwing an odd pop bottle at Hitler it would come out better for everybody. Maybe we'd be in better shape to do something afterwards." Nolan thought again. "Anyway," he said, "going to war is a hell of a big step for a country. It's not so much of a step for a young guy like me, without any family or much of a job. But it's a big step for a country, and I don't know as there's any call for us to take it."

Mike shrugged. "I wouldn't argue with you," he said.

"That's a mighty big ocean," Nolan said again. "Both of 'em. Two big oceans."

Nolan lifted his skinny frame from the bed and stretched the stiffness out of his shoulders. "Guess I'll write a letter myself," he said.

"Say, what's the date?" Mike asked, picking up his pen again.

"Saturday."

"What day of the month, I mean?"

"Sixth," Nolan said. "Saturday December the sixth. Nineteen forty-one."

CHAPTER

5

For a while Mike fought against the Word. He fought it not because he was moral or squeamish, but simply because its grating monotony offended his ear. The fight was hopeless; soon he was using the Word as generously and indiscriminately as everybody else.

The Word was less a part of their speech than an obbligato to it, a steady undertone that beat time for their speech as the angry "Lef-Ri! Lef-Ri! Lef-Ri!" of the corporal beat time for their feet. You could use the Word any place, in any context. You could use it as a verb or a noun or an adjective or an adverb, and in certain situations you could use it by itself as a complete sentence. You could use the Word as a demand, as a plea, as a prayer or a cry, or as a question or a simple statement of fact. You could use it as a challenge or an invitation, as a negative or an affirmative, as a sob of despair or a declaration of faith. The most eloquent of them used the Word to lend stress and power to their speech, and the most inarticulate of them used the Word to cover up their fumbling and give them time to put their speech in order. All through the war it was the hardest-worked word in the English language. The British Tommy and the American

G. I. used it with the same soaring lavishness and for the same disparate purposes.

Some of them were afraid of the Word. Even Lister, the most profane man by nature in the hut, said: "I've gotta quit saying Word all the time. If I don't I'm gonna be sitting at home some day and I'll say: 'Pass the wording butter'." But when they went away on their first forty-eight-hour passes, they found it was as easy to exclude the Word from their homes as it was difficult to exclude it from the barracks. When you came into contact with polite society, you turned off a master valve somewhere in your subconscious mind and the flow of the Word dried up. When you returned to the barracks, the valve opened again and the Word gushed forth again in all its resiliency and volume. It was practically automatic. You didn't even have to worry about it. You soon forgot that the Word lost its original meaning, which was direct and closely connected with biology.

*   *   *   *

Mike got home for Christmas, smelling faintly of Creosote and feeling harder and healthier than he had felt since he quit playing ball. He jammed his thick Melton cap on the baby's head and sat back trying feebly to disguise his delight from Tina while Joey stumped around the room shouting: "My Daddy's a soljer and Joey's a soljer! Bang! Bang!"

Tina brought him his breakfast to bed and when she came to get the dishes he would pull her down beside him, holding her body close to him and drawing her face up to his, hungrily studying every detail of it until, embarrassed, she buried her face in his shoulder.

"You're more beautiful than ever, baby," he announced.

"That's the animal in you talking," she said affectionately.

As she drew her Junoesque body erect, his eyes dwelled with respect on its long curves. "You know, I'm not as worried about you as I should be," he grinned. "If the worst comes to the worst, you can always get a feature spot at the Casino."

They went dancing. They ate in Chinatown. They drank a little too much on Christmas Eve and ate a little too much on Christmas afternoon. They gave the baby the right presents and the baby said the right things when he saw the tiny apartment-size tree. It was a good Christmas.

A letter came from Mike's brother in the last delivery before Mike went back. Joe wrote:

"Marje and I have decided to get married. It looks as though I'll be getting my call in a few months. We thought of waiting, but maybe I won't have to go overseas right away, and we both think we ought to take a chance."

Tina said: "I feel sorry for kids like that. A lot sorrier than I'll ever feel for us. We've got a lot behind us, and it's been good enough that we know what's ahead of us too. But so many of them may not even get anything."

Mike said: "Don't worry about Joe. He seems to be able to look after himself. A lot better than he used to anyway."

Tina glanced at him quickly. "Mike," she asked, "you're not mad at Joe, are you?"

"Don't be silly," Mike said. "Joe's got the same right as anybody to work it out for himself. I'm living right in the same hut with fifteen or twenty guys who are in the army already and still won't sign up to fight. But I'm not even very mad at them. Why should I be mad at my own brother just because he's waiting for his call-up papers?"

Tina wondered silently if there wasn't too much conviction in his voice. "Let's not talk about the army anyway," she said.

                    *   *   *   *

No one was really aware how or even when the almost invisible line that had marked the difference between the A men and the R men grew and thickened until it was a wall of suspicion and hostility. Almost every evening another man would be sitting on his bunk stitching a set of Canada badges on the shoulders of his battle dress or rubbing a coat of dried Silvo off a new cap badge. Two or three A men would stroll over and look down to see what kind of badge it was. They would say: "Ordnance, uh? That's a good outfit. You'll learn a lot. Good chance for trades pay." Or they'd say: "Engineers, uh? They work you too wording hard there. Me, I'll take my chances in the wording infantry." Nobody would congratulate the man or make speeches at him, but from then on, when it was time to break for a smoke he would be with the A men, and when they were munching chocolate bars in the canteen he would be with the A men, and when the solvent residents of the hut were strolling down town for beer between supper and lights out, the new convert would be with the A men then too.

By New Year, thirty-four of the original R men in the hut had signed for active service and the other eleven were living in a little society of their own, a society that was neither completely isolated from the larger society of the hut nor completely united with it. More and more the eleven kept to themselves. They still fell into their old places for foot drill, but at meal parades they shuffled into position together at the end of the line. During the ten-minute breaks for smoking, the little gap that had separated the A men from the R men was wider than it had been in the first days, and now nobody crossed it to borrow a light. Just before PT periods broke up, there was usually a game or a relay race, and when sides were being chosen the eleven R men were always chosen last, and as soon as the R men entered the game or the race, the noisy cheering stopped.

You could not have told whether the gulf was a spontaneous growth of life in the hut, or whether it was something that had been cultivated by the permanent staff of the camp, the officers and N.C.O's who would remain in the camp to train the next

draft after this draft had gone. The R men began to draw more
fatigues than the A men. In foot drill, the little lance-corporal
continued to squall impartially at all blunderers, but when the
offender was an A man, the lance-jack's voice would shrill: "Pick
it up, that man in the centre file!" and when the offender was an
R man the lance-jack would identify him by name, announcing
his shame to the whole squad and through it the shame of R men
in general.

And now, on inspections, the little coterie of live-stock judges
would usually walk quickly past the A men. But almost every
morning, the company commander would stop before at least one
R man and point his swagger stick at an exposed gaiter buckle
or a protruding shoe-lace and say: "Mr. Johnson, this man has
spoiled your whole platoon." Sometimes the company commander would say: "What's this man's name?" The subaltern
would say: "Forsee, sir," or "Sumner, sir". The company commander would stare hard at the man and say: "Yes, I know that
name." Once, the company commander commented on the
unshined shoes of one R man, the muddy gaiters of another, and
the unpolished cap badge of a third and as he returned the subaltern's parting salute, he said loudly, so that the whole platoon
could hear: "Mr. Johnson, most of the men in your platoon are
playing ball. But I won't put up with this sloppiness by a few.
You will please confine the entire platoon to barracks for the next
two nights."

Almost every day two or three of the R men would be fallen
out of the squad and told to report to the company commander's
office. They would return sullen and silent. Lister or Gerbchuk
or perhaps one of the newest converts to the ranks of the A men
would look at their faces as they fell in again and snigger: "It
looks like the old pep talk missed again." But by the middle of
January there were only eight R men in the platoon.

It was the lance-jack who first taught the A men to stare

meaningfully at the cap badges of the R men and then chant tauntingly: "The Maple Leaf Forever!" It was the full corporal who taught them that even such broad subtleties as that weren't necessary.

Most of the R men had already learned that self-assertiveness was not expected of them. Sumner, nevertheless, walked into the cubicle after the duty roster went up late one evening and complained about being put on fatigues for the third day in a row. He came out in a minute and went straight to his bunk. The corporal followed him and stood in the centre of the room beside a table of card players and said noisily:

"So you don't like washing dishes?"

Sumner was lying on his bunk, his flabby face shielded by the mattress above. When he answered he made his voice low, trying to keep the matter private.

"I'll do my share," he said.

"You're wording right you will!" the corporal said. The card game stopped and the players looked fixedly at their cards, holding everything but their ears in a state of suspended animation.

"What else do you want to do but wash dishes?" the corporal demanded.

The man on the bed did not reply.

"Maybe you'd like to be a soldier," the corporal said loudly. "Well, we can wording soon fix that for you. I got pull around here. I could get you in the army. I got friends in the army," the corporal said.

One of the card players tittered.

"Word!" the corporal said disgustedly, glaring at the silent bunk. He stamped back down the room and disappeared into the cubicle.

Another time Forsee, the pale, blinking youngster who slept in the bunk above Mike, was dragging dirty laundry out of his kit bag behind the bed. The corporal came up to the bed and put his elbows on the sill so that he could look down at Mike on the lower bunk and so that his elbow was between Forsee and the main aisle of the hut. The corporal was a big, sloppy man, with a big, sloppy face. He almost filled the space beside the bed.

"You two fellows getting along all right?" the corporal said to Mike.

"Just fine," Mike said, putting his book down. "Of course we're still waiting for the silk sheets. Aren't we, Forsee?"

Forsee said nothing.

"I was just wondering," the corporal said, "Forsee don't seem to be satisfied."

Forsee tried to move past the corporal with an armful of laundry, but the corporal kept his elbow across the narrow alleyway. "What's your hurry, Forsee?" he said. "That can wait."

The corporal said to Mike: "Forsee don't seem to figure you're good enough to bunk with him. He wants to move down with Drayton."

"It doesn't matter," Forsee said, "I only asked. I didn't mean anything against Tully."

"It looks like you A guys aren't good enough for the R boys," the corporal said.

"Forget it," Mike said, "I probably snore."

"Or maybe him and Drayton just want to hold hands before they go to sleep," the corporal said. "The ole boogey man might get them."

"What's the fuss about?" Mike said. "Drayton's his best friend. Why shouldn't they be in the same bunk? It's all right with me."

"Well, they're not wording well gonna be in the same bunk!" the corporal snapped. "Do you get that Forsee? And if you're as smart as I think you are, Tully, you'll get it too. It may not mean anything to you that we got a few gutless worders around here that are trying to play the rest of us for wording suckers and——"

Mike scrambled to his feet and stood in front of the corporal, between him and Forsee.

"Look corporal!" he said angrily, "you've got your job to do around here, and maybe you're doing it the best way you know how. But leave me out of it. Go do your job somewhere else. And don't ask me to help you. Forsee and I are getting along fine. Suppose you just leave it that way."

The corporal stared at him and then dropped his eyes. "There's no call for you to get sore, Tully," he said. "I got nothing against you." He walked away.

*　　　*　　　*　　　*

That night Mike was still awake long after midnight. He lay in the darkness watching the red glow of the pot-bellied stove and the bronze bar of reflection it threw against the metal cross-support at the foot of his bed. A shadow shuffled through the door from the ablutions room and stopped at the stove. The damper clanged hollowly and the shadow shuffled on. Mike reached over his head and extracted a cigarette and a match from the trousers of his battle dress hanging behind the bed. He struck the match on the floor, cupped it quickly over the end of the cigarette and then lay back again.

"You awake, Tully?" The voice lowered itself from the sill of the upper bunk, cautiously and deliberately, as a climber who is not very sure of himself shins down a pole.

"Uhhuh."

"Thanks for what you did."

"That's all right, Forsee."

Mike finished the cigarette, carefully ground it out on the floor, returned the butt to the pocket of his trousers, and dispersed the ashes over the floor by sweeping his hand across them.

"You must think I'm an awful heel, Tully."

"Why should I?" Mike muffled the words through his arm, making his voice sound as sleepy as he could, hoping that the conversation would end.

Forsee's head appeared over the sill, dark and shapeless against the night.

"I hate this place," the boy whispered. "I'll be glad when we're out of it."

"Guess we've all had enough of it," Mike grunted.

"I don't mind what they say. It's just that they're all so damned sure they know how to run everybody else's life."

Mike stirred noisily on his pillow.

"It's all right for them," the boy whispered. "But we're not all the same. A lot of them were never so well off in their lives. You just have to look at them to tell. They never ate better. They never got paid better. Somebody even does their thinking for them. Why shouldn't they go active?"

"Go to sleep," Mike growled. But the boy's voice was a muted little tempest of excitement now and it ran on unheeding.

"That's all right for them. But I gave up a good job for this. I was making forty-five a week. I've got a wife. I've got a lot to lose."

Mike swung himself erect, clenching his hand around the edge of the bed frame under the dark oval of Forsee's face.

"Listen, you wording little sparrow!" he whispered fiercely. "I'm not interested in your snivelling little life or any part of it. Just because I wouldn't help that wording slob of a corporal push you around, you think I'm on your side. Well, I'm not! You had a good job. I had one twice as good. You've got a wife. I've got one of those too, and she's probably twice as good as yours too. Word! I've got a kid damn near as big as you. And there are lots of others like me," he whispered savagely, "and they don't whine about it either. I guess the corporal was right. You do think you're too wording good. Well, from now on, you're on your own as far as I'm concerned. You and the other wording snivelling little sparrows."

He threw himself back on his pillow and pulled the coarse blankets over his head. It was nearly reveille before he got to sleep.

CHAPTER

6

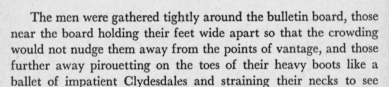

The men were gathered tightly around the bulletin board, those near the board holding their feet wide apart so that the crowding would not nudge them away from the points of vantage, and those further away pirouetting on the toes of their heavy boots like a ballet of impatient Clydesdales and straining their necks to see above the cluster of heads in front.

At the top of the chart there was a typewritten line in capital letters: TESTS OF ELEMENTARY TRAINING. And below, in upper and lower casing: No. Nine Platoon. The chart was ruled off in squares, and in nearly every one of the squares there was a check mark in black ink.

"Hey, Lister, how'd I do?"

"Quit crowding a minute! Let's see. Gerbchuk. Got 'em all."

"Hey, look up Rogers."

"Rogers. Rogers. You missed your gas. You got to take your gas again."

"What about Seznyk?"

"Seznyk. You're O.K. Got 'em all."

"Well, word! How in the word did I ever get that map readin'?"

"How in the word did anybody get anything?" Kennebec's jeering voice was so familiar by now that no one even looked around. "These wording plumbers they got running this place couldn't teach Einstein to add two and two.

"Sure!" Kennebec mocked, "you'll all get 'em all. You're all great soldiers now. You can recite the three rules of aiming. Of course most of you couldn't hit a bull in the ass with a handful of buckshot, but what's that matter? You know all about the Lewis gun except how to shoot it, but what's that matter? They don't use the Lewis gun anymore anyway. You know all about the anti-tank rifle and you'll never use that either. You know how to stick a bayonet through a sack of sawdust without falling on your faces. You know the difference between an easting and northing, if you think real hard. You can whip on a gas mask, pardon me, respirator, in nine seconds, and you know that tear gas smells like floor wax. My wording nerves!" Kennebec snorted. "And you still think they brought you here to learn something about soldiering. Word! You fired fifteen rounds out of a twenty-two on a twenty-five yard range. You haven't even seen a Bren gun or a real rifle yet. You still don't even know why you're here," Kennebec jeered. "Well, I'll tell you again. Half us are here to help them get recruits and the other half are here to get recruited."

"Aw dry up, Kennebec, you give me a wording pain."

The corporal clumped out of the cubicle. "That's enough, Kennebec!" he said indignantly. "If you wanta stay here, just keep talking like that. You'll stay all right—right in the guard house."

Kennebec smiled sourly and walked away.

"Never mind that jerk, corporal," somebody said sympathetically.

"I never mind anybody," the corporal said pompously.

"Hey, corporal," Lister asked, "when do we go out?"

"What's your hurry?" the corporal bantered. "Don't you like it here?"

"Oh, it's been dandy. Just dandy. But when do we go? We been here away over two months now. We nearly all passed our T.O.E.T.'s. We ought to be going soon."

"Maybe you'll hear this afternoon," the corporal said grudgingly. "The old man is going to talk to you on the first parade after lunch. Maybe he'll tell you then."

*   *   *   *

The major walked with a permanent list. He stood with a list, his whole left side adroop under the weight and prestige of his old campaign ribbons. His sharp sallow face seemed to list beneath the scraggly gray counterbalances of a moustache which he allowed to grow too long because it would not grow thick enough. His speech listed; he began his longer sentences strongly and confidently, but they trailed off and fell away in threshing shadows. Some of the individual words listed. He pronounced "ing" like "een".

The major was smiling and his yellowing teeth listed humorlessly beneath the smile. "Well men," he said, "I have good news for you. At least I think it will be good news for you. You've been traineen hard and workeen hard and I know you've found companionship and in spite of the hardships you have experienced, I know you have profited by the experience of the ah experience."

The major paused. "And now," he said, "you will soon be goeen away. I shouldn't tell you when you will be goeen, but you have been such good soldiers here that I was just sayeen to Mr. Johnson I don't believe there has been a finer platoon in camp than Number Nine and I have been watcheen men come and go ever since."

Kennebec, lounging in the rear file, scratched his ear ostentatiously and whispered out of the side of his mouth: "Good old Wylie!"

"You will be goeen on to your advanced traineen centres in

five days from today," the major said. He waited indulgently
for the ragged cheer to subside.

"Some of us," with a great effort the major adjusted the list
of his body—"Some of us will have to stay. We envy you. I
think all of you know a bit about my record and when I think
of the humble part I have been able to play as a soldier of the
British Empire I can't help thinkeen of the humble part and
envyeen, yes envyeen."

"A heart as big as all outdoors," Kennebec whispered.

"But you don't want to hear a speech," the major said. "There's
just one thing I want to say. You will be goeen on to other camps
where you will find that they are not as generous in giveen you
leaves as we have tried to be here. And before you go, as a reward
for your fine performance here, I want you all to have a leave with
your families because you may not for a long time. I have put it
up to the colonel."

Under cover of another cheer, Kennebec said aloud: "When
they made old Wylie, they threw the mould away. And none too
soon."

"The colonel consented," the major said, "on one simple little
condition. It's a fair condition. It applies to all the other platoons
in the camp and they will be getteen leaves too if they meet."

The major's voice grew sentimental. "We are proud of the
record of this camp," he said. "When we can send out a draft
that is one hundred percent active, we are proud and we know that
you are proud too, because in the final analysis. Today is, let's
see, Monday. You'll have to be back here Friday to join your
drafts to your new traineen centres. So that leaves two days. If
good old Number Nine platoon can show a one hundred percent
active service roster by Wednesday morneen, the whole platoon
will leave on forty-eight hour passes at noon and I'm confident. It
just means all pulleen together and talkeen it over among yourselves. I know that some of you, perhaps for what seem to you

like good personal reasons, haven't been as fast as the rest to decide about goeen active, but I know that no man in Number Nine would want to deprive his entire platoon of the last leave they'll be getteen for a long time and I know even if they did. So talk it over among yourselves and pull together among yourselves, and that's the British way, the way that means so much to all of us."

The major smiled affably and listed to attention. "That's all, Mr. Johnson," he said.

Before the subaltern called them to attention, Mike glanced down the length of the platoon's rear rank. Most of the men looked the same; their eyes were bright with excitement, their lips were parted above their teeth, and their breathing had become a silent steady panting. It was not the same with the three R men he could see at the end of the rank. Sumner had dropped to the parade ground on one knee and was conspicuously absorbed in adjusting a gaiter. Drayton had taken off his dark-rimmed glasses and was polishing them jerkily with a dirty handkerchief. Forsee was staring straight ahead and his pale eyes were dull and without feeling.

Kennebec turned to Mike.

"God bless our happy home," he said.

"God damn our happy home!" Mike said savagely.

CHAPTER

7

The hut was nearly empty. The beds were silhouetted flat and naked in the sludgy bath of starlight from the windows. There was no sound but the complacent crackling of the stoves, and now and then a muffled cough. The room smelled empty; it was warm, but much fresher than usual. The washroom door was closed, but a slab of yellow light fell through its crack across the middle of the floor.

Mike put one hand on the floor and pivoted his body halfway out of bed into the slab of light from the door, holding his head and his free hand close together in the light. His wrist watch said a quarter to one. He swung his head back to the bunk and half sat up, searching the other bunks in the semi-opaque gloom.

They were all there. That was Sumner on the third bed down, across the room. And Drayton two more beds away. He could hear Forsee breathing in the bunk above and see the light bulge of his body through the mattress. They didn't even have guts enough to go loose. They were just lying there, pretending to be asleep, and listening to the minutes drag by.

Maybe they knew going loose would be no use either. Maybe they knew they could either take it or give up, and there was no third alternative. They knew how far Miczawicz got. Miczawicz knew his rights. He went running to the major with his black eye and his two loose teeth, and the major threw him out. And Miczawicz walked back into the cubicle and said: "All right, I'll go active." Barton, Judson, Crowther and Denman — they knew when they were licked too. . . . "Eight little R Boys, scared as they could be. One got his kisser smacked, then there were three" . . . . That Lister was a riot.

It would be worse tonight. Last night the corporal was in, and they had to be quiet enough that the corporal could pretend he didn't hear. But the corporal wouldn't be in at all tonight. He'd made a point of telling them. There was no bed check and no roll call tonight. The sentry was still on the gate, but they all knew the way over the fence anyway. They should be coming any time. And they'd be drunk tonight. Some of them anyway. That was the idea. That was what the corporal meant. Or the lieutenant. Or the sergeant. Or the major. All of them, probably. Kennebec knew what he was talking about after all. They'd played it the same way right from the first day, now that you looked back.

He wanted to say something to Forsee, but what could he say? He couldn't say he was sorry for what he'd said the other night, because he wasn't sorry for saying it at all. The only thing he was sorry about was that Forsee happened to be what he was. No, not that exactly either. He was sorry that the others were what they were and that he himself was what he was, and that what they all were, the others and himself and Forsee, would have to be exposed and proclaimed for all of them to see. He knew what they were going to do. They had told him, and asked him to help. He had said he wouldn't help, nor would he hinder them. And perhaps that made him worse than any of them. It was all right deciding there was no use, but if it was wrong you still had to try and stop it. But was it wrong?

There was nothing he could say to Forsee. But he could ask Forsee for a match, and perhaps asking him for a match would tell Forsee something that he could not tell him in any other way. It might tell him, at least, that the matter which was about to begin would not really be a matter of personalities, however much it must seem to be. It might tell him that the matter had been ordained by forces far beyond the control of anyone in the hut, and that it would be as ridiculous to take it as a personal matter as to take the war itself as personal.

He slapped his hand softly against the mattress above his head. "You got a light, Forsee?" he said.

The clothing hanging behind the bed rustled and a grey arm sheathed in a woollen undershirt reached down over the sill.

"Thanks."

"If you're short of cigarettes, you'll find some in my half of the kit box," Forsee said.

Mike stopped in the act of striking a match. . . . They were coming now. . . .

Their feet were scuffling in the frozen gravel outside the hut. The door creaked open and their boots rang hollowly through the vestibule. They wouldn't all come in together. Three or four or half-a-dozen at a time.

"Not so much noise!" the voice at the end of the room was thick and sententious.

It was answered by a high giggle, and then two tearful voices were singing low from the black corner bunk beside the vestibule:

"If I had my way, dear,
"You'd never grow old—
"A garden—"

A shadow lurched down the hut, threw open the door into the washroom as the doors shuttered back on the sudden flare of light. The bed creaked thinly as Mike felt Forsee's body relax against the upper bunk.

A babel of noisy whispers broke out at the far end of the hut, and a bottle rang a hollow High C against the iron rail of a bedstead. The whispering stopped, and a swaying file of shadows moved down the hut through the slab of light from the washroom door, past the glowing stove, and merged in an uncertain knot near the middle of the corridor between the beds. Mike swung his legs to the floor and padded on his bare feet to the fringe of the knot. He recognized the bulky form of Lister at its centre.

The knot dissolved away from him and he followed it. A bed creaked heavily in the darkness ahead. Mike looked down at the bed. There were three men sitting on each side of it, hunched together in the darkness like merging black mounds. The covers between them stirred blackly and then were still.

A glaring beam of light stabbed through the darkness, played whitely on the white corner of a pillow for a moment and then moved across the pillow and focused on a face. The eyes in the face were a single slash of copper, like the eyes of a cat caught in headlights at night. The face was white and flabby.

"Wake up, Sumner!" The words shivered roughly through the silence.

"Shut up, Davis! I'll handle this." Mike could make out Lister's heavy features now, thrust close behind a flashlight, close to the white face of Sumner on the pillow.

"It's me, Lew. Al Lister."

"Hello, Al." Sumner's eyes were closed tight now against the light. His voice tried to duplicate the casual warmth of the other. It failed; it sounded scared.

"Good old Lew." Lister leaned forward with the torch. His own body and the other bodies on the bed pressed hard against each other, wedging tightly into the shapeless contours of the blankets. Lister's free hand reached down and patted the right cheek of the face on the pillow. And then, lightly but sharply, it slapped each cheek three times. There was no sound of protest.

"Like a drink, Lew?"

"No thanks, Al."

"Sure he does. Give him a drink. Who's got the jug of goof?"

Another hand thrust the neck of a bottle into the beam of the torch. It glinted purple in the light as it probed for the lips of the man imprisoned under the blankets and the wine spilled over the lips and rolled down Sumner's flabby chin in a red smear. Sumner tried to rub it off with his shoulder, but the six men holding him in the vise of their bodies leaned forward again, pinioning him closer than before. Lister curled a loose fringe of blanket into his free hand and swabbed the chin dry with delicate, over-solicitous stabs.

"All right, Lew?"

"All right, Al."

"That's not the first drink we've had, Al." Lister turned his head away from Sumner, but still held the flashlight close to Sumner's face. "Me and Lew used to kick around a lot when we first come here," he said. "Me and Lew are pals. Ain't we, Lew?"

"Ain't we, Lew?"

"Ain't we what?" For the first time Sumner spoke with a hint of spirit.

"Pals."

"Sure."

"Sure what, Lew?"

"Pals."

"Pals, who?"

"What do you mean, Al?" Sumner no longer spoke with spirit.

"That's what I mean. Al. Al. Just Al. You remember my name, Lew. You just said it. It's Al. Tell them what we are, Lew. Tell the boys right."

"We're pals, Al."

Lister patted one of the cheeks again and then slapped the two cheeks again, three times on each side, as he had done before.

"Well, Lew," Lister said, "I guess you know what the boys have been saying." He moved the flashlight closer, so close it was almost touching Sumner's nose.

"The boys have been saying you're yellow, Lew," Lister said. "That hurt. The boys say you're not only yellow, but you don't wanta play ball with the rest of us. The boys say you don't care if we get our leave tomorrow or not. The boys say you'd do us out of it."

"I don't like that kind of talk, Lew," Lister said. "And that's not all, Lew. The boys were real mad at you. They wanted to toss your stuff outside in the snow. And then they wanted to throw you in the shower. I said you can't do that fellahs. You can't throw a man in the showers at this time of night. It's too cold. The water's just like ice. You can't do that to my pal Lew. That's what I said to the boys, Lew."

Lister said: "And that's not all, Lew. The boys said if that wasn't enough, they'd get rough. Real rough, Lew. I said they couldn't do that either. I said it was all right to have a little fun between friends, but rough stuff don't go. I said it was all right to do like this."

Lister's foot scraped against the floor as he bent his body forward on the bed. He removed the flashlight a little way from Sumner's face and drew his free hand back to the level of his shoulder and then slapped Sumner hard across the mouth, twenty times or more. Each slap made its own sick crash.

"That's all right, Lew," Lister said when he was done. "That's between pals. I told the boys you wouldn't mind that."

The man pinioned in the bed tried to twist his face toward the pillow. His tongue ferreted across his swollen lips but there was no moisture on it.

"I told the boys you'd go active in a minute, Lew," Lister said. "I told the boys if we'd put it up to you man to man there wouldn't be any argument. And there wouldn't either. Would there, Lew?"

Sumner tried to open his eyes, but the harsh light from the torch ground them shut again.

"Would there, Lew?"

Lister waited for a minute. They all waited. Their waiting ceased to be an abstract thing. It was physical and it possessed the whole room; you could hear it and you could smell it. The six soldiers sitting on the bed leaned forward to look at Sumner's face and the springs of the bed drew together under their shifting weight with a constricted, half-throttled twang. The sound was like an unfinished sigh. A man standing behind the bed coughed primly. The only breathing that could be heard was Sumner's; it was heavy but even, like the breathing of a man taking ether. The unheard breathing of the others soaked and deadened the air with the stale sick fumes of cheap wine. The men were sweating, and the sweet musty smell of their sweat mingled with the smell of the wine, drenching the room with the heavy odor of climax.

Under the flashlight, Sumner's loose face was relaxed and bland, like a weathered marble statue seen by moonlight. The harsh light cleansed his face of all line and expression. He had ceased screwing his eyebrows toward the little jowls of fat beneath his eyes to shut out the glare of the torch, and his closed eyelids were smooth and round. You could not have told by any of the conventional yardsticks whether he was afraid or not, and yet every inch of his face spoke of fear. If you could hear the waiting in his breathing and smell the waiting in the air, you could see it still more clearly in Sumner's face.

"Lew!" Lister said at last, "the boys are tired of waiting."

"All right," Sumner said lifelessly. "All right. I'll do it. I'll go."

The torch snapped out and the room was black again. There was a congestion of bumping shadows and the smothered ring of clothed bodies lurching against metal bed frames.

A new voice said: "How do we know he'll go through with it? How do we know he won't wording double-cross us?"

"He won't. Because if he wording double-crosses us, we don't get our leave. And we'll all be here together for three more nice long days."

Drayton was sitting erect in his upper bunk, waiting for them. When Lister sprayed the torch on him, he looked for all the world like a juvenile and highly Nordic Gandhi, sitting cross-legged under his blankets with his absurdly large issue undershirt billowing away from his skinny neck to lose his skinny chest under its glazed white folds, and his short-sighted eyes blinking nakedly in the bleached sacs of flesh that had been pinched out under them by a lifetime of wearing glasses.

"Go ahead," Drayton said, shrilling out the words in a fractured parody of resolution and defiance. "Do whatever you want. It doesn't matter what you do. I still won't."

"All right," Lister commanded, "let's have a look at his stuff."

Drayton watched immovably while they dumped his kit bags on the floor, swept the clothing behind the bed into a bundle and rolled it into a pile on the floor with their feet and methodically dumped the contents of his brushes box into a smaller pile beside the bed.

Davis rummaged through the debris but found nothing that seemed of interest. Dubiously, he held a white envelope up to the beam of the flashlight.

"Let's have that," Lister said.

"Give it back!" Drayton said fiercely. "You can't take that." He squirmed free of the blankets and made a grab at the letter across the edge of the bed, but another man threw him back on the bed and three others ringed themselves around him, pinning his skinny body against the mattress with their arms. Drayton kicked for a while and then lay still, panting malevolently.

"*Dear Ernest,*" Lister read. And then he repeated prissily: "*Dear Ernest.*"

The others chorused: "Dear Ernest."

"*We received your letters sixty-four and sixty-five today. It hardly seems like sixty-five days, even though we have seen you since, but in some ways it seems longer.*"

A high sniggering voice interrupted, with mock approbation: "Ernest writes every day!"

"*I am glad you are not finding the life too hard,*" Lister read, "*or at least that you think you are not finding it too hard. But you were always inclined to take things too robustly.*"

Another interruption: "Just look at that robust ole hunk of man!"

"Lister!" Drayton panted desperately, "Stop! Please stop, Lister!"

"*I am sending another bottle of milk of magnesia along with the cod liver oil, the cake and the woollen scarf. I know it will do you good and if the other boys tease you about taking it, all I have to say is they ought to be ashamed of themselves.*"

A sharp smack interrupted Lister again as one man hidden in the darkness slapped another's wrist and squealed: "There! That will teach you not to tease Ernest again."

Drayton was crying. "For God's sake, Lister, don't. Please, Lister. It's from my mother."

"*I think it's wonderful about you passing all your T.O.E.T.'s. They sound terribly hard and complicated. How did the other boys make out with them? I'll bet not many of them finished ahead of you.*"

"Ernest finished ahead of everybody," a man behind Lister said triumphantly, "That is, if you read from the bottom up."

"*It's nice that you get along with the other boys so well,*" Lister read. "*I know that somewhere deep down in your secret self you have always considered yourself a little bit backward,*" *especially in sports. But there are other things besides sports and I'm sure that when the other boys get to know you better, you'll be still more popular with them."*

"Boy, is Ernest popular!" the man behind Lister said. "We're going to make him Queen of the May."

"Jesus!" Drayton was crying softly and hopelessly. "Oh Jesus!"

"Your last letter worried me just a little," Lister read. *"Now I know most of the other boys are going overseas, Ernest, and I can understand why you want to go with them. I don't want to hold you to your promise against your will, but I know it's for the best. You're not as strong as the others. I shudder to think what might happen if you ever got over to England, in all that damp, and eating that terrible food, not to mention the other things."*

"Ernest might get hurted, Ernest might get hurted," the man behind Lister chanted.

"There are plenty of important jobs to be done right here in Canada," Lister read, *"and goodness knows, if everybody was needed over there we'd have had conscription long ago."*

The man behind Lister beat time with his hand on the end of the bed and uttered a nasal, "Ta-ra-ra-ra-ra-ra-ra-ra", apeing the playing of a fanfare by a band.

Lister read on: *"Dr. Purvis was out today with a specialist from Toronto to see your father. The pain has become worse in the last few days, and I think your father knows now too, although he will give no hint of it. It is no worse and no better than Dr. Purvis feared. At the most your father still has six months left. We must still try to pretend—"* Lister's voice died away emptily.

The man behind him tittered nervously but afterwards, for a while, nothing could be heard but the naked sobbing of the boy on the bed. Lister's hand dropped to his side and the letter slipped out of his fingers to the floor. You could not see his face, but a pale hint of light reflected back on it from the wall, from the flashlight, and it was enough to show the sudden sagging droop of his mouth, a dead sag and yet as live as pain. The light was not enough to show his eyes, but it was enough to show the shamed narrowing at their corners; his whole face was a silhouette of shame. The light could not have been crueller to Lister if it had been turned away from the wall and focused full on him.

"Let go of him," Lister said.

"Let go of him," he said.

The men standing beside the bed obeyed and Lister said to Drayton: "We'll leave you alone now. You don't have to do it."

Drayton's sobbing had stopped. He sat up in the bed again and held his arm over his face like a garment thrown across his unclothed hurt.

Drayton said: "It's too late. I want to do it now."

Lister said doggedly: "No. Forget it. It doesn't matter."

"I'm going to," Drayton said. "Whether anybody wants me to or not. I thought nobody could make me, and now nobody can stop me."

"No," Lister said, "Forget it."

"It's no use telling you what you've done," Drayton said. "You wouldn't understand. But you've done what you set out to do. I'm going active. We don't have to talk about it any more."

Lister turned and shuffled stupidly away from the bed, into the dark aisle of the hut. The others followed him. They knew he would not stop at Forsee's bed now, and the wish to stop there had drained out of them as it had drained out of Lister. But two of them, Davis and another, paused uncertainly.

"There's only Forsee left," Davis whispered. "It's all wasted if we let him go."

Forsee heard them, and they heard Forsee drawing his body in on the bed, and the uneasy dregs of ferment that were left in them by the dispersing mob began to stir again. Davis and the other man moved close to the bed and two more men came up and stood close beside them.

Mike found himself still on the outskirts of these uncertain figures, standing barefooted in the middle of the floor, almost exactly where he had been when he first stopped beside Sumner's bed. For the first time, he felt thoughts taking shape in his head again. He wondered what had rooted him like this so long, rooted not only his body but the workings of his mind, and more acutely still, he wondered what he would really have thought of the things he had heard and seen if his mind had been less deadened by them. The answer would not come, but he found a part of it. This was the way he had felt, one night years before, when he left a stag party with some other men and went to a house where they featured something called an "Exhibition." The mechanical, a-thousand-times-rehearsed eroticism of the exhibition had left him horrified and physically sick. Yet, while the grisly burlesque was on, he had been unable to tear his eyes away from it. He had sat through it all, fascinated and sick, and then gone outside and spilled the contents of his stomach.

This night was much the same. Standing barefooted in the middle of the floor, he wondered abstractly, without putting his wonder in words, whether there was such a thing as having carnal knowledge of a man's soul. He wondered if it was less right that men should look with too much detail at women's bodies than that they should look with too much detail at the hearts of men. The shame and revulsion of the night struck and engulfed him in one swift overpowering wave; his body trembled with it.

For the first time since the others had come into the hut, he spoke aloud. His voice was tired, but it rang out loudly through the black room.

"That's enough!" Mike said.

He walked back to his bed and shoved his way through the gathering knot of men to the top of the bed. He felt in the darkness for Forsee's shoulder and when he found it, he sank his fingers into it and dragged it up from the pillow until Forsee's face was close to his.

"We've all had enough, Forsee," he said. "We're not going to have any more arguments and we're not going to have any more trouble. You're the only R man left in this whole hut and you're going active in the morning. There's no use talking about it, Forsee. That's what you're going to do."

Forsee's body tautened and tried to pull away from him. But Forsee said: "You don't have to do anything Tully. I'm going active. I was going anyway."

The platoon went on leave at noon. In the officers' mess, the colonel stood the company commander a double whiskey and the company commander stood the platoon commander a beer. A few days later a tiny set of fresh statistics passed across a chain of desks at Ottawa and the owners of the desks observed that the recruiting policy was continuing to work very well.

CHAPTER

8

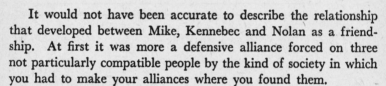

It would not have been accurate to describe the relationship that developed between Mike, Kennebec and Nolan as a friendship. At first it was more a defensive alliance forced on three not particularly compatible people by the kind of society in which you had to make your alliances where you found them.

Nolan liked everybody in the hut. Mike liked almost everybody. Kennebec never said so in words, but his attitude indicated that he despised each member of the platoon from the marker to the blank file.

These were the three oldest men in the hut. In some ways their maturity was a bulwark against the harsh and nagging encroachments of the new society, and in some ways their maturity magnified the encroachments and made them harder to bear. This, at least, they had in common: they resigned themselves to things more quickly. Kennebec disguised his resignation by remaining the noisiest and most offensive beefer in the platoon, but he was really more resigned than either of the other two; if he had been less aware of the hopelessness of doing anything about anything, he might have been less unpleasant.

Kennebec belonged to a small class which is at least as common inside an army as outside. He was a man of words who had the power to dominate men of action with his words, even though he did not always make his words intelligible. He had developed the insult to such a level of savage competence that victims who normally responded to an insult with an old-fashioned punch in the nose sensed that the normal defenses and retaliations were inadequate. They writhed under his insults. They cursed him for his insults and hated him for them, but they bore them. Kennebec was a small man, almost frail. There was scarcely a man in the hut who had not at some time expressed a determination to perform certain lurid renovations on his pinched, condescending little face, and there were not more than two or three who would not have been capable of doing it, if they had ever summoned the will to try. But nobody ever did try. "You're all afraid of me," Kennebec used to taunt them, and in a manner of speaking, they were.

Nolan was everything that Kennebec was not. He was tall where Kennebec was short. His face was open and humorous where Kennebec's was secretive and angry. Nolan took things easy. His favorite relaxation was a form of colloquy which he called "barbering with a dull razor," a non-incendiary type of repartee in which you could say anything you liked to your vis-a-vis, and he could say anything he liked to you, always provided it was understood neither party meant a word of it. He was least successful with Kennebec. Kennebec always gave the impression of meaning what he said.

The truce between Kennebec and Nolan hinged on so improbable and evanescent a factor as the Y.M.C.A. cup-cake. One Saturday afternoon after dismissal, Mike and Nolan were in the canteen buying cigarettes. The room was crowded and the queue was long and as they shuffled toward the counter in the queue the leaden soggy pathos of the place swirled up around them in a suffocating geyser of melancholy. There was no particular reason why they should have seen it on that particular day, among all days, nor why they should have seen it simultaneously. They had both been in the canteen a hundred times before and never seen anything but its physical properties, which is to say they saw it as a sticky, congested, dirty, badly lighted and otherwise unpleasant centre of commerce presided over by a bored young civilian who obviously felt he was cut out for higher things.

But this time they saw deeper. They saw the two rows of morbid-looking youths sitting bolt upright on two rows of kitchen chairs around the walls, each youth staring emptily to his front, each with a bottle of milk or soda-pop in one hand and an iced cup-cake or chocolate bar in the other, each feeding his robot-moving jaws with robot motions of his hands, none really tasting the food and drink and none failing to taste in them the tasteless-ness of his emasculated, boneless life. They saw the youth three places ahead of them in the queue sweep two bottles of chocolate milk, a nut bar and three date squares into one clutching armful and then, with a desperate gait that was half walk and half trot, beat another similarly burdened youth to a vacant chair in the corner of the room, settle into the chair with a desperate plop and begin cramming his mouth and emptying it again in desperate gulps. They saw that it was neither hunger nor greed that made this sad charade. They saw that the men were doing as they did because there was nothing else for them to do. They all had lacks to fill, and it was as necessary to fill their lacks as to fill their stomachs; they were trying to fill both in the same way. In the haunting awareness of their lacks, they had turned to the hobby of eating as some men with other lacks turned to stamp collecting or raising peonies.

In that moment Mike hated the army more fiercely than he had ever hated it before, and almost as fiercely as he would ever hate it again. He glanced over his shoulder and guessed that Nolan's thoughts were roughly the same as his own. But neither of them could put his thoughts in words and in the face of so much sadness their inarticulateness made them uneasy. They were grateful when they heard Kennebec's high contemptuous squall behind them, saying what they might have said themselves.

"Jesus!" Kennebec was saying. "Look at them! Dope fiends! Slaves! If the narcotics branch knew what went on in these places every wording canteen in Canada would have been padlocked long ago.

"Cup-cakes!" Kennebec jeered. "As the Russians forgot to say, cup-cakes are the opiate of the people. Their girl forgets to write them, so they have a cup-cake. The sergeant bawls them out, so they have a cup-cake. They don't get their pass, so they have a cup-cake."

A young soldier hurried past with a bottle of chocolate milk, two round fruit pies done up in waxed paper, two chocolate bars, and a package of chewing gum.

"Look at that guy!" Kennebec snorted. "From the amount of junk he's packing, he's got more wording trouble than Hitler."

"God, Kennebec!" Nolan said respectfully, "you're a miserable son of a bitch. I guess you're the most miserable son of a bitch in the whole wide wording world."

"You know," Mike said, "it sort of makes a guy pine for a nice greasy mess of pork chops and a long bottle of rot-gut whisky."

"Well," Nolan said, "what's holding us back? I got dough."

At the door, Mike looked to see if Kennebec was following them. He wasn't. Mike went back.

"Why not get out of here?" he said to Kennebec. "Nolan and I are going downtown to buy a jug."

Kennebec looked surprised. "Sure," he said, "I'll come. Everybody can't get drunk on cup-cakes." Of such slender fabrics are alliances formed in any army.

Mike was the cornerstone of the alliance. Kennebec and Nolan still didn't get along too well, but Mike smoothed over most of their crises with a mixture of tact and brute stubbornness. Occasionally, when straight pacifism failed to work, he would thrust an artificial bond on the other two by deliberately antagonizing them both. It was a lot of trouble, but most of the time Mike thought the trouble was worth while. Nolan was easy to like, and although it was almost impossible to like Kennebec, there was something fascinating in his undefeatable superiority and wrath.

They moved on to Camp Borden in the same draft, and when they were being documented at the advanced training centre, they asked to be allowed to remain together. They were assigned to the same platoon for training as infantry reinforcements and were told that with normal luck they would eventually find their way to the same battalion in England.

The novelty of the army wore off for Mike and Nolan; Kennebec had never admitted there was any novelty in it for him. The accepted measurements of time ceased to have much significance for any of them, except when they were on pass. In camp, the difference between a day and a week was no more significant or memorable than the difference between greasy roast beef and boiled potatoes and greasy pork and turnips. They learned the same things week after week and became so weary of learning them that they forgot them and learned them all over again.

The thing that kept them interested in the army, if interested was the right word, was the knowledge that some day they would be going to England, and some day after that, they would actually be going to war. All the kit inspections, all the foot drill, all the panting over obstacle courses, all the P.T., all the lying on the dusty ranges under the hot sun, could not alter the fact that some day their being in the army would have a meaning. They thirsted for the return of meaning to their lives as animals thirst for an issue to their blood. They did not know what it was they thirsted for; they thought they thirsted for a change of scenery, a change of routine and the excitement of being nearer to the war, but what they really thirsted for was meaning. They swallowed endless rumors about imminent drafts for overseas. The rumors always failed them, but at least, in a small way, they relieved the tedium of waiting. Four months after they arrived at Borden, Nolan burst into the hut with the announcement: "Big overseas draft positively going out Friday. Got it from a fellow who works in the orderly room."

"Word!" Kennebec snorted, "you're still not going for that stuff?"

"No," Nolan said thoughtfully, "but it's the only game in town."

In the spring they voted on what they thought was a national plebiscite for or against overseas conscription. Mike and Nolan marked their ballots in the affirmative, but Kennebec maintained his position as a perpetual minority by voting the other way. "They started to raise the army as if they were running a frat rush," Kennebec explained sourly. "Let 'em finish it that way. Besides, all the wording little R boys have worked themselves into such a stew by now that they wouldn't be any good anyway. I don't want to wind up sharing a trench with a guy that had to be dragged over by his heels screaming for mamma."

While Mike was waiting in the queue at the polling booth, a corporal came out of the booth waving a pencil and gloating: "Bang! And another zombie bit the dust!"

"What's a zombie?" Mike asked.

"Haven't you heard it yet?" the corporal grinned. "That's the new name for the R boys."

One night early in September the platoon sergeant went around the hut and made every member of the platoon sign a paper that announced itself as a "warning for special duty." Any soldier who was absent from his quarters after the twelfth would be liable to punishment as a deserter, not as an ordinary A.W.L.

The sergeant grinned: "No, they didn't tell me what it means either. But my guess is the same as yours."

They went on embarkation leave and then remained in camp, sitting out what Kennebec called "the automatic wait."

They sailed on the Queen Elizabeth. Mike, Kennebec and Nolan crammed their kit into three of the four tiers of a bunk in E deck and watched the other tiers fill up like a dark and foetid honeycomb. The loading of the ship wasn't finished until two days after their draft embarked. Kennebec said he had no interest in ships, but Mike and Nolan explored every cranny of the liner that wasn't barricaded by the M.P.'s and spent hours looking at her ancient guns and banks of rocket frames.

Hour after hour, struggling columns of men tugged up the gangplanks with their heavy kit, disappeared through the holes in the grey sides of the ship and debouched among its labyrinthine entrails. There were airforcemen and soldiers of a dozen regiments, the best part of one whole division and odds and ends of several others, and as they seeped into the last corner of deck space, the resting ship seemed to throb with vitality and dynamism. There was strength to this and direction—above all direction—and Mike was part of it; whatever happened they would never be able to take that away from him.

The ship muzzled away from the dockside at ten o'clock in the morning, moving cautiously and crabwise into the harbor in the wake of her straining tugs. It was a bright morning. The decks were jammed. There was no band and there were not many people on the docks to see them off, but those who were there waved.

Mike leaned on the rail and looked out over the docks to the grey city and its green backdrop of hills, and told himself that this was the last he would see of Canada for a long time. He felt a current of nostalgia running through him and he fed the nostalgia deliberately, with a kind of planned gourmandizing, doling out little morsels of memory and repining one at a time. The valley at home was one, still parched and yellow now from the heat of summer, sloping beneath its yellow prairie grass toward the tarnished silver filament of the river. His brother Joe was another, striding down the valley and swinging an empty berry pail. School and playing ball were one and the bakery and the people he had got to know there another. Pop, sitting in the big blue chair, talking, was one. And Joe Junior, taking his first step.

He saved Tina until near the last. He dwelled lingeringly on their parting and how she had looked when he said there would be no other women and how she had whispered: "Don't promise. But try. Try hard, Mike."

A woman in a red dress was standing on a wooden pile at the end of the dock, waving a white handkerchief, waving good-bye. And it could really be good-bye. Perhaps he would never come back at all. The thought was too big to encompass, but toying with the filmy shining edges of it was not unpleasant. He put his hand across his eyes and felt an unmistakable drop of moisture.

"That's right." Kennebec's rasping voice stung through his solitude like a jet of acetylene. "That's right," Kennebec said, "have a real good cry. It'll do you good."

He glowered down into Kennebec's mocking face and then shoved his way angrily down the rail. Some day, he promised himself, he would punch Kennebec's wording face for him. Hard.

CHAPTER

9

Mike spent a year, seven months and two days in England. Among the people who specialized in the study of world relations at the basic levels, there were some who would have said the experience made him an anglophile and others who would have said it made him an anglophobe. In truth he became neither; on the day he left he was of substantially the same species as on the day he arrived—he was a foreigner doing his best to understand a foreign country and not succeeding any better or any worse than the circumstances made it reasonable to expect. He knew the English better at the end of his stay than he had known them at the beginning. He had even been influenced, in certain minor respects, by their ways; he said "cinema", "petrol" and "lift", for example. But they were not the same people as his people, nor was their country the same as his country, and although he liked to tell himself that his understanding of both the country and the people matched his knowledge of them, the very evanescence and instability of his views should have been proof enough to him that it did not.

Being a foreigner, he disliked the English for the most implausible of reasons and liked them for reasons which, in

appraising his own countrymen, he would have considered trivial
or irrevelant. He disliked them for the blackout and liked them
for the flat half-section of ruin between Ludgate Circus and St.
Paul's. He disliked them for their Brussels sprouts and liked them
for their Sunday movies. He disliked them for making him press
Button A before he could make himself heard on the telephone
and liked them for providing policemen who always knew the way
to Marble Arch. He disliked them for Lady Astor and liked them
for Nathaniel Gubbins. He disliked them for the way their officers
said "Ectuelleh," and liked them for the way the barmaids said
"Dearie". He disliked them for closing the pubs at three o'clock
in the afternoon and ten o'clock at night and liked them for having
pubs at all. He disliked them for the taxi drivers who overcharged
him and liked them for the bus conductresses who wouldn't take
his money. He disliked them for the way they said "You cawn't
miss it," and liked them for the way they called him "Canader."
He disliked them for the B.B.C. and liked them for the Windmill
and Phyllis Dixey. He disliked them for their dingy N.A.A.F.I.
canteens and liked them for the Lyons Corner House. He disliked
them for Aldershot and liked them for Trafalgar Square.

In fact, his view of England never really reached the full
stature of an opinion. It was a shifting bed of prejudice, for and
against, which always rolled away from him just when he felt he
was getting his feet planted in it. For long periods sometimes—once
when the Eighth Army was driving across the North African
desert, another time after he had been caught in an air raid in
London—he was filled with the same reverent awe which exposure
to the standard school curriculum of Saskatchewan and to the
columns of the Toronto Telegram and the Globe and Mail had
induced him to believe was the only possible attitude for a right-
thinking Canadian to adopt toward the English. And for other
long periods the English filled him with that unanalyzable mixture
of distrust, suspicion, jealousy and condescension which was the

more or less inevitable result of discovering that somebody had been trying to foist a lie on him and that the English weren't a damned bit better than he was.

Once, in a bar, a prosperous-looking stranger bought him a drink. Mike asked the man politely if he had ever been to Canada. The man said: "No, but I've knocked about the other colonies a good deal." It was a week before Mike was ready to quit hating the English again.

Another time, he met a Canadian air force sergeant who said he worked in public relations. The air force man told him that as far as most of the R.C.A.F. was concerned, Mike could have the Limeys.

"Look at their wording papers!" the air force man said. " 'Lancasters and Halifaxes of the R.A.F. bombed the German Baltic port of Stettin in great numbers last night'. Listen to the B.B.C. 'The R.A.F. were out in force over the Ruhr last night'. R.A.F.! R.A.F.! Nothing but the wording R.A.F.!" the air force man fumed. "More than half the guys on every mission are from Canada or New Zealand or Australia, but the way the Limeys put it in the papers, it's nobody but the Limeys up there getting their guts full of flak night after night. It's bad enough that they won't tell their own people how much the Canadians are doing—they won't even let us tell Canada what they're doing. My boss has been fighting for months to get the Air Ministry censors to pass a statement that nearly forty percent of all the air crew flying out of R.A.F. stations are Canadians. There's no security in it, but they just wouldn't pass it. They finally let him say it was twenty-five per cent and even that was a struggle." Mike hated the English for another little while.

It was usually Nolan who, so to speak, took his more violent prejudices off his hands. Nolan's approach to the English was much less complicated than his own; from the start, Nolan simply patronized them. He spent most of his first furlough in London

in and around the American Red Cross Rainbow Corner on
Shaftesbury Avenue, looking for and occasionally finding soldiers
he had known at home, and he returned to Aldershot with a neat
little file of phrases and sayings for all occasions.

"England! The white man's burden!" Nolan used to say.

And, in the days before it had become a cliche: "Some day
us Yanks are gonna cut the cables on those barrage balloons and
let this whole wording island sink back into the ocean."

Nolan's tone of barbless banter, and the innate affection for
people that sat on his features like a sandwich board made it
possible for him to say things like that, even to Englishmen, without giving offense. Nevertheless, Mike felt a queer compulsion to
answer him.

"Hell!" he would snort, "These wording Limeys had the war
won before you Yanks even knew it was started."

And: "Word! If it wasn't for the Limeys you'd be saying that
in German."

For all three of them, for Mike and Nolan and, surprisingly,
even for Kennebec, the only real penetration that they made
beneath the surface of England was forced on them by a Sunday
evening supper in the home of an Aldershot greengrocer's clerk.

The supper itself was forced on them by one of the incurable
busybodies of the Army Auxiliary Services who had arranged to
have twenty-four presumably lonely soldiers partake of official
"hospitality" and then found himself with only twenty-one candi-
dates. He pleaded with Mike, Nolan and Kennebec to avail
themselves of the invitation of Mr. and Mrs. Robert Stansgate.

The Stansgates lived in a small brick house with their daughter
Pamela, aged eighteen; their son Richard, twelve; a photograph
of their older son, Harry, a member of the Eighth Army; a few
plush parlor chairs whose color had once been purple; a sagging
oak dining table; an equally sagging sideboard surmounted by a
slightly chipped plate bearing the likeness of King George the

Fifth and a porcelain beer mug made in the image of Winston Churchill; a lacquered sea shell inscribed "Souvenir of Blackpool"; a wall portrait of Mr. Stansgate; another wall portrait, in color, of the winner of the nineteen twenty-three Epsom Derby, on which Mr. Stansgate had wagered two pounds, ten shillings at odds of a hundred to seven; a W.C. that leaked; and numerous closely affiliated relics and rewards of an honest lower-middle-class family life, not the least of which was the subdued but ageless odor of boiled cabbage.

Mrs. Stansgate was a small, drab, friendly woman whose hair, it was difficult to avoid feeling, would have been more becoming if it had abandoned its foredoomed struggle to remain the color of moleskin and turned white instead. Mr. Stansgate was on the small side too, but except that he wore glasses and smoked a pipe, it was difficult to notice anything in particular about him. The daughter Pamela had a pleasant face and a clear complexion, although her teeth were somewhat too large. The son Richard was big for his age, and better looking than his sister.

The Stansgates greeted them heartily and they sat down to supper right away. Mrs. Stansgate said she always liked to serve a meal piping hot. Mr. Stansgate said that in more than twenty years of married life he had only been asked to eat one cold supper and that was when Mrs. Stansgate was at her sister-in-law's helping to nurse her through an illness. Mr. Stansgate said he didn't know how some men put up with it the way their wives neglected things around the house. Mrs. Stansgate blushed and said maybe she'd surprise Mr. Stansgate one of these days. Nolan said he liked his meals served hot too, and the trouble in the army was that the food was often cold. Kennebec said half the cooks in the army didn't care whether you ate your food hot or cold, just so long as they got through in time to go to the pub.

Mr. Stansgate said Mrs. Stansgate called the dish spam rissole but he called it plain old eggs and spam. Mr. Stansgate added that whatever you called it, it suited them all right.   Mrs. Stansgate said the last time she made it she had more powdered egg, and personally she liked it better that way.   Mike said it tasted just right to him.   Mrs. Stansgate said she had been going to serve pilchards, but tinned pilchards went up three points last week and the fresh ones weren't in yet.   Nolan said he liked pilchards too, but he really preferred spam, if it was cooked nice with a bit of sauce on it.   Mike said he liked spam better than pilchards too.   Kennebec said they would have to get Mrs. Stansgate to give their battalion cook the recipe for spam rissole.   They all laughed.

Mrs. Stansgate asked if they noticed anything about the greens. Kennebec said all he noticed was that they were mighty good.   Mr. Stansgate said, see Mother, what did I say.   And then Mr. Stansgate revealed that Mrs. Stansgate had cooked the greens American style.   Mrs. Stansgate said it was really quite simple, anybody could do it, you just put less water in with the greens and didn't boil them quite so long.   Mike said he knew there was something about the greens.   He said he hadn't tasted cabbage like that since he left home.

After supper Mr. Stansgate brought out three quart bottles of Whitbread's Ale.   Mrs. Stansgate said she didn't think she'd have any because beer always made her sleepy right after a big meal, and Pamela said she didn't think she'd have any either. Mike and Nolan helped Pamela with the dishes and when they were finished they came back and sat in the room where they had eaten, and drank some more ale.

Mr. Stansgate asked how the beer in England compared with the beer over home.   Nolan said it was a lot better.   He said American beer was only around four percent.   Mike said Canadian beer was stronger than that, but he liked English beer.   Mr. Stansgate said there wasn't enough grain to make real beer any more, but if American beer was like Nolan said it was, he was

just as pleased he'd never gone to America. If the beer was like
Nolan said, Mr. Stansgate said he'd start a revolution. Mrs.
Stansgate said the funny thing was he would.

Mrs. Stansgate asked if any of them had ever been to Blackpool and they said they hadn't but had always wanted to. Mr.
Stansgate told them about the trip the Stansgates had taken to
Blackpool three years before the war. Mrs. Stansgate interrupted
him near the start to say that she thought it was four years before
the war. Mr. Stansgate said he was sure it was three years, and
they referred the matter to Pamela, who decided her father was
right. Mr. Stansgate finished telling about Blackpool.

Mrs. Stansgate asked if it was right about the high wages in
America. Nolan said they were probably higher all right, but
living was higher too. Mr. Stansgate asked what a greengrocer's
clerk would get in America and Nolan said he might get thirty-
five dollars a week. Pamela said that was eight, almost nine quid.
Mr. Stansgate said, lumme, that was almost three times what he
was making before the war. Yes, Mrs. Stansgate said, but remember what he said about it costing more to live. Well, for instance,
Mr. Stansgate said, what would rent cost you in America for a
house like this. Nolan said it would cost forty or forty-five dollars
a month. Mr. Stansgate asked what it would cost in Canada.
Mike said it would cost about the same. Kennebec said it might
cost five dollars less. Mr. Stansgate looked pleased and asked
them to guess what he was paying for this house. Nolan said it
must be a good seven pounds a month, even allowing for cheaper
rents. Mike and Kennebec said it must be at least that much.
Mr. Stansgate said well, he would tell them and they could believe
it or not as they pleased. On second thought, Mr. Stansgate said
he would let his wife tell them. Mrs. Stansgate told them the
rent was sixteen bob a week. Nolan said he wouldn't have believed
it. Mike said he wouldn't have believed it either. Kennebec said
that was less than half what you'd pay at home. Mr. Stansgate

said they were a little slow over here, no doubt about that, but you generally found things evened out wherever you lived.

Mr. Stansgate told them about their son Harry in the Eighth Army and Pamela read them part of Harry's last letter where he told about drinking goat's milk from an Arab's goat. Mrs. Stansgate said she wondered if they would like to see the parcel they were just about to finish doing up for Harry. They said they would, and Pamela brought the parcel out of the sideboard and showed them what was inside.

There were twelve packages of Capstan cigarettes and eight packages of Woodbines. There was a small tinned plum pudding and two jars of home-made pickles. And at the last Pamela showed them a small tin of salmon.

Mrs. Stansgate told them how she had happened to find the salmon. She told them how many points the salmon had cost, and how difficult it was to get salmon these days even if you had the points. Mr. Stansgate said well they'd better hurry up and send it or the salmon wouldn't be there very long. Mrs. Stansgate said Mr. Stansgate liked salmon almost as much as Harry did. Mr. Stansgate said that was plenty. Mrs. Stansgate said even when salmon was easy to get, she could remember that boy eating a whole tin of it just for a snack. Pamela said she bet Harry would just die when he opened the parcel and saw the salmon.

They left at ten o'clock. The Stansgates saw them to the sidewalk and made them promise to come again. Mike and Kennebec and Nolan all said they would, but they knew they wouldn't and the Stansgates knew they wouldn't too.

"Why do they do it?" Kennebec said fiercely as they walked back through the quiet moonlit streets. "I'll bet they've been through that same wording performance every Sunday night since Harry went away. The same performance every week, right from the last sick little joke about the beer and the last shred of testimony whether it was nineteen thirty-five or nineteen thirty-six they went to Blackpool, right down to the last mouthful of spam rissole. And I don't suppose it ever did work. I don't suppose anybody ever did walk out that gate without feeling they'd just been let out of jail. And I don't suppose those people ever hung over the fence and said good-bye without feeling the same way. You could see it; we kept thinking, Jesus! these people are boring, and they were thinking the same thing about us."

Mike said: "I guess that wording spam rissole cost them a week's points too. They'll go on short rations all week just to feed three strangers who'd get a better meal by staying in barracks and more entertainment out of a hanging."

"The thing that got me," Nolan said, "was that song and dance about the tin of salmon. I could have cried. It nearly made me bust out and cry."

"I think I know what makes them do it," Kennebec said after a while. Kennebec's voice was not as it usually was; it was a little puzzled and almost respectful. "I think it's because somebody has persuaded them it's the right thing to do. From then on it doesn't matter whether it works or not. It's the right thing to do and by word, they'll do it, come hell or high water. Maybe the vicar told them, or somebody in the Salvation Army, or maybe they figured it was something they had to do for Harry. It doesn't matter where the idea came from. They accepted the proposition that what they were doing was the right thing to do, and after they got sold on that, nothing could stop them. You could curl up and die before their eyes with spam rissole coming out of your ears. You could fall into a fit in the middle of the old man's story about Blackpool. You could get so desperate that you'd rear up and shout: 'My God! The dam has burst!' or 'My God! The Germans have just dropped eight divisions of paratroops at Horsham!' but that wouldn't stop them either. There is no power this side of the grave that would stop them."

"It was the salmon that got me," Nolan repeated. "I wanted to cry."

"Yes," Kennebec said, "and it was second-grade salmon at that. Everything was second-grade, their house, their furniture, their conversation, their cooking. But that's all right, it's good enough, it suits them. Even their dreams are second-grade. You remember how the old lady said yes, it's a nice little house but she did hope they'd be able to get a nice rug when the war's over. And how the old man said, well they had hard times in the past all right, but now it looked as though they were going to get Beveridge and it would be a different country for everybody. How he was worrying about what Harry would do when he got back but now he didn't have to worry so much because Harry would never really be up against it if they got Beveridge. What's Beveridge? Two pounds a week, or is it one pound ten? I forget. The brave new world boils down to twenty-five bucks a month and a thirty-two dollar carpet and that's good enough too." Kennebec's words were not overlaid with the chronic superiority and contempt, but only with respect and wonder.

"Be careful, Kennebec," Mike said, "you sound almost humble."

"I guess that's the way I felt," Nolan cut in, "I guess that's why I wanted to cry."

Mike said: "I don't know that people like that need our pity. I don't know that they need our approval either. But from now on they can have either one from me, or both, if they need it."

Nolan said: "I'm still not going to get excited about them. I'm still glad I don't have to live here. But from here in anybody that wants to sell me on the idea that they're greedy and scheming and that my country ought to steer away from them is going to have quite a sale on his hands. Maybe it's true that the people who run the country for them want to fix it so the world will always be eating out of their hand. But I'm wording sure that's not what the old man and the old lady back there want. All they want is two quid a week and a new rug, like Kennebec said. And

Harry back home from the desert. I guess that's all they ever did want. It's not much. It's less than our janitor gets."

From then on they were less preoccupied with the complexities of the English character. They took the English the way the English had taken them, indulgently and companionably, although a little gingerly and with the unspoken understanding that when all was said and done it would be much better for everybody when they could go home.

Nolan formed a series of highly transitory alliances with a series of barmaids, shopgirls, lady munitions hands and red cross workers, and rendered it as his considered judgment that "These dames aren't bad once you get used to their chattering and chirping." Kennebec went steady for almost two months with a school teacher, but fell out with her on the joint issues of free love and Munich. Mike remained faithful to Tina, but admitted the project wasn't as easy as he had thought it was going to be.

At the end of their first spring in England, all three were posted from their reinforcement unit to an infantry battalion of the Third Division. As they moved into their new bivouac in a forest near the South coast, Mike felt again, for the first time since he had roamed the crowded decks of the Queen Elizabeth, a galvanism and suspense, as though he were queueing up before a turnstile to history. The queue was long and a little confusing; you couldn't see what was at the end of it, but you knew it was something big and important and you felt big and important yourself. It was still a secret that the Third Division would be one of the assault divisions when the second front was opened, but it was an open secret. Everybody in the division knew it. The division had been training for the job for almost two years.

Mike worked hard. He learned to handle his rifle, the Bren gun, the PIAT anti-tank projector, the two-inch mortar, the grenade and the bayonet, and learned not merely to the satisfaction of his instructors but to his own. While they toiled and panted and cursed and groaned through the wracking drudgery of battle school, he drove himself even more relentlessly than the instructors did, and finally he was as well content with the condition of his body as with the condition of his aptitudes. He was a good soldier in those days—such a good soldier that Nolan and Kennebec took to casting knowing leers at him and making rude smacking sounds with their lips. The prophecy implicit in this popular form of barracks comment was duly fulfilled. Mike acquired one stripe and then a second, and finally a third. And before he had been eating very long in the sergeants' mess, he was being considered for an officers' training course.

His career in the higher strata ended one day in the colonel's office after he had come back two days overdue from a nine-day leave in Scotland.

"There's no explanation, sir," he said miserably, "I just slipped. I'm sorry, sir." And there was no explanation that would have meant anything on a charge sheet. They couldn't put a girl with red hair, four thousand miles away, on an army charge sheet. They couldn't put a little boy on it, or a village in Saskatchewan, or a four-room flat in North Toronto. They couldn't put the nights of lying alone in an army cot, or the ache in your empty arms, the nights of wondering what you were doing here, in this strange lonely place, waiting to fulfill the strange lonely tasks that you had set out upon a million years ago. All they could put was "A.W.L. Reduced to ranks."

When Mike moved his kit back from the sergeants' hut, Nolan said: "Welcome home, general." And Kennebec said: "Don't look now, sir, but I think you're on kitchen fatigue tomorrow." Mike growled, "Go to hell!" but it wasn't bad to be back at that.

In the summer he got a letter from his brother saying that Joe had been drafted at last.

Excitedly he wrote back: "When you get over here, let me know right away, and I can claim you into the regiment. It's a good outfit. You'll like it."

Joe's reply was a long time in coming and when it did come, it was evasive. "I don't figure I'll be over there for a while yet," he wrote. "There'll be plenty of time to make plans then."

They went on several schemes, living on compo rations, kit pared down to battle order, and rumors. The rumors were not just ordinary, private, army rumors. They were public and epidemic. By the time winter ended the whole country throbbed with them, as the sky above it throbbed with the bombers crossing the Channel by night and day. Eisenhower and Montgomery were back from the Mediterranean. They began to see the gaudy flash of SHAEF everywhere. The streets of London filled and overflowed with American soldiers and then, with a subdued and ominous drama, the streets began to empty. And then England was sealed off from the rest of the world and the coasts of England were sealed off from the rest of England. And into the coasts, through the barbed wire and past the sentries, as into the slavering maw of destiny, the men and weapons poured.

For a while they thought their last exercise was going to be the real thing. But the landing craft scudded back to the coast of England and they splashed ashore again to storm imaginary objectives in the face of imaginary resistance from an imaginary enemy. They dried out feeling half relieved and half defrauded.

And then, in May, they went to their marshalling area. There was a new set of loading tables to be studied, a new job of waterproofing to be done on their vehicles, a new assembly line of letters to be dropped into green envelopes, beginning: "Well, by the time you get this, I guess . . ."

They sat in a ring beside their tents on the bare dusty floor of a forest and heard the official news from a twenty-two-year-old boy with two faded diamonds showing on each shoulder of his battledress where he had cut the officers' pips away.

"It's the real thing this time," the boy said. There was no cheering, but still a noise went around the ring of men, a mass ejaculation that was part sigh and yet not all sigh, that was part gasp and not all gasp, that was boasting and challenge and triumph and fear, and being all of those was really none. In the silence that followed, a soldier sitting near the back of the ring uttered a shrilly doleful cry: "Well, word!"

Everybody laughed. Walking back to his tent, Mike told himself it was just as well that posterity got its dope on great happenings from the official files. Twenty years from now, they'd be teaching his kids that when this monumental adventure was launched, somebody stood up with his hand over his chest and said: "Don't shoot until you see the whites of their eyes," or "Lafayette! We are here!" or something equally appropriate to the importance of the occasion. But he would know better. He'd know that among the men who had to do the shooting, the only observation that had found expression was: "Well, word!"

Maybe it was as intelligent an observation as any, at that. He sat down on the edge of his mattress and started writing a letter to Tina.

CHAPTER

10

He wished Rinowski would stop talking.

He rubbed a damp hand across his wet forehead and then carefully wiped the sweat away on the bristly nap of his tunic. He loosened another button of the tunic and reached behind him in the dark to adjust the inflated rubber life belt beneath his head. The air was hot and thick, as it had been aboard the liner almost two years ago, but now and then a little gust of freshness plopped past the blackout curtain and brushed its soothing breath against his face. You could smell the sea in these gusts, faintly, as you heard it stroking at the thin bulkheads. The force of the sea was not sufficient to rock the ship. It pitched a little sometimes and slipped when it changed course, but the motion was slow and steady. Stealthy. The motion was almost as stealthy as the stealthy thrum of the motors, cut to half speed and thrumming through the night silence in a conspiratorial, wary undertone. You could imagine the ship was listening for something and did not want to make too much noise lest it fail to hear.

The men were not in bunks. They were lying close together on their blankets on the floor, unrecognizable and formless and, for the time, uncomprehending. Most of them were asleep or lying

quietly in the darkness and willing sleep to come. Mike was sure
he would be able to sleep if Rinowski would stop talking.

Rinowski had a monotonous voice. It was high-pitched and
almost childish in tone, the voice of a boy, and although he was
trying to keep it low, it carried. His attempts to keep it low
merely made it flat. There was no inflection in it, and Rinowski
sounded like a schoolboy reciting, droning his words by rote without fully understanding them.

"The wife and me used to bowl a lot," Rinowski said. "That
was when she was working for Eaton's. The wife's a good bowler.
She can still beat me as often as I beat her nearly. She's good at
picking up splits. She don't get as many strikes as I do, but she
spares up them splits. Well this night we went bowling. I forget
if she beat me or I beat her. It's funny I don't remember. Usually
we had a bet. I used to bet two bits against her fifteen cents. She
beat me a lot. I'd get more strikes than her but she picked it up
on spares."

Mike turned on his side and pulled the life-belt into the U of
his neck, allowing his head to loll back across its bloated curve.

Rinowski was saying: "This night we went to the drug store,
the one near Coxwell, and we were just sitting there talking when
I told the wife she was going to marry me. I forget what we were
talking about. About the bowling most likely. We'd had a couple
of beers and I guess I was feeling kinda cocky and I just said:
'You're going to marry me,' just like that. The wife said after
you could have knocked her over with a feather. She let on she
didn't take me seriously but I said I meant it and finally she said:
'Well, if you do, ask me again tomorrow and see what I say.' I
didn't know if she wanted me to ask her again or not. I nearly
didn't. I kept thinking all the next day, 'I'll bet she's laughing
at me', and I nearly didn't ask her again at all. The wife comes
from a real good family. One of the best families in the Beach.
Her uncle was an alderman. Everybody knew him. He run for

board of control one year but got beat. He nearly won but when
he got beat he just dropped out of it. He had a good job anyway."

Mike twisted his head away from the life belt. He half raised
his body and dragged the blanket across the deck under him until
there was enough of it above his shoulders to roll into a little
pillow. The steel deck was like bone pressing against the bone
of his hips, but his head rested easier. He listened to the motors
and the slapping of the sea on the bulkheads, trying to make them
exclude Rinowski's voice, but it was no use.

"The wife and me had a big wedding," Rinowski was saying.
"We had the reception afterwards at her uncle's place. That was
the alderman. Alderman Harry Aitken. The wife's got all kinds
of friends. We had all kinds of little things on trays at the reception. We had six jugs of whisky and three jugs of gin. No beer
though. The wife said a wedding was no place to serve beer. My
old man pretended to be real sore about it. He said if any son of
his ever got married again and there was no beer they could count
him out. My old man likes his beer. He don't drink any more
than he can handle, but he likes it. He don't like whisky. I don't
like it much either. I'd rather have beer."

Mike raised the upper part of his body on one hand and levered
himself to his feet. He stood erect for a minute, swaying with the
easy motion of the ship and peering down at the dark deck until
his eyes had picked out a channel among the sleeping men. When
he was sure of the channel, he walked through it to the steel
companionway and up the steps past the blackout curtain into a
dark corridor. He guided himself along the corridor with his
hand, turned his body sideways and edged it through another
blackout curtain. The air hit his face fresh and strong and he
bent his head away from it, opening his mouth to expel the first
draught, which had splashed into his lungs with the sharp force
of a cold douche. It was a while before he could bring himself
to raise his face into the wind again.

At first all he could see was the sky, which seemed as uniform and obdurate in its blackness as the heavy canvas curtain at the end of the corridor. Then he saw that it was shot with smears of slate-grey, and with something like a thrill he saw a star hanging close to one of the smears. But the main expanse of the sky was sulky and remote, as if it saw a portent and wished to withdraw itself from what was about to happen and have no part of it.

Mike moved to the side of the ship and put his hands on the wet rail to brace himself. Until his eyes were drawn into harmony with the darkness, he did not look across the sea, but into it, peering straight down over the rail to the slanting ruff of phosphorous that flared away from the bows, gleaming like neon on the ebony of the sea. He watched this until, just beyond the edge of the phosphorous, he distinguished the flabby black shoulder of a wave shrugging gangway to the ship. Then he searched the sea, carefully and painstakingly, probing into all its latitudes and corners. The first companion ship he saw was level with the starboard bow and not far away. It had no shape or being of its own; it was independent of neither the sea nor the night, but was like a tumor of them both, a black formless growth that clung to the sea and the night and could go only where they willed to take it. He did not dare to take his eyes off the ship for fear that he might not be able to find it again, but at last he left it and looked for others.

There was another directly behind the first, and another further away, abreast of the stern. And suddenly a fourth stood out bravely against the barely visible line between the sea and the sky. This one stood out not as a growth or a shadow, but as a ship; it had funnels, and the black triangle which moved above it along the dim backdrop of the horizon was unmistakably a gun turret. This was a warship. It might be a battleship and at the least it was a cruiser. Moreover the warship had volition and power of its own. Its course was not the same as the courses of the other ships and it moved faster than they did; it was not a creature of the sea or the night. It could go where it chose, it was beyond the run of the sea and free of it, the ship was a sign— no, a proof, a promise—that there were still men abroad who were not bound in hostage to the sea and the night, who could still will where they were to go, who could still will whether they were to live or die and make their will bear fruit. The warship could plunge on in the swell of the sea or it could cut across the swell and turn back. As though to confirm the point, it changed course again and was soon engulfed in the darkness.

A sentry walked up behind Mike and told him: "Nobody allowed up here, mate."

Mike explained: "I couldn't sleep. It's stuffy."

"All right. Watch out for officers."

Mike moved toward the stern of the ship and stood for a while looking at the inky sled-like bottom of an assault boat which hung from davits above the rail.

A man in a shallow woollen toque and a heavy turtle-neck sweater came and stood beside him.

"You for that one, mate?" the man asked.

"No," Mike said, "Mine's on the other side."

"First time, I guess?"

"First time for keeps."

"It's never as bad as they think", the man said. "It never has been anyway."

"You Navy?" Mike asked.

"Combined Ops. This is our fifth."

"That's a lot," Mike said.

"Torch. That was North Africa. Sicily and Messina and then Anzio. We get in and out," the sailor said apologetically.

Mike asked him: "How do they seem, going in?"

"Them things?"

"No," Mike said. "The men. The army."

"All right," the man said. "Good."

"I mean do they—" Mike said, "Do they seem—"

"Afraid?" the man said. Mike was grateful to the sailor for using the word for him. He had not wanted to use it himself. He was not afraid and did not want the sailor to think he was. But the subject interested him. He wanted to hear about it.

The sailor stood unspeaking for a moment, while they listened to the stealthy hum of the ship's motors and felt the gentle vibration of its decks under their feet.

"A lot of them, yes," the sailor said. "But it doesn't seem to make much difference. Sometimes the ones that are afraid are better than the ones that aren't. And none of them ever know they won't be afraid. Some of them know they will be, but nobody ever knows he won't be, right until the last. Some people say you can tell which way they'll be from their eyes or the way they talk. My mate says you can tell from their hands. But you can only tell if they're going to be afraid. If they're not going to get the wind up there's no way you can tell. It's like putting a beer in front of a stranger. If he picks it up and holds it to the light, you know he's going to drink it. But if he doesn't pick it up right away you don't know he's not going to drink it. I'm always windy," the sailor went on. "But I never know when it's coming on. All of a sudden there it is, and there's nothing you can do about it."

A glow of impatience came over Mike, an urge to get back to the hold, to the privacy of the floor and his blanket. He wanted to lie in solitude with this new discovery and to try to winnow a meaning from it. It seemed a good discovery to him and an important one, and he wanted to examine it.

But the sailor was still talking.

"It's no use worrying about whether you'll be windy or not. I'll tell you one thing to watch, though. They never watch it the first time, but it's worth watching. They gave you two paper

bags to spew in. Don't forget them and don't lose them. It's
no use deciding you won't be sick. In a good swell nearly
everybody is sick. Some of them say it doesn't matter, if the
worst they get on them is spew they'll be bloody lucky. But there's
no use spewing on yourself if you can help it. It doesn't do any
good and it stinks like bloody hell."

Mike thanked him and left. "Well, I've got to try and get some
sleep."

"Good luck," the sailor said.

"Good luck."

He paused at the outer hatchway and listened while a plane
muttered in and out of hearing in the distance. Then he felt his
way back down the companionway to his blanket, groped for the
little ball at its head and lay down again. At first he thought
Rinowski had gone to sleep, but the toneless litany began again,
blending a third monotone with the hum of the ship's throttled-
down motors and the stroking wash of the sea against her plates.

"The wife always had a dog," Rinowski was saying. "I never
liked dogs. But this dog she's got now is no trouble at all. It's
just like a person some of the things it does. Not tricks. It don't
hardly do any tricks at all. But it's smart and some of the things
it does you can see it thinking just like a person. It's an airedale.
Airedales are supposed to be mean but don't let anybody tell you
that. Our dog's name is Spike. The wife named him that. She
said she named him from his hair. His hair is spiky. Wherever
the wife goes the dog goes, but if she don't want him to go in she
just tells him to wait outside and when she comes out, if it's an
hour or five hours, he's there sitting and waiting for her. Maybe
it's a store where they won't let dogs in, or an apartment of some
girl that don't like dogs around. It don't matter. The dog just
sits there and waits if it's an hour or five hours."

After a long while a new man came down the companionway
and stood at its foot for a few moments, looking uncertainly at the

sleeping men, as though he could not make up his mind to disturb them. Then he said loudly: "All right!" He repeated it, more loudly still: "All right!"

The new man played a flashlight around the room. Now and then he would catch a soldier full in the face with the light and hold it there while the soldier blinked his eyes open, stared vacantly into the light until he remembered where he was, and then stumbled to his feet. When there was enough room for him to move about, the new man walked across the hold and turned a switch on the wall. A single electric light bulb winked to life, yellow and very dim, and as the men rose from the floor, stretching and scratching and tugging the twists out of their battle-dress, their shadows danced between the steel ribs of the bulkheads like deformed giants in some silent tribal rite.

Soon they were all on their feet and soon they all remembered where they were. At first no one spoke in anything but the lowest undertone. Finally a man belched. It was a firm and deliberate belch and it produced such a satisfying ring that its author belched again. This second belch was even better than the first. It was solemn without being pompous, eloquent without being flowery, rueful without being downcast and droll without being flippant. The belch said a great deal. It said, for instance: "Ho hum, what a way to make a living!" It said: "Come! Now let us to the task!" It said: "Our dog's name is Spike. The wife named him that." It said: "Our Father which art in Heaven; hallowed be Thy name."

Under the familiar impetus of the belch, the fractured hush disintegrated and the hold became almost cheery, with the half-forced, half-grumbling cheeriness of any reveille. "Hey sarge!" someone shouted. "When do we get our wording breakfast?" The man who had come in and turned on the light shouted back, for everybody to hear: "You eat in five minutes. Everybody eat a good meal whether you're hungry or not. It may be a long time before you get hot grub again."

"Is it light yet?" somebody asked. "Has anybody been outside?"

"Not yet," the sergeant shouted back. "In about an hour it'll be light."

"How's the weather?"

"Pretty cloudy, but it ain't so bad. They say we'll still get the air. The cloud's high enough that they'll still be able to see the beach."

Somebody asked, daringly: "Where's Hitler? What happened to them subs?"

No one answered this, or acknowledged hearing it, and the talk drifted to wry little jokes like: "Hey, Gus, here's the ten bob I owe ya. Do you want it in shillings or francs?" and "Baby! If mother could only see me now!" and "Hey, Harry, you still sure you don't wanta gimme the phone number of that dame in Brighton?"

A man was singing, in a boisterous undertone:

"Oh give me a home
"Where the buffalo roam,
"And the DEER and the Anta-lope play . . ."

Another man was singing, more quietly:

"I touched 'er on the knee, how ashamed I was,
"I touched 'er on the knee, how ashamed I was,
"I touched 'er on the knee, she said, Sir you're
      mighty free,
"Lord God Almighty, how ashamed I was."

Another man sang plaintively:

"I've got sixpence,
"Jolly, jolly sixpence,
"I've got sixpence to last me all my life,
"I've got tuppence to spend
"And tuppence to lend,
"And tuppence to send home to my wife."

Several others joined this last man in the muted chorus:

"Rolling home, Rolling home,
"By the light of the silvery moon,
"Happy is the lass
"Who will ta ta ta ta ta
"By the light of the silvery moon."

Three soldiers started a crap game under the yellow electric light, shooting for wads of green invasion currency and calling loudly on the dice to treat them with favor. But it was plain that they were less interested in the dice than in having it known among their companions that they were shooting dice, here in the swaying lower decks of a ship, here beside its humming engines, here on the greatest D-Day of all D-Days, here on the way to a beach in Normandy. They soon ended the game and gathered in their money, scarcely knowing who had won and lost.

Mike carried his kit and webbing across the hold, arranged it in a pile beside the bulkhead, stacked his rifle alongside, and fell into the line that was forming at the entrance from the hold to the ship's galley. In a moment Nolan came and joined him, yawning and rotating the stiffness out of his shoulders.

"How d'you feel?" Mike asked.

"Good," Nolan yawned. "You get much sleep?"

"Some," Mike said, "I was up top for a while."

"What's it look like?"

"Kind of eerie," Mike said. "Quiet and black as hell. I could only see about four other ships. I guess they're all there, but it wasn't like it was coming out of harbor."

Nolan said: "I didn't think there was that many ships in the world. They must have seen us at Southampton. They must know we're on the way."

"I guess they know we're coming," Mike said. "But that doesn't mean they'll figure out where."

"They got nothing on me," Nolan said, "I don't know where we're going either. The only name I remember is Nan Green. Funny thing, I used to know a girl back home named *Anne* Green." Kennebec came up and stood behind them in the file. "Hey, Kennebec!" Nolan said. "What's the name of the town at our beach? What's the right name for Nan Green?"

"Bernières," Kennebec said. "Bernières-sur-Mer."

"That man knows everything," Mike said with mock admiration. "Just everything." He waited for Kennebec to pick up the cue, but Kennebec made no response. Mike glanced at Kennebec and then wrenched his head away quickly, feeling a sharp little chill, so abrupt and penetrating that it contracted his throat and made him cough. Kennebec was staring at his right hand and slowly rubbing the ball of his thumb across the tips of his fingers and then rolling it back again, studying the performance with leaden fascination. *Some people say you can tell from their eyes or the way they talk. My mate says you can tell from their hands.*

When they came above decks it was almost light. The clouds hung low, but they were breaking, and past their dissolving edges they could already see the first hint of blue swallowing the last wan struggling stars. The sea was a vast sweep of grey water, covered with vast reaches of grey ships, but it was something more than that, it was something so big that it could only be grasped in the abstract. It was a mighty rush of wind, a giant beating of wings, it was a thirsty slaver of an awful god, the stirring of a universe.

Everywhere they looked there were ships. Long gaunt warships, swashbuckling through the grey swell, wheeling and turning through their own spume, flexing their leashed muscles in the dawn after their long night of vigil. Fat little minesweepers and tank carriers and clumsy LSI's toddling up to the horizon, hanging there momentarily, and coasting out of sight down its slope. Tiny torpedo boats darting in and out among the slower craft at thirty

knots and flat steel barges wallowing at three. Tugs and merchant-
men of a hundred designs, recruited for a thousand different ends.
A blowzy side-wheeler threshing doggedly ahead, her decks piled
high with supplies.

Their colored rows of signal pennants stood out bravely from
their masts, and the signal beacons on their bridges winked companionably across the water. The ships could not be counted.
They could only be measured by the acre and the township. As
he looked at them and tried to guess how many they might be,
Mike's heart expanded with hope and gratitude and something
close to downright cockiness. In the same degree that it had
seemed evil and hostile in the dark of a few hours before, the sea
now seemed good and friendly. It was no longer a fetter dragging
the imprisoned ships to some fearful unknown. It was a staunch
ally which lent its hard grey flesh to the ends of their flesh and
entwined its sinew with their sinew and heaved and rushed beside
them toward their common future, sparing nothing, withholding
nothing and portending nothing that was not ordained already.

"They can't stop us!" Mike whispered exultantly to Nolan.
"They'll never stop us."

"I've quit worrying about us," Nolan answered with heavy
dolefulness. "What I'm worrying about now is me." But Mike
could see that Nolan felt good about it too.

An officer came above deck, moving stiffly in his corset of
webbing, and walked slowly through their lounging ranks, asking
each man the same set of questions.

"Water bottle full?"

"Rations O.K.?"

"Any questions about our objectives or your assignment?"

A few Spitfires sang overhead and a man near the rail yelled,
"Look!" and pointed ahead past the bows of their ship. In the
far distance, beyond the horizon, a bleary ripple of gunflash faded
out of sight and a jet of tracer, brighter than the gunflash, cascaded

up a bank of cloud, hung there for a moment, and then faded too. The sound was too far away to be heard. The officer looked at his watch. "The real stuff starts in fourteen minutes," he said.

The ship gathered itself and stretched out in the heaving sea. The hum of its motors became a quick growl as it left its place in the pattern of moving vessels to hurry through the sea with the abstract intentness of a man hurrying through a crowd when he is late. A few other ships stirred and began to hurry in the same way and as these speeding vessels surged by, the men aboard the vessels that had more time looked at them with a mixture of envy and compassion and called and waved across the water. "Good luck infantry!" they called faintly. And: "Give 'em hell!"

The officer said: "Here goes the first team!" and the ship rushed on until the traffic thinned out a little. Abruptly it cut its motors and idled.

"Look!" the man near the rail yelled again. This time it was the land he pointed to, a low blob of purple looming through a far haze, mysterious and indistinct. The men stared at the land, not anxiously or apprehensively, but with great absorption. Thin little V's appeared at the corners of their eyes and their eyebrows came together in little paunches of flesh as they stared across the sea into the haze, searching for some link between this distant shadow and the land they knew from their maps and photographs, the land of Nan Green, Mike Red and Oboe Amber, the land of the Normandy beaches. They saw none of the detail they were looking for, but they continued to stare.

And now, high above them, above the Spitfires and the Typhoons that raced back and forth from the ships to the land, they heard and partly saw the first wave of bombers. The clouds muffled the sound of the bombers' motors and hid them from view except in brief, scuttling, microscopic dashes from one cloud to the next. But in a little while, after the first of them had gone and others were overhead, a hollow hoom-hoom-hoom rolled back across the water. They stared at the land again and saw its dingy outlines stir and quiver and finally rise in a black blend of smoke and shadow, like a genie summoned from his rest.

"The poor bastards!" Mike whispered, "The poor bastards!"

But as the first hoom-hoom-hoom rumbled into a second and then a third, a fourth and a fifth, and as the smoke above the land became a thick billow, his eyes grew bright with excitement and he was possessed by a savage exhilaration. He felt the pores opening under the rubber band of his steel helmet and he squeezed the stock of his rifle until his hand was numb.

"Give it to the bastards!" he cried hoarsely. "Pour it to the bastards! Powder them to hell!"

As the ship idled closer to the land, they saw the first buildings and soon they picked out two little towns, gleaming whitely against the black smoke, like naked corpses lying on their shrouds. Away off their bow a drifting battleship squirted a huge ball of flame toward the towns and before the sound that went with the flame reached their ship, it was lost in the mighty retching and hammering of a thousand guns. The whole fleet erupted in one cosmic belch and threw its thunderous vomit at the beaches in bucketfuls. When they listened for it, they could distinguish between the throaty roar of the battleships and the tearing b—rrack of the field guns that soon began to fire out of the metal crucibles of their landing craft, but the nuances of sound were unimportant and the understanding of them made them no less stupefying. The men on the ship put their hands over their ears and moved their faces close to one another and shouted. When they found they could not make themselves heard, they grinned and shook their heads with uneasy satisfaction. They looked at the shore again. The white towns were grey smudges now, and their surest landmarks were the new tufts of fire that glowed through the darkening smoke. There was no sound of answering salvos from the shore, but half a mile off their starboard bow a small craft, half the size of their own, abruptly and dramatically dissolved in a single gust of flame. And as a rocket ship edged in toward the shore to rake the beach with its close-toothed harrow of death, a Typhoon, swooping down for a look, cut straight across the high grey parabola of rocket trails and disappeared in a ball of orange vapor.

Mike scarcely remembered boarding the assault boat. But the steel plates of the boat acted as a cushion against the pounding tumult of the guns and as the boat pitched away from its mother ship, he found that he was able to put aside the drugging indulgence of thinking about the bombardment and think again about the trivialities that he knew he must not forget. He settled on his haunches, wedging his life belt between his back and the plates of the boat, and carefully slid open the bolt of his rifle. There was a cartridge in the chamber. He closed the bolt, put the catch to safety and reminded himself that the last thing he must do before leaving the boat was to move the catch again. He felt for the handle of the adze-like trenching tool strapped to his back beneath his small kit bag, and wrenched at the cork of his water bottle to make sure that it was pushed down tight. He opened the two ammunition pouches above his breasts and closed them again. He counted the grenades hanging from his belt. Then he unscrewed the valve on his life belt and blew an extra lungful of air into it. The last thing he did was open the mouth of a heavy paper bag and place it on his knees.

The boat had found its course and was reaching swiftly toward the land, yawing and slipping and rolling in the swell, then shaking itself doggedly and plunging on ahead. Mike's stomach heaved, as though under the massaging of a fleshy unseen hand. He dropped his head on his chest and closed his eyes. With his free hand he moved the paper bag to his mouth and tried to empty his stomach into it, but nothing came except a series of dry, aspirate coughs, from deep in his chest, and a trickle of thin bodyless saliva drooling across his lips. He lifted his head again and drew a lungful of salty air out of the small rectangle of space that hung above the sides of the boat. The color seeped back into his face and he knew he wasn't going to be sick after all.

He looked across the boat to the row of men squatting or standing inside its flat steel haunch. They were close together, and yet each man was now alone. Some were grey with seasickness and some were grey with a sickness of the soul. No one talked. There was no need to talk now. There was no need to sing or pray or curse or to dredge tough little wisecracks out of the toughened recesses of their quickening hearts. Those who were afraid had no need to hide their fear and those who were not afraid had no need to show their fortune off. For there was enough fear in them all, or near them all, to give them the knowledge that fear or the lack of it was not a matter for shame or pride, but only a matter of chance.

The man across from Mike was sitting with his legs wide apart, staring with a mixture of distaste and proprietary appreciation at a pool of fresh vomit on the lurching plate of steel beneath him. Each time the boat pitched across another wave, the man doubled over and quietly replenished the pool, then resumed his study of it.

The man next to him had dropped his head far back across his shoulders and was gazing straight upward past the flat line of the boat's side into the empty sky. The next man seemed to be asleep; the edge of his steel helmet had slipped down across the side of his head and was cushioned on his shoulder. His face was relaxed and peaceful, but when the boat pitched his head forward off his shoulder and he opened his eyes to right himself, he looked around him with the stunned wild fixity of a hospital patient coming out of an anaesthetic. The man next to him was vomiting into a paper bag.

And then three or four men were on their feet, looking over the top of the starboard plate across the sea. The next man was Kennebec. All the muscles of Kennebec's narrow face were in a state of drunken inertia. Each time a high wave sent a fresh shudder through the frame of the racing boat, his pale cheeks quivered lightly, like subtly changing shadows. His jaw hung slack and the tip of his tongue lolled sensuously in the moist runnel between his lower teeth and his lip.

Mike looked away from Kennebec and searched the line of figures for Nolan. The American held his rifle upright between his legs, his two hands tightly on the barrel and the top of his helmet resting on the rifle just above his hands. His face was hidden.

The boil and rush of sound that beat around the hurrying assault boat faded into a distant growl. The barrage was thinning out, preparing to lift from the beaches and grope further inland toward the secondary defenses. It was possible to hear the stuttering grumble of the adjacent landing craft driving toward the shore and the liquid ping, like elastic breaking under tension, of an occasional enemy shell landing in the sea nearby. And in a while, from what seemed to be very far ahead, a machine gun chattered.

"*Oh God!*" Mike formed the words in his mind without uttering them. "*Make it now. Make the boat stop now and make the ramp open and let us out, on the beach. I'm all right now. But a minute from now I might not be any good at all. I might not be any good in thirty seconds. Make it now. I could do it all now, exactly as they told me to. But in thirty seconds I might not be able to do anything. I might just sit here and watch the others go. I might not be able to lift my arms or move my legs. Make it now. Make it now.*"

A rivulet of sweat ran down his cheek from the narrow gap between his forehead and his helmet. He ground the sweat away with hard sweeping strokes of his forearm. The rough cloth of his sleeve stung as it scraped across his face and he continued the rubbing after his face was dry.

A new compulsion seized him and he lifted his body to the edge of a thick kapok life raft and hauled himself up the side of the boat until he could see beyond it, across the jumble of assault boats pitching toward the shore like wreckage arranged in geometric order. He was just in time to see the nearest boat blow up on a mine, sundering itself in one black sledge-hammer clash of sound and vision. One soldier from the boat was thrown across the sea, almost halfway to the edge of Mike's craft. In a quick, unfinished stab of horror, like a dreadful motion picture scene broken off in the middle, he saw the man's face turned upward to the sky, saw the punctured tatter of his life preserver trailing after him in the water like a grey intestine, saw the man's arm twitch, saw his eyes roll whitely in his bloodless, unbelieving face, and then saw no more.

Mike's fingers slid away from the edge of the boat. He sat down again on the life raft and tried desperately to draw into himself, to expel all awareness from his mind. The sweat lay on his face in pools, filling its lines and overflowing its contours. His fingers were stiff and leaden as he curled them around his rifle and his stomach was a jagged icicle pressing on his thumping heart. Beseechingly he looked across the boat again to the row of soldiers he had studied before. Again all he saw was their aloneness and through it, his own. In a minute they would be doing vast unfathomable things for each other, he and they, pooling the vast unfathomable resources of their spirit in the only pure and perfect community known to their race, the community of battle. But in these last moments each of them was on his own. There was nothing any man could do for his neighbor or that his neighbor could do for him.

The boat jarred and a tremulous grating shook its hull as it came to a stop on the gravel floor off the shoreline. The shivering impact threw Mike heavily into the man beside him, but when he caught his breath it was with a sob of gratitude. He heard the impatient clanking of the opening ramp and stumbled toward the square of daylight that had replaced the boat's flat bow, shoving at the man ahead of him in his haste. Above the loud scrape of his hob-nailed boots on the ramp, he heard a sailor's voice call from above him: "Watch out—sand bar!" He held himself at the crest of the ramp for an instant, and in the same instant the man ahead of him on the downward slope of the ramp turned and looked past him into the emptying belly of the boat. The face was as set and naked as the face of a child awakened in a nightmare, and the realization that it belonged to Kennebec did not register until its owner, with a kind of hopeless shrug, had turned his back and slithered quietly into the sea. Mike slithered after him, took a step on the edge of a sandbar and then found himself waist deep in water. Holding his rifle above his head, clear of the waterline, he half ran and half pushed his way straight ahead until he felt the heavy warm grip of the water drop by degrees from his waist to his hips and finally to his knees. Then, when he was able to get his feet clear of it he quickened his gait to a high-kneed lope.

He did not see much at first. His attention was focused partly on the back of Kennebec, a few steps in front of him, and partly on the back of the man immediately ahead of Kennebec. As he splashed through the shallowing water, the panorama of the beach rationed itself out to the corners of his eyes in small glimpses, without much pattern or cohesion. He saw some more soldiers spilling out of a boat that had driven straight up to the dry sand. He also saw several dead men, as well as one man, badly wounded, using his arms like flippers to drag a mash of crushed legs and shredded battledress back from the shore into the water. He saw any number of black mines and yellow shell cases bobbing in the water on big wooden stakes. He saw concrete blocks and iron tank traps at the water's edge in great profusion, some of them broken and twisted by the bombing and shelling or by the demolition parties, but many of them still intact. He saw much barbed wire, some of it lying in rusty whorls and spirals and some of it staked out neatly in little garden patches.

Straight ahead and very close, not much more than a hundred yards away, he saw the main beach position of the enemy, a straggling settlement of tall pill boxes and squat machine-gun turrets anchored to a high continuous concrete breakwater and sprawling back through a grey-brown belt of low dunes and marshes to a village. The nearest building of the village appeared to have been a waterfront hotel of fawn stucco; now it was a smoking fossil, its face eaten away by shell holes, the red tile shingles of its roof lying in front of it in untidy piles and tiny waves of flame lapping against its wooden beams. There were several other fires in the village and most of the houses he could see were shorn and broken by concussion.

The fading hammer of the shifting and diminishing barrage made the beach seem, not exactly quiet, but unreal, as the street outside a great and noisy factory seems unreal after you have left the factory and can hear only its dim echoes. As his feet hit the sand, Mike scarcely noticed the thwack-thwack-thwack of Bren guns merging with the quicker slurp of German Spandaus and Schmeissers from the back of the breakwater. But then, in quick succession a rifle bullet sang hard and high above his shoulder, like a violin string plucked almost to breaking point, a heavy mortar broke nearby with a testy crump and a German eighty-eight-millimetre shell fused the last split second of its warning swish with the cruel smack of its explosion in one venomous package.

He made no conscious catalogue of the things he saw and heard in those first few seconds. The real centre of his world was the two backs ahead of him, which he must follow. Suddenly the second back straightened out of its crouch, stiffened momentarily and then pitched to the sand. Kennebec swerved and lunged to the left and then he was running straight down the beach under the curve of the breakwater. As he reached the lee of the worn rampart, Kennebec twisted his body into a crabwise jog and lobbed a grenade over the top.

Mike involuntarily shifted his eyes to follow the flight of the grenade, and swerved to follow Kennebec's path a second too late. Something thin and hard kicked across his shin with brutal force and he plunged headlong into the sand. As he fell a hot claw raked through his battledress into the flesh of his thigh and wet sand jammed into his nose and mouth in a stifling jet. As he spat and blew it out, he tried to roll back to his feet, but from the hip to the ankle one leg was pinioned as in a vise. He squirmed and tried to reach his leg with his hand. But his hips lay between a tangle of wire, which sealed off the whole lower part of him in a jagged impenetrable corral. He cursed, bitterly, despairingly and supplicatingly, and then raised himself on his elbows, brought his rifle to his shoulder and waited.

He waited almost calmly. He waited alertly, far more alertly than he had waited in the ship in the long night and the long morning, and with a far better understanding of what it was he waited for. Up to now, he hadn't quite known; it might have been fear he waited for before, or courage, or adventure, or the reluctantly unfolding knowledge of what kind of man he would be when all these things called to him at once. But now there was no doubt. Now he waited for death. To this final waiting there could be no other fruition.

It could not be long. Already it was staked out for him, neatly and precisely, like a problem in calculus. The breakwater hung above him, forty yards off, just far enough away that it gave him no shelter from the enemy sitting on top of it and behind it, and just close enough that no enemy hidden there could miss. And he knew it was no mere part of the fortune of war that after Kennebec and half-a-dozen other soldiers swung off to the left under the breakwater, no other soldiers had appeared within the narrow orbit of his vision. He had been told enough about his battalion's plan of attack to know that there would be no frontal attack on this part of the enemy defenses. Later they would take this part from the flanks. They would tidy up the barbed wire in front of it, and that would be much too late for anyone caught in the wire now. It was already too late to pretend that he was dead. His first frantic attempts to free himself had committed him; if there were any Germans on the breakwater or the dunes ahead of him, they must have seen his movement.

He kept the rifle at his shoulder until his arms began to ache with the weight of his body and the back of his neck was a steady agony. In this time his instinct was conscious of many things that merely hovered at the outskirts of his senses. As much through instinct as through perception, he was conscious of the man who had run up the beach ahead of Kennebec, now lying dead a few feet away. He was conscious of the snarling little eruption of grenades and Sten guns on his left, where Kennebec and the others of their section who remained were trying to take out a Spandau. He was conscious of the noisy Donnybrook on his right, where the rest of his company swarmed through the fresh wet shell-holes on the beach and spat their tracer off the thick hides of three connecting casemates, like glowing hornets attacking a herd of elephants. He was conscious of an amphibious tank growling in from the sea, half swimming and half waddling in its square water wings, and poking its gun through the giant loophole of a pillbox straight into the protruding muzzle of a German 105. He was conscious of the continuous V of spraying sand behind him, at the rendezvous of two German machine guns sweeping the beach from opposite ends on fixed lines of fire.

At last, when it seemed he could support the rifle and his body no longer, he saw what he was waiting for. Over the sand-coated barrel of his rifle, a low pimple of earth rustled against the far shoulder of the breakwater. The barrel of a rifle nuzzled warily across the cement plateau of the breakwater and behind it, hugged close to the pimple of earth, the unmistakable black flare of a German helmet, a dark smudge of flesh and a patch of grey-green cloth.

This was the first German soldier Mike had ever seen. He turned his left wrist a fraction of an inch, bringing the sights of his rifle in line with the smudge of flesh. The black wen at the end of his rifle wavered, hung, wavered again and then steadied itself into the sharp notch of the hindsight. The man on the breakwater began to move again. Mike squeezed his right hand into the stock of his weapon and the hard kick of its wet, sand-grimed barrel sent a shiver all the way back to his pinioned thigh. If the German made a sound, it was lost in the enfilade of noise from the other parts of the beach, but his dropped rifle rang with finality on the concrete.

Mike slid back the bolt of his rifle and hammered another cartridge into the chamber. He hoisted himself on his elbows again and resumed his waiting.

This time the wait was not so long. The threat he had been watching most intently when he first saw the German rifleman was a small two-man pillbox sitting squarely on top of the break-water a few yards further down, a round shallow boulder with two shallow loop-holes cut into its face and staring out to the beach like empty eye-sockets. Now, in one of the sockets, he saw the thick short funnel of a machine-gun muzzle feeling carefully along the lower rim. He fired quickly this time and heard his bullet splatter against the side of the pillbox. The machine-gun muzzle disappeared hastily.

In a moment it poked back into view again. Mike fired once more and worked the bolt of his rifle. But this time the bolt came back sluggishly and when he tried to shove it forward, it thwacked against the palm of his hand and would not move. Feverishly he pulled the bolt back again and clawed with his finger nails at the scarred cartridge case wedged into its grimy bore. His nails tore away on the base of the cartridge and left the ends of his fingers raw and bloody. He fumbled for the big issue clasp-knife at his belt, stuck the edge of the largest blade in his teeth, and tugged it open with his hand. But the cartridge was driven home as firmly as a rivet. When he tried to pry the knife under its base, he could get no leverage.

He let the useless rifle drop into the sand, and yanked the grenades out of his belt and laid them in a pile beside his right hand. He rolled over on his side, pulled a pin from a grenade, and lobbed it blindly over his shoulder, toward the pill-box. Without waiting to hear its flat metallic splash, he threw the next in the same way, and then the next, the next, and the next, and finally the last. He did not expect to hit anything with the grenades, but each of them would keep the German machine-gunner's head down a few seconds longer. And, as a corollary, with the last grenade gone, the German would be free to bring his head up and keep it up until he had done his work.

Mike rolled back on his face, tugged one last time at his imprisoned leg, and lay still. With his hands he slid his steel helmet forward to cover the top of his head, and then he cradled his face in his hands, smelling the wet sand close to his nostrils as he filtered the air into them between his fingers.

I should be crying, he told himself. *I should be praying. At the very least, I should be saying something brave and corny. This is it, maybe. Or what's the holdup? I should be lighting a cigarette and lifting my head up into the sun and blowing smoke right into that bastard's face. I should be saying:* "Well, anyway, I took one with me." *I used to dream about this sometimes, in my crazy, big-shot dreams. Me lying somewhere on a beach, and taking it, and then the others standing around afterwards and saying:* "That was Tully. They didn't come any gamer." *I wonder if the others lying here ever had dreams like that. It doesn't matter*

*anyway. It doesn't matter how we die. The only person who will
see me is that bastard up there in the pillbox and all I'll be to him
is a sack of khaki caught in a piece of wire. And pretty soon he'll
be dead too.*

Mike cupped his fingers around his nose and began rubbing
his nose, feeling its high bridge and the long flare to its nostrils.

*Christ! I've got a big nose. How did Tina ever get to think
I'm good to look at?*

He was trying to keep himself relaxed, perhaps because of some
subconscious pride or vanity. But slowly and inexorably, like the
pull of a rack, the suspense drew him taut. And then, when all
his muscles had contracted into tight, waiting knots, poised for
some final convulsion, a sound as harsh and sudden as terror itself
split the air beside his ear. He threw his body away from it in
one writhing lunge, and above the sound he heard his own voice
scream.

The new sound stopped and a voice called anxiously, very
close to him: "It's me, Tully. Rinowski."

He threw his body back on its side. Beside him in the sand
and level with his thigh, the muzzle of a Bren gun pointed across
its stubby spraddling bipod toward the pillbox on the breakwater.
Rinowski, sprawled beside it, kicked a leg across the sand toward
him, briefly exhibiting a tatter of khaki cloth and bleeding flesh.

"I got caught too," Rinowski panted. "I'm all right now."

Mike looked at him stupidly and then, with a great effort, not
because he thought it was the thing to say, but because he thought
nothing else would be any use, he shouted above the disorder of
sound from the rest of the beach: "You better get out of here,
kid. There's a machine gun covering us."

"I seen him," Rinowski panted. "He'll keep his head down a
while. That last burst scared the wording Jesus out of him. If
I could put one through that little loophole it would shut him up
for good."

Rinowski dragged himself forward a few feet, lifting the legs of his gun's bipod clear of the sand and inching it ahead in tiny cautious bounds. When he was even with Mike's shoulder he carefully moved the gun over to him. "You take it," he said. "Where's your knife?"

Mike pulled the gun into the crook of his shoulder, trained it on the closer of the two fissures in the pillbox and stretched his free hand across his back with the knife. Twice while Rinowski was hacking at his battledress with the knife and untangling the wire from his foot, the muzzle of the German machine gun appeared in the aperture of the pillbox and drew back again as Mike squirted the Bren.

"Try it now!" Rinowski shouted. Mike pulled the numbed leg in with the muscles of his thigh. It came easily; he was free.

Rinowski squirmed up beside him again and said: "I'll take it now."

"I'll take it," Mike said. "You hit for the breakwater."

"No," Rinowski said doggedly. "It's my gun. I can't leave it go." His voice was high and childish again, as it had been when Mike lay listening to it in the hold of their ship. It was the voice of a boy, an earnest boy claiming his place in the world of men.

"Jesus Christ!" Mike shouted. "Let's do something." He allowed Rinowski to tug the gun back. His face was pale with excitement and doubt, but in spite of himself, in spite of what he knew was implied in the transfer, he had no power to argue further.

"Go when I say," Rinowski shouted. "When he shows again, I'll give him a burst and you can run for it. I'll give him another before you get there."

The two men lay together in the sand. Mike felt there was something he should say to Rinowski, but he could think of nothing that would have validity or meaning.

In a moment Rinowski shouted: "Get ready!"

When he heard the quick stammer of the Bren again, Mike scrambled to his feet and ran for the concave wall, running low and digging his feet into the sand like a football plunger. When he was halfway there he heard the Bren hammer again and heard the bullets biting at the concrete. He fell into the sand, lay there for a moment, and then backed into the breakwater and dropped on one knee, looking across the beach to where Rinowski was stretched out beside the gun. There were more dead on the other parts of the beach than he had thought. He spent an instant appraising the flung litter of bodies and the litter of landing craft disgorging their streams of men across the smoking shoreline. But Rinowski, alone in the microscopic eddy of his one-man battlefield, re-claimed his attention at once.

Rinowski lifted the bipod free of the sand, threw it forward a few feet and then hastily hauled his body up the side of the gun-stock and picked up his aim again on the pillbox. He repeated the action twice before he had to fire his next burst. Altogether he had come perhaps six yards closer to the shelter of the curving wall.

He crawled a little way further and paused again. He was so close now that his head almost reached the pale line of shadow made by the wall in the sand. He fired a third burst. This burst was shorter than any of the others had been. And after it coughed out, Rinowski did not advance the bipod again. He glanced anxiously at his chest and began grappling with an ammunition pouch, quickly and furtively, aware that what he was about to do must be done without delay and without being observed.

"Oh, God," Mike whispered, "his magazine is empty." Mike prayed, not to God, but to the boy fumbling in the sand with his gun and ammunition. *Run for it, Rinowski*, he prayed. *Don't try to put on a new magazine. You're so close he can hear you. He'll hear you and know he's got you. Run for it, Rinowski.*

With great stealth, the boy drew a flat, chopped-off crescent of black metal from his bullet pouch and held it in his right hand beside the stock of the gun. Then he lowered the other hand from the stock and stabbed swiftly at the body of the gun with a quick two-handed motion, like a boxer throwing a one-two punch in a close clinch. The first punch knocked the empty magazine forward and away from the gun into the sand, and the second brought the new magazine up to its place in a hard metallic clatter. There was no firm click as the magazine slipped into place. Instead, into a tiny vacancy in the uneven racket of the beach, there crept a furtive scraping. It was a sound that Mike had heard many times on the ranges, the sound of a magazine missing its slot and being dragged across the top of a gun in hurried, probing stabs.

The German in the pillbox recognized the scraping too. Before Rinowski could jab the magazine home, the German's gun opened up in a long rippling purr, throwing a low curtain of sand around Rinowski and kicking his whole body back from the Bren as though someone were yanking at his heels with a rope.

The boy shook himself and slithered back to the gun, fondled it unsteadily with the magazine, and fired back. The pillbox was quiet again.

Rinowski was badly hurt. No new blood showed on him, but he was breathing in long, sucking gasps, which even the steady rivet-beat of fire from the two ends of the beach could not submerge. His hold on the gun was weak and uncertain and its muzzle waved rather than pointed at the pillbox, like the accusing finger of a drunk.

Mike, flattened against the saucer-like face of the breakwater, rose and took a half step toward the struggling boy. But when his hips came clear of the concrete he could go no further. Every muscle in him jarred to a stop on a single impulse. He stood as though grappled in a strait-jacket and then turned his head a little and, with a look that was close to pure cunning, guided one hand back behind him until it rested on the concrete, feeling the concrete's solid strength and reaffirming its power of sanctuary. He remained thus while Rinowski resumed his painful grovelling up the shallow slope, but the cunning disappeared from his expression and was replaced by a stiffened mask of horror, of shame, of pity and, above all, of fear.

For the first time since his unit had been ordered into its marshalling area more than three weeks before, Mike's mind was fully concentrated. His thoughts were no longer diffused and obscured by the strange complexities of watching an Army prepare for this day, of preparing himself for it, nor by the mighty tremors of the day itself. They were focused with cruel and ruthless clarity on the boy in the sand, rejecting as extraneous everything that did not bear directly on the boy. And because he was not extraneous to the boy, he was able to examine himself with the same clarity as he examined the tragedy unfolding in the sand. The horror and shame and pity and, above all, the fear with which he made the examination were as much for himself as for Rinowski. His reason ruled him now. It told him what he ought to do. It also told him brutally that he could not do it, and, more brutally still, it told him why he could not do it. He could not do what he ought to do because he was not quite the man he had hoped to be, and his reason did not add that no man ever is.

Rinowski was still pawing feebly toward him, inching forward with his hands and elbows and clumsily driving the gun ahead of him with his shoulder. The Spandau lashed at him again. It might have hit him or it might not. The boy squeezed on the Bren and kept coming across the sand with the slow doggedness of a sick animal that is close to home.

When the distance between Rinowski and himself was no more than twice the boy's length, Mike was still frozen to the breakwater like a badly synchronized mechanism in which both the controls and the working parts are in perfect order, but the circuit between them simply will not function. But as Rinowski clawed the sand again and began to haul his limp body another hopeless foot or two, the circuit closed. Mike felt it happen. The sensation was physical. It stung his muscles and his flesh and filled his head with rushing blood. His throat choked out a cry of gratitude and challenge. With his hand he threw himself away from the breakwater and hurtled across the sand to Rinowski's side. He stooped and grabbed the boy around the armpits, shook him into a rough state of balance across his hip, and lurched back across the slope with him, the gun trailing after them in the grip of Rinowski's dangling hand.

The machine gunner in the pillbox stuck his head up again just in time to see them fall under the eave of the breakwater, and his parting tattoo chunked wildly into the furrow left by Rinowski's dragging legs.

Mike put the boy down, slid his steel helmet forward off his head and ripped a big wad of shell dressing from under the green camouflage net which covered the helmet. He jerked a black Commando dagger out of the boy's webbing and cut away the khaki waterproof cover on the dressing. He squeezed open the buckle at the front of Rinowski's web belt, peeled the bullet pouches and their straps back over his shoulders and began to slash his jacket with the knife.

He rolled the boy gently away from him and began feeling with the dagger for the seam at the top of his right sleeve. In a moment he stopped what he was doing and ran his eyes up and down the boy's right side from his thigh to his shoulder. Rinowski's whole side was a soggy drench of blood, and set in the red drench, like black buttons on the jacket of a London coster, a row of bullet holes ran the full length of his ribs. Mike counted the holes. There were nine.

He turned Rinowski on his back again and lifted his head off the sand, cradling it across his own legs. He opened a water bottle and spilled a little water across his lips. Rinowski was breathing hard, fighting for every breath in liquid gurgles. His face was drawn and yellow and the yellow deepened with every breath. His breathing reached and passed its climax in one gasping tremor and then became slower and more even. The yellow faded from his face and became a luminous green, the color of decay stealing up on life. Mike felt the racked body loosening and falling away from its struggle.

He bent his head close to the boy's ear. "Rinowski!" he shouted wildly. "I'll write your wife! I'll tell her how you talked about her all night long, about getting married and your dog and where you live." There was no sign that the boy heard and soon there was a sign that he was beyond hearing. His broken body tightened into a hard knot, quivered two or three times, and then unwound and relaxed like an uncoiling spring. Mike laid the boy's head in the sand, pried the Bren gun from his loosening fingers and stood up against the breakwater.

He snapped the magazine off the gun, stooped over Rinowski's body to remove a fresh magazine from one of the bullet pouches and slapped it into the gun's thin dorsal cavity. He stood for several minutes beside the body, debating what his next step should be. He could creep down the breakwater with comparative safety and perhaps find his section in time to help with whatever the section was doing now. He could stay where he was and if the battle went according to plan, the machine gun above him on the breakwater would eventually be cut off and smashed from the rear by other men, some of whom might die.

Or there was a third choice. This last choice was the hardest of the three. It was as hard as the choice he had had to make when the boy at his feet was crawling toward the haven where he now lay dead. And yet, unlike the other choice, he could accept this one or reject it; whatever the compulsions were, for and against it, they were not stronger than he was. His fear had not diminished; if anything it was more insistent than before. But his fear was only one part of him. In a way that he could not understand, the dead boy had released him from some dimly comprehended bondage and restored to him the freedom to do such things as he believed to be necessary. He made his choice.

He slithered a few yards down the breakwater until the flat appendage on its morning shadow told him that he was directly beneath the pillbox. He picked out a place on the sand just outside the shadow and measured the distance to it in his mind. Three long steps would do it, but four short steps would be better. He would have to make the pivot on his left foot, so that the weight of the gun would be rolling with his body, and that meant that he would have to take the first step with his right. He would begin firing as he made the pivot. The gun would have to be pointed at the correct angle and he must not turn too far. He would have to make an allowance for the fact that when he ran he would be facing downhill but when he had made his pivot he would be facing uphill. He would have to hit the loophole with his first burst. And of course, everything depended on the validity of his theory that there was a lot of chicken in the German, that the German still would not dare to stick his head up and keep it up.

He did not hurry these calculations. After they were finished he gave himself an instant to think how well Kennebec had done, how, with the terror so thick upon him you could have scraped it off with a knife, Kennebec still did his job exactly as though this were another scheme.

He checked his calculations again. When he was satisfied with them, he folded the legs of the bipod, grasped them near the top with his left hand under the barrel, curved his trigger finger around the grip, and punched the butt of the weapon into his hip with his right elbow. He filled his lungs with air, like a trained sprinter who senses the impending report of the starter's gun.

Then he catapulted himself off the breakwater, with his back squarely in the line of vision of the pillbox, and ran out into the naked sand of the beach.

He squeezed the trigger while he was beginning his pivot, hosepiping an uneven arc along the wall until the loophole was full in his face and startlingly close. It must have been the first ricochet or the second that hurt the German, because his head came up almost at once, unmarked but lolling stupidly, and then, while the last bullets from Mike's magazine gnawed through the steel and bone, it turned away, slowly and petulantly, as a man turns his cheek from a sudden gust of rain.

When the rest of him dropped out of sight, the German's arm twitched angrily on the ledge of the pillbox and pointed the nose of the 42 out to sea. The German fired only one shot, and that after he was dead.

CHAPTER

11

Not counting attached engineers, artillery observers and specialists, Mike's company had landed with an assault strength of a hundred and twenty-seven officers and men. It was almost dark when he found his company headquarters hastily digging into an apple orchard three miles inland from the beach, and by this time the company's strength had been cut to one captain, one lieutenant, two sergeants, one full corporal, two lance-corporals and thirty-four riflemen. No one knew or had found time to care how many of the eighty-six others were dead and how many wounded or missing. But Kennebec, who was among the survivors, told him that Nolan was believed to be on his way back to England with a not very serious shrapnel wound.

Kennebec said: "Everybody thought you must have bought it." He put no special inflection in the words, and when Mike said: "I was wondering about you," there was no special inflection in his words either. They were merely two casual acquaintances discussing a matter of some slight mutual interest, but of no great importance to either. They had already begun to make their first adjustment, the adjustment of looking on death not as a theory, but as a fact. In the last few hours death had

become the core of their lives, and while their hands set up
physical defenses against death in the poppied fields, their
minds were preparing slit-trenches against death too.

You could still have friends. In some respects your friends
would be more valuable in this new world of death than they
had ever been in the old world of leaves, women, beer, parades
and pay-days. But you could not make yourself dependent on
them. You learned quickly, in a few hours, to look on the
possession of a friend as you had once looked on the possession
of a wrist-watch or a radio. The possession was a handy one,
and you would miss it if it were lost. Nevertheless, you must
be prepared to lose it, and go looking for another.

That night their company was brought up to strength by
reinforcements and stood guard against an expected attack
by German paratroops. The paratroops didn't come, but the
SS did. These were a new breed of soldiers, far different from
the able but somewhat cautious troops they had met on the
beaches. These were the Hitler Youth, the beardless killers whose
highest aim was to die and whose only God was an evil little
man in a moustache. They came just before dawn, rustling
through the dark fields of spring wheat, with a screaming curtain
of mortars just ahead of them and the fearsome clanking of
their tanks behind. They overran the first outposts and strode
on through the wheat, Hoching and Heiling and pausing only to
die, until they had chopped through to the company headquarters. Then it was every man for himself. Mike lost contact
with his platoon, but beat his way back to Battalion with the
help of a Sten gun and a considerable amount of luck. He found
the battalion itself preparing to retreat.

But by dawn their brigade's reserve battalion went through
them and by nightfall the situation was restored, which meant
that Mike was back in the same slit trench, in the same orchard,
standing the same watches, but with different people around

him. Kennebec was still there; so were a sergeant named Coombs, a corporal named Jenkins and four riflemen named Jones, Smallman, Gilbert and Giovanni. Except for these, his platoon was composed of strangers. Nine days later, after a brigade attack had advanced the line two thousand yards, he helped to bury some of the men who were not strangers. The most profound thought he permitted himself on this occasion was that maggots were decidely unpleasant.

He had been taught that modern warfare was a sweeping fluid process of thrust and manoeuvre, but everything he saw and did here was a flat denial of this doctrine. On D Plus One his division had succeeded, after a rough and tenuous fashion, in establishing a continuous front. On the left this front began in the fields and orchards overlooking a triangle of villages called Buron, Gruchy and Authie, and swept to the southwest in a shallow crescent which ended near a railway bridge on the right of a town called Bretteville L'Orgeuilleuse. For the first thirty-three days there was no consequential change in either the shape or location of this crescent. Two or three times, Mike's battalion was moved from one part of the crescent to another. And once, it was withdrawn from the rim of the crescent for a period of forty-eight hours.

One part of the crescent was as much like the next part as one day was like the next. The villages looked the same. In the early days they were only gaunt and empty and ridged with scars but not broken by them. The swift erosion of the daily barrages changed them, but they changed as one; when the destruction of one became so complete that even its church steeple melted into the growing pile of rubble, the village was still without distinction, for the same thing had happened in the next one.

The wheat grew no taller in one field than in the field adjoining. The red poppies ripened and began to drop their petals no earlier. The legs of the dead cows pointed no straighter to

the sky, nor did their bellies swell faster in the summer heat, nor
was the smell of their rotting flesh more violent or unclean. The
shell holes were no thicker and the slit-trenches no deeper.

Sometimes there would be a small attack to make, seldom
more than a mile in depth or wider than the frontage of a battalion.
These attacks had little to distinguish them from one another
either. Sometimes the objective would be the outskirts of one of
the villages, endowed for the occasion with the code name of
Tallulah or Bette, and sometimes it would be an orchard named
Flute or Piccolo. The guns behind the attacking battalion would
split the uneasy night into loud, livid fissures, and after half
an hour, or an hour, or three hours, the barrage would creep
forward with the infantry behind it. The German mortars ringed
around Bette or Piccolo, as the case might be, would pour their
own shells back through the barrage on the hypothesis that a
barrage that moved was likely to have men moving behind it.
And for the last quarter of a mile or half-mile, the infantrymen
making the attack would walk through the wheat, through the
mortars, taking the trenches of the enemy one by one, sometimes
with the help of tanks, but more often with their rifles, Sten guns
and grenades. They almost never failed to capture their objective,
although now and then the enemy would take it back from them,
either by retaliating with a similar attack or, if the position were
an exposed one, by blanketing it so thoroughly with mortars that
it became impossible to live there long.

Inevitably, these small local attacks were accompanied by a
fairly high index of what the upper echelons called battle wastage.
To the men who participated in the attacks, the wastage nearly
always seemed disproportionate to the results. They had been
told that their first main purpose was to capture the city of Caen,
and Caen looked no closer from Tallulah than it had looked from
Flute and no further away from Bette than from Piccolo. They
had not yet been told that the larger purpose of these bloody little

actions was to draw the enemy's main strength toward themselves
and weaken him for an American breakout almost sixty miles
away. If they had been told, it wouldn't have made much difference. "Strategy," as Kennebec said later when he heard what
they had been doing in those early days, "always looks lousy to a
stiff."

Some nights there were patrols, but for the greater part
of the first month, they did nothing but sit in their slit-trenches,
each man in his own little unpeopled hell, each man weighing
and assessing, according to his own private standards, his own
capacity for misery and constantly wondering at its magnitude.
"A man can stand anything," they sometimes told each other with
desperate pride, and they were in a fair way to proving it.

They proved to themselves that a man could go without sleep
until the rims of his eyes were swollen and sickly red, like
strips of putrefying bacon rind, and his brain was a blob of amoebal
pulp that could distinguish light from dark, noise from silence, and
a remark from a command, but little else. They proved that the
human body can go without warming, the human stomach without
feeding, the skin without washing, the bowels without emptying,
the heart without encouraging, the soul without uplifting and the
mind without nourishing, all for periods that would have seemed
spectacular to a scientist and impossible to a layman. Even the
least hardy of them soon learned to look on rest and food as
luxuries. That is not to say that they learned to dispense with
either, but only that they learned not to expect them in regular
or uniform allotments.

In the fields and orchards and in the villages turned to
stinking fossils by endless rounds of shellfire, the days lay around
them like the beads of a tarnished necklace spilled in mire. They
forgot the names of the days and the happenings that set them
apart from one another. This was less the result of eating or not
eating the same food, serving on or escaping the same stand-tos

and patrols, and snatching or missing the same cramped and brittle fragments of sleep, than the result of being hit or not being hit by Moaning Minnie. That was the name they gave to the German multiple mortars that stonked their positions, wherever they were, a minimum of twice and a maximum of several dozen times in each twenty-four hours. Minnie was the most continuous and urgent factor in their lives, outside death itself.

It was Minnie who chained them to their narrow slit-trenches, robbed them of their sleep even when they were nominally free to sleep, interfered with the arrival of hot meals from the company cook-house, and gnawed and lacerated their nerves until the brave envied the fearful and the fearful envied the dead. The six-barrelled mortar was less dangerous than it sounded. Its sick, low wail always gave fair warning and there was usually no excuse for not being in a trench by the time the second shell arrived, even if the first got the jump on you. Nevertheless, it occasionally happened that a shell scored a direct hit on a trench, and the casualties always seemed harder to accept than the casualties the battalion took in battle.

One day a dud shell dropped near the company position. After an armorer had removed the fuse, the men looked at it. It was the size of a small oil drum, a hard glittering monster that was as foreign to their conception of a mortar bomb as a 5.5 projectile to a Mills grenade. They talked about it for a while, marvelling that this was what they had associated with so long on such familiar terms. The next stonk came a couple of hours later. It was short and not particularly accurate, only eighteen rounds. When it was over and Mike stuck his head out of his close-fitting envelope of earth, the man in the next trench, a soldier who had hitherto enjoyed a modest celebrity because of the steadiness of his nerves, was babbling over and over again, in an awful toneless harangue: "It's too wordin' big. They never told me it was that wordin' big. It's too wordin' big. They never told me it was that wordin' big." Mike himself was far more shaken by his look at that single, monstrous dud than by two weeks of barrages. And for more than a month afterward, his nightmares were not of bursting shells or mutilated bodies or of SS men walking across the wheat fields, but of a fat cylinder of steel gleaming in the sunlit grass.

*   *   *   *

These were weeks of melancholy and paradox. The paradox was that although their melancholy permeated their souls as completely as the cold night earth permeated their bones and the endless M and V permeated their blood cells it did not rob them of their humor, but rather, reinforced it. The heroic sweep of their abjectness, without limits that they could discern in either time or space, was an invitation to humor. It was not the desperate humor of a Pagliacci, but slow and gentle and utterly without malice: the only really perfect kind of humor, the kind in which everybody sees the joke and nobody is sure whether the joke is on himself or someone else. Their humor did not call for wit or cleverness, nor very often for laughter. It was enough to say, after a salvo of enemy shells or a dangerous patrol: "Word! I thought I was sent for that time!" The eyes of your listeners would dwell on your face with affectionate approval for a moment, and that was better than a belly laugh. It was enough to say: "Word! What I'd give for a bath!" or "Hey! Let's go down to the corner and get a bottle of Labatt's," or "I dreamt a woman crawled into my trench last night." There was humor in the very preposterousness of their yearnings and in the very boundlessness of their melancholy, and hence humor was never very far away.

*   *   *   *

It took only a short time for them to begin hating their enemy. Most of them didn't get started on this project until some minutes or hours after they had come into physical contact with the first

German soldiers. Up to then, in spite of the impassioned indict-
ments of the enemy which they had read in their newspapers,
heard over their radios and even delivered to each other occasionally, they had not really narrowed the war down to personalities.
They judged themselves to be fighting for various causes: some
for their country; some for a system; some against cruelty and
injustice; some simply for the approval of society; some because
they could think of no more interesting and fruitful way to spend
the time. Most of them were here for none of these reasons
singly, but for all of them, mixed in various proportions according
to the forces that made them individuals. They landed on the
beach fully prepared to kill anyone who challenged these various
ends. It was not until somewhat later, nevertheless, that they began to consolidate the abstract promptings of their ideals, con-
victions and conventions and find their common denominator in
a simple primitive hatred of the German soldier. Their hatred
became as vivid and venomous as the tracer from their rifles, and
it shot as straight. Its target ceased to be an improbable gang of
sadists in Berlin, a turgid philosophy or a physical though distant
menace. The target for their hatred was Hans Schmidt, soldier
of the Wehrmacht, the man sitting over the next knoll in a Norman
wheat field.

The hatred came easily. On the beaches, the Germans and
their conscripts from Poland and Russia had sat in their pillboxes
and their trenches in the surrounding dunes chopping their long-
range rifles and machine guns through the assault waves with the
zest of shooting-gallery patrons in on a pass. But when the pass
ran out, when the luckiest of the invaders scrambled over their
own dead and won a few positions from which they could fight
back on something approaching even terms, the Germans and their
conscripts began hoisting handkerchiefs and little white flags that
appeared to have been prepared for just this occasion. And as
they walked out with their hands up, they cast smirking sidewise

glances at the beaches which seemed to say: "Look how many we killed. And now they can't kill us."

The SS troops they met further inland fought with no such reservations, and perversely they were hated worse for the manner in which they died than their comrades on the beaches were hated for the manner in which they lived. From the line of its secondary objective to the end of the battle for Caen, Mike's battalion was in constant contact with the Zoot Suit Kids of the Hitler Jugend. Their sullen, boyish faces became as familiar as their mottled brown-and-green camouflage uniforms. Their trick of leaving snipers behind, some in civilian clothing, and some in uniform, to shoot despatch riders, runners and truck drivers in the back, became as familiar as their trick of throwing live grenades under the flag of surrender. The Zoot Suit Kids died as bravely and miserably as their Fuehrer had taught them to, and their respect for the rules was no stronger than his. On D-Day plus three, a liaison officer from the battalion on the right flank told the adjutant of Mike's battalion that an officer and eighteen N.C.O.'s and riflemen from his unit had been lined up and shot by an SS detachment after being taken prisoners. Long before an official investigating tribunal confirmed the story and announced its details in a special order, the enmity between the Third Canadian Division and the 12th SS had distilled out its last adulterant and left a pool of purest venom.

Mike killed his first German without feeling, to save his own life. He killed his second in a spirit of atonement and gratitude to young Rinowski. He killed his third in a berserk passion.

A sniper was operating somewhere around the heavy stone barn that was serving his company as a headquarters. A sentry coming off duty pitched dead in the farmyard on the way to fill his tin helmet at the stone water trough. Their platoon commander led Mike and the sergeant named Coombs to the corner of the barn. "He must be out in the wheat field there," the platoon commander said. "We've been over it once, in a hurry, and about all I can tell you is that there don't seem to be any mines in it."

"I'll use a Sten," Coombs told Mike. "You take your rifle and a few grenades."

They went back into the barn and came out another door, on the side away from the field. Another sergeant saw them leaving and said: "Going somewhere, Jack?"

"Duck-huntin'," Coombs said. The other sergeant nodded. It was part of the humor of their existence.

Coombs and Mike worked around to the edge of the field quickly, making their way down a sunken dirt road in a spraddling squat, like arthritic frogs. They lay at the edge of the field for a minute, discussing how they would go about the next part of their job.

"I been out there a couple of times," Coombs whispered. "I know where there's three snipers' holes. They're just like slit trenches only they got little steps dug at the end of them. They hop from one to the other when they think they're spotted. There's lots of ordinary trenches too. We better go over them one at a time, but I figure he'll be in one of the snipers' holes. I think I can find them. When I think we're gettin' close I'll give you a whoa with my hand. Keep as far away from me as you can and still see me. If I see him and figure he don't see me, I'll give you a come on, and you try to work around behind him. Don't do no shootin' till you hear my first burst unless you're sure you can get him. If I see him and I figure he sees me, I'll fire right away. I can keep his head down till you take a go at the other side."

Coombs felt his way head first into a shallow furrow between two rows of wheat, carefully patted down a channel in the adjoining row of wheat with hands, and squirmed off into the heart of the field. Mike followed, a little faster, taking advantage of the irregular rut left by the sergeant's body.

It was slow going. Mike thought his watch must have stopped. When it said they had been on their way only twenty minutes, the time seemed like two hours.

The sergeant paused for a long time, peering at something hidden by a screen of wheat. He worked his way to it, an inch or two at a time, and then waved Mike past an empty trench.

Mike lay near the trench while Coombs crawled on a little further. How long was it now? Forty minutes? Well, how many days? He wasn't sure. It was either D Plus Three or D Plus Four. That would make it Saturday or Sunday. He tried to make a more exact estimate by calculating how much sleep he had had. It was either sixteen hours or eighteen. There hadn't been any the first night. Two hours the second, four the third, and then the long sleep in the barn, ten hours. But there was another two hours last night for sure. Then it must be D Plus Five now. Hell! It was Monday.

Anyway, it wasn't much sleep. Some of them said the shelling helped the going without sleep, and some of them said it only made it tougher. The sergeant-major, who had nearly a year in Italy, said he didn't know which was the worst, but he knew there wasn't a man living who could take shelling and no sleep both.

There didn't seem to be any way of telling when you were going to be beat. Some of them would be fine, like Gilbert, and then a minor thing like looking at a dud mortar would break them right up. It wasn't just the tension building up either. You didn't feel tense after the first few days at all. You felt numb. Your body didn't seem any slower, but your mind was slower. If it was relaxation, it was a funny kind of relaxation. Right now you were relaxed. It was peaceful here in the wheat field. You could go to sleep in two seconds. And yet the smallest noise, the breaking of a twig maybe, and you couldn't be sure you wouldn't fall right apart and start to cry or yell, or fire your rifle at the first moving thing you saw, even if it was only a blade of wheat.

With an effort, Mike pulled himself out of his reverie and began bellying through the young grain again toward the sergeant. A small noise made him stop—a high-pitched whing terminated by a flat clunk, like a tuning fork suddenly brought against wood to end its vibration. A fierce chill seized him and his mind uttered a startled oath. A silencer!

He peered through the miniature jungle of wheat stalks to see if Coombs would move. The sergeant was as motionless as the drowsing wheat itself, and he was not frozen in his immobility, he was slumped into it. Mike pulled himself off the winding rut the sergeant had left in the caking loam and circled slowly in a rut of his own making until he could see the upper part of Coombs' face and the gelatinous ooze of blood filling the tiny wedge between his head and the earth. He crept a little closer, gently tugged the sergeant's Sten gun from beneath his lifeless arm, and backed away.

He was not sure what to do next. He didn't give it much thought. His nerves had tightened and gathered inside him, like a tangled ball of quills. Some powerful, nagging reflex usurped the functions of his brain and it drove him on, deeper into the heart of the field. He moved quickly. He did not altogether abandon caution, but he drew his knees up under him and shoved his body ahead two or three feet at a time with his heels. The filling heads of wheat waved recklessly over the shallow arch of his back.

Perhaps it was because he moved more like a patrol than like one man that the sniper decided to give up. His cry of "Kamerad!", rolling across the floor of the field, was as close and intimate as a cough heard in a telephone booth, and when his soiled handkerchief waved above the wheat it was not more than twenty yards away.

Mike stood up, snuggling the skeletonized butt of the Sten gun against his hip. The German was tall and thin and his torn camouflage suit flapped off his bony shoulders like a smock. His young face was haggard and a little afraid, and his blond hair was streaked with brown earth stains. He held his hands clasped together in his hair.

Mike made a motion with the gun and pointed it at the German's middle. The German began moving toward him, keeping his hands on his head. His gait was a weary shamble; he scarcely lifted his feet at all and once or twice he stumbled on the uneven floor of the field.

The two men's faces held each other until the gap between them was cut by half. Each face seemed to draw poison and malevolence from the other, and when they were close enough to see into each other's eyes, each face was a mirror of hate, a replica of the hate in the other.

Mike measured the German's body again as he shambled closer. His torn uniform had now flapped completely open, leaving his belly naked above his sagging trousers. His belly was brown and lean, and from the gouged curlicue of his navel a minute hedge of silky hair spiralled upward to his chest. As yet the hair had no color. It was lighter than the lean flesh to which it clung.

Mike counted his prisoner's steps now from the motion of his belly, and counted his breathing from the slow heaving of his naked flesh. He could distinguish the individual hairs of the German's belly, shimmering in the sunlight like wisps of fine thread.

He pressed the trigger. The German gasped. Above the gasp and the quick hammering of the Sten, the slugs from the mouth of the gun dug into his belly in wet thuds, like stones thrown hard into fresh concrete. For an instant the force of the bullets held the German's belly erect and in line with the gun. The bullets chewed it into a red slush, and then the slush slumped out of the line of fire. Mike held the gun steady and watched the German's chest sag into it, and heard the slugs biting louder as they hammered into bone. At the last, the German's head sagged into the path of the bullets and then swayed away from it. Mike moved the gun so that the last rounds in his magazine crunched between its staring eyes.

Mike studied the mangled body at his feet for a moment and choked out a tortured sob. "Rot!" he sobbed. "Rot, you wording bastard! Rot in hell!" He turned and walked across the field, dredging out a new sob with every breath. When he was near the edge of the field he began to run.

CHAPTER

12

Mike shrugged off his bulging entrail of webbing and threw it in a corner of the violated farmhouse parlor. He sniffed the stale air. "Jerry was here too," he announced confidently. "Funny how they all smell the same. I guess they've got even less time for taking baths than we have."

"I don't figure it's that," Kennebec said. "It's probably those rotten little sausages they eat. You get a whole batch of men eating the same things for months on end and even if it's rose petals they're bound to stink. We probably stink just as bad to them."

"Anyway," Mike ventured, "this looks like a pretty fair go. Look! There's not a hole in the whole wording roof."

Kennebec was dubious. "There must be something wrong," he said, "or company headquarters would have grabbed it first."

"The major's probably found himself a chateau," Mike thought. "I hear we're in reserve till Tuesday."

"Sure!" Kennebec said. "What's that mean? Instead of Minnie, we get the Eighty-eights and 105s. I'm gonna look for a hole."

"Let's case the joint first."

"What for?" Kennebec shrugged, examining scornfully the

meagre contents of the parlor: a round hardwood table, a few kitchen chairs, a splintered rosewood buffet lying half in and half out a gaping shell-hole in the thick plaster wall, and a litter of broken dishes and masonry fallen at the edge of an ancient patterned rug. "They get out in a hurry," Kennebec said. "But they're never in such a hurry that they leave anything behind."

Mike was more optimistic. "You never can tell," he said hopefully. "One place, Three Platoon found eight bottles of Calvados and a whole cellar full of cider."

Mike disappeared into an adjoining room. Kennebec stretched out on the floor, pillowed his head on his haversack, and lighted a cigarette.

In a few minutes Mike called through the doorway: "Hey, Kennebec! Here's that old worder again."

"What old worder?" Kennebec called back lazily.

Mike appeared in the doorway.

"Petain," he said. "Only this time it's not just his picture. They've got the flag draped around it and a fancy ribbon with that slogan of his about work and family and all that stuff. Oh well, so what?"

"So the hell with 'em," Kennebec was indignant. "This is the third place we've hit where they've had that old worder's kisser stuck up on the wall like he was Joan of Arc herself. I'm beginning to think the major's right. Half these people aren't on our side at all."

"Some of them," Mike conceded. "Not half."

"I wouldn't be too sure," Kennebec said. "You remember when the major said—when was it? D Plus Two or Three or somewhere back there—that we ought to keep away from the Frogs? When he said he'd just as soon trust a German as a Frog because at least the German wore a uniform. I thought the major was a wording fool. But I'd hate to bet on it now. I'm just beginning to wonder how many of the women that tossed roses at us when we came off the beaches had just climbed out of bed with a Zoot Suit Boy. And how many of the old boys that shoved wine at us were shoving wine at Jerry the night before. And how many of the poor old ladies that lit out from these farm-houses headed straight for Germany, clutching their framed pictures of old Petain to their withered old boobs."

"You're in a hell of a state," Mike said in mock commiseration.

"Yes," Kennebec said, "and how many of those snipers that we never catch are the people we came over here to bail out?"

"You're seeing things too," Mike said. "You know damn well two-thirds of the sniper flap is our own guys shooting at shadows and scaring hell out of each other."

"I suppose it was a shadow that got Coombs and that other kid."

"No," Mike said, with annoying reasonableness. "It was a German. In uniform. You're not blaming the Frogs for that?"

"Maybe I am," Kennebec said. "How did he manage to live a mile behind the lines for nearly a week? Who hid him? Who fed him?"

"Probably he did," Mike said.

"All right," Kennebec said. "How about the two women I saw in the POW cage yesterday? I suppose they were there for peddling their skirt? The hell they were! Just to make sure I asked the provost. They were caught shooting on a convoy out of a church steeple."

"That's two."

"Yes and there's more," Kennebec said. "I saw a copy of the Express the other day over at Battalion. Monty had his first press conference and he talked about women snipers too. He didn't say how many we'd caught, but if it had been only one or two, Monty wouldn't have talked about it."

Mike said: "From what I hear, Monty needs less to start him talking than you think."

"Well, let's forget the wording snipers then," Kennebec said. "But you've got eyes, Tully! You've seen the change in these people. At first they were all cheers and waves and smiles. Sure! They thought we'd be gone in a day or two. But when we didn't go, they stopped cheering damn' fast. As far as they're concerned now we're just a wording nuisance. We draw shell-fire; we're even a little careless about where we shoot our own guns. They won't even give you a thimbleful of cognac any more unless you show your money first. Oh sure!" Kennebec said hotly. "It was all right for us to come over and lose a few thousand men grabbing their wording country back for them. They just don't like us to leave our stiffs lying around so long."

"What have they got to cheer about?" Mike asked. "You've got eyes too. You've seen them scrounging through the ruins of their houses, dragging their furniture out in those little go-carts and sometimes not finding anything worth dragging out but their dead kids. I don't know that there's any call for them to keep cheering forever. You were through Caen. You know what happened there. The wording BBC kept telling them for months that they should be ready to get out when they got a warning. They got ready and waited for the warning and the warning never came. But the planes did. You saw what it did to their town, and if you didn't see what it did to the people who lived there you must have smelled it. And yet when we went through Caen they were still cheering and tossing flowers. But you're sore because they don't take it up as their full-time business. Jesus! I'd think I was doing pretty fair if I could raise one feeble little croak."

Kennebec asked: "How long have we been here?"

"Six weeks, I guess," Mike answered.

"How many Frenchmen have you seen doing any fighting?"

"A few," Mike said. "How about the old guy that came out on his bike and led the battalion into Caen? How about the farmer that walked out on the airport at Carpiquet with that eighty-eight sniping at him over open sights and told us where that mortar battery was? How about all the air force guys we've seen who say the only reason they're alive is because the underground took charge of them?"

"You said it right first," Kennebec said. "A few. Damn few. Oh, once the Germans are gone, they get their arm bands up fast enough. They get out the Sten guns we gave 'em to use on the Germans, and round up a few broken-down whores and shave their hair off. They beat their breasts and holler about the dirty Allemands and come sneaking in to denounce each other as collaborators. But how many of them come right out and fight when the Germans are in the neighborhood? A few, like you said. Damn' few."

"Maybe that's true around here," Mike said. "But how about over on the other side where the Yanks are? We're not moving much here. The best the underground could do if they got too randy on this front is stir up the Zoot Suit Boys till they started massacring everybody in sight. But the Yanks have bust loose and given them a chance over the other way. And even the Yanks say the underground is writing off almost as many Jerries as they're writing off themselves. That's what the BBC says, anyway."

"In the meantime," Kennebec said, "I'll wait till they show me. Personally. Resistance!" he snapped. "Listen: I talk their language. I've talked to a lot of them. I'll tell you what resistance is! It's that little cafe owner in Bayeux who hid his champagne from the Jerries so he could sell it to us for four hundred and fifty francs a bottle. It's that little wart with the beard who owns the novelty store. He told me himself he spent nearly four years smuggling in silk and dye from the black market in Paris so he could make flags in his basement, and then when De Gaulle came he sold the flags for five times what they cost him. And both those guys are heroes, according to their own miserable lights.

"Word!" Kennebec snorted. "It's bad enough fighting for them without having to pretend they're something that they're not. I've talked to a lot of them. And I haven't found three people whose understanding of the war wouldn't disgrace a Cree fishing guide back in Algonquin Park. They think we're here for one reason, and one reason only. To drive the Boche out of France. And they don't give a good God damn for one other thing: not for Poland or Belgium or Czechoslovakia or Holland, or least of all the dead we leave around to clutter up their fat little farms. The day I went into Bayeux for my bath, DeGaulle was speaking there. I guess he's a great man, but he's also a smart man. That was his first speech in France, and he was smart enough to tell them what they wanted to hear. He didn't waste his time talking a lot of irrelevant cock about a better Europe or a better world. He talked about France, about the complete sovereignty of France. Those were the words he used. He said, 'The victory which we shall gain shall be the victory of liberty and of France.' France! France! La Belle France! La Belle balls!"

Mike said: "Well, how would it be in Canada? Suppose the Japs took over Canada? What would be eating the heart out of every good Canadian? The Phillipines? Pearl Harbor? The starving Chinese? You're damn right it wouldn't. It would be getting the Japs out of there and getting our country back to the place where we could vote for Willie King or the CCF, where we could go down to the corner movie or hole up in a beer parlor and make speeches about how we fought the Japs by sticking thumbtacks under the automobile tires. We'd stack up to it just about the way the French stacked up when the Germans were here. Most of us wouldn't like it, and some of us would risk our lives trying to make it so uncomfortable for the Japs that they'd have to move out. But there'd be a Petain in Canada, some respectable Senator maybe, or one of our most solid business men. He'd form the kind of government the Japs wanted and run it the way the Japs said. And he wouldn't find too much trouble getting people to work for him. No, and there'd be lots of scared or greedy people willing to put his picture up in their front parlors. And there'd be women in Canada willing to crawl into the hay with any Jap officer who could show them where to get silk stockings or a little extra food, if food was scarce. And there'd be lots of staunch Church-going citizens willing to do business with the Japs. And when the Yanks, or the Limeys, or whoever it was, came and bailed us out, a lot of others would wave at them and throw flowers at them and sell them rot-gut whisky at twenty dollars a bottle."

Kennebec conceded grudgingly: "You could be right, you know. But you've still missed my point. My point is that I'm not quite as enthusiastic about this proposition as I used to be. You know, Tully, I used to think I was a hell of a guy. I read the Nation and the New Republic like some people read the Bible and I let liberal with a small l roll off my tongue like a monk telling his beads. I went to Spain with the Mac-Paps. I thought it was as simple as the alphabet. You fought the Fascists and if you were good enough to lick them, everything was going to be all right. Well, we lost in Spain. That was all right, though. We tried. I did, anyway. When I got back they made me report once a month to the Mounted Police. They figured I was a Communist. But that was all right too. It made me feel bigger than the rest of them, a kind of martyr I guess. I tried to get back into the army and for a while they wouldn't take me. Nobody came right out and said it was because I was supposed to be a Red. The chances are I was only too old and skinny. That didn't matter much either. I got in finally, and it still looked pretty much the same to me. You fought the Fascists and if you were good enough to lick them, things were still going to turn out swell. But every time I look a little closer at this thing, I get the feeling I'm threshing around in some God-damn swamp. Everybody's

eyes are full of mud, including my own, I guess. It doesn't look
half as clear as it did. The truths are only half-truths, and,
something worse, the lies are only half-lies."

Mike was almost certain he had won the argument. For once,
at least, Kennebec's astringent logic hadn't routed him. But he was
still glad there wasn't time to brood too deeply over what Kennebec had said.

*　　　*　　　*　　　*

It was months, in fact, before he thought of it at all. The
pattern of his war went on through the summer and the fall
without substantial deviation, and the orbit in which his mind
moved was no less cramped and confined than the endless series
of slit trenches through which he hounded his body. In August
his battalion helped to seal off the Falaise gap. In one attack
its four rifle companies took sixty percent casualties. In another,
the whole battalion walked into an ambush, and in the space of
six hours it was so badly cut up that it had to be withdrawn from
the line and completely reorganized.

For a few days, on the way through the noisome slaughter
pen of the Falaise gap, the German bodies, lying in pungent
clusters around the wreckage of their guns, lorries, wagons and
horses, almost seemed to say the same thing that everyone who
didn't have to fight the Germans was saying. Falaise had finished
them. They could never recover. Patton was on the outskirts of
Paris and still making his own pace. The British were on the way
to Brussels.

In those few surging days, Mike's battalion rushed all the
way to the Seine and beyond and hardly fired a shot on the way.
And then, with cruel abruptness, the vision of a quick victory
disappeared, and the war again became the size and shape of a
small rectangular hole dug in a shell-scarred field. Somehow, the
Germans recovered, reorganized after a fashion, and stood again.

Painfully, one at a time, his division began cleaning up the by-passed channel ports. The higher echelons drooled with confidence, but the inconvenience known to them as battle wastage continued.

When Boulogne and Calais had fallen, they moved up to the Scheldt, and here the fighting was as bad as ever. It was fall now, and the season matched the country. Cold wet winds and cold wet polders, grey forbidding rains and grey forbidding dykes, stretching endlessly through the smoke of endless battles. They splashed waist deep in the icy flood waters, sometimes riding out into the Scheldt itself in black amphibious Buffalos. These bleak dangerous months insulated and localized their minds as effectively as the strategy of the campaign insulated and localized their battles, and if their minds often left the Scheldt it was on personal business, to dwell on how wonderful it would be to be somewhere else, to be lying in clean beds perhaps with their women beside them, or to be steaming into a harbor with a band playing under a summer sky.

Late in October Mike went to Brussels on his first forty-eight-hour leave. Nolan went with him; Nolan had come back to the battalion, shortly after they crossed the Seine, fully recovered from his D-Day wounds.

As they jostled through the perpetual football crowds on the Boulevard Adolph Max, they stared in wonder at the uniformed doormen who stood at the intersections leading to the shady bar-strewn side-streets and called to the passing soldiers, like circus barkers: "Like nice girls, boys? Lotsa nice girls, good music, dancing, lotsa fun. Half a block boys."

"My wording nerves!" Nolan said. "I'll bet this is the only city in the world where the pimps wear uniforms."

The city seemed incredibly gay to them, and after the interminable ruin in which they had been living since June, its glossy wholeness was easy to confuse with prosperity. The only glimpse they caught of the lean ferment beneath the surface was vouch-

safed them by a seedy and mildly drunk civilian who lurched up
to their table in a bar and made a theatrical speech at them in
English: "Long live the Allies! Long live Belgium! Long live my
wife, who is ill and can buy eggs and milk and meat only on the
black market. Long live the peasants, who are feeding their butter
to the pigs because they are not allowed to sell it for five hundred
francs a kilo. Long live the Communists, who know if the hunger
grows sharp enough they will have their coup. Long live the
government, who would rather punish the patriots of the underground than bring justice to the collaborators."

Their forty-eight hours in Brussels cost them a month's pay
each, plus ten thousand francs which they had extracted from
a German officer before sending him on to a prisoner of war cage.
They didn't regret paying the equivalent of twenty dollars a bottle
for champagne, but on the morning they left, Nolan read something out of an army newspaper that made them both feel a little
sheepish about the various toasts they had drunk, in various bars,
to La Belle Belgique.

"My wording nerves!" Nolan said. "Did you know they've
got a coal strike on in this country?"

"What for?"

"Wages. Food. The government. Everything. They need the
coal and we need it for the war. But the first thing they do
after the Huns are gone is go on strike. They dug coal for Jerry
though."

Nolan read another item in the paper. "Do you know what
those tanks were doing we saw roaming around the streets yesterday? They were supposed to be guarding the government against
some kind of a revolution."

"I never saw anybody that looked like they wanted to revolt
except that screwball in the pub," Mike said. "What's the
trouble?"

"Maybe that screwball knew what he was talking about,"

Nolan said. "The government wants the underground to give up their guns. And the underground say they won't unless the government starts cracking down on a few collaborators. According to the underground the government is protecting a lot of big shots who got fat when the Germans were here. Whoever's right, it looks as if they're all a lot more interested in grabbing power for themselves than getting the war finished."

"Oh well," Mike said, "what's the difference so long as we can get another drink before the truck pulls out?"

Nevertheless, he was more disturbed and impressed than by anything Kennebec had said in their conversation in the battered farmhouse before Falaise. Walking down the soggy shoulder of a dyke to join his platoon again, he remembered the hordes of side-walk hawkers he had seen in Brussels, openly trading in Army cigarettes. He remembered the shabby grocery store where he had seen Army rations openly on sale at prices only a millionaire could afford. He remembered the friendly English provost sergeant who had warned him and Nolan: "Look, chums, if you're buying any cognac be careful where you buy it. Some of these people will sell you methylated spirits—at two quid a bottle. Two of our blokes died from it this week." He remembered the brittle floozies, the noisy bistros, the shop windows crammed with shoddy souvenirs at high prices, all the hallmarks of a newly liberated city on the make for its liberators. These were the only things he remembered of Brussels, for in his hectic, hurried forty-eight hours they were all he saw. Was this what Rinowski had in mind when he grovelled up the beach, he asked himself. Was this the end Coombs en-visaged when he went into the wheat field after the sniper, back in Normandy? He counted the dead men he had known well enough to call by their first names. The number came to more than a hundred already. Was this the root product of their bloated, mutilated flesh?

He communicated some of his forebodings to Tina's father

in an air mail letter. Pop's reply was so long that it came by surface mail. Pop wrote:

"*I see what you mean. Since I missed the only war they were thoughtful enough to make me a contemporary of, I can only answer from the doubtful perspective of an ivory tower.*

"*But it seems to me there must be something over there, if you can only find it, that will help you to come back knowing that what you did was good and essential and that the good of it can never be altogether lost. I can't suggest where you ought to look for it. Maybe it will just sneak up on you sometime. Maybe you'll find it in the face of some Belgian kid or some Dutch woman throwing flowers at you. Maybe you won't find it until you get to Germany. Perhaps it's waiting for you in a concentration camp or a jail. Maybe some day the man you're living and fighting beside will show it to you.*

"*I know it's very important for you to find it. Once I told you about my brother and me in the last war, how he went and I didn't and neither of us ever forgave himself. It might have sounded just like putting words together, but it wasn't. My brother had a bad time over there, but the worst time was when he got back and discovered that he couldn't show himself either sufficient cause or sufficient effect to justify going through it. That made it hard for him to live with people, and harder still to live with himself.*

"*One time, Mike, even before the war started, you said something that I've often thought of since. We were talking about the world's troubles and I thought you weren't excited enough about them. You asked me if I thought you should be parading under home-made banners. The context has changed a lot, but I think it's still a good question. And whatever the right answer was then, I think the right answer now is yes.*

"*If we only knew it, or were honest enough to admit it, Mike, I guess a lot of people are parading under home-made banners these* days. Oh, I know it's the store kind that make the biggest splash, and everybody is so dazzled by them that it hardly ever occurs to anybody to question their right to fly right up there at the front of the procession beside the drum major.

"But the store banners aren't quite all they seem—the trouble with them is they're just a little too gaudy and a little too neat. They try to make things too bright and simple. When Mr. Churchill or Mr. Roosevelt or Uncle Joe hands another one off the assembly line, we look at it with open mouths and we feel things running up and down our spines, and we repeat the words on that fine store banner with gratitude. 'United Nations', it says. Or, 'Democracy'. Or 'The Brotherhood of Man'. Or 'Lasting Peace'. Or 'Our Way of Life'.

"These are good banners, Mike, given to us by good, sincere men. They're good enough for most of us. For most of us, they supply courage and a hope that we sorely need. But for some of you, their very simplicity and brightness is a drawback. I mean those of you who are marching right up near the head of the parade. At first you see the banners more clearly than anybody; that's why you're marching near the front. But you also see a lot of other things more clearly than the rest of us. And after a while these other things make you suspicious of those fine bright store banners.

"You begin to see, ahead of any of us, that once you start to fight a war, the ends you're fighting for are never as bright and simple as they looked at first. You see that, although you may still be fighting for what is proclaimed on your banners, war is such a mixed-up business in its nature that a lot of opportunists and hitch-hikers have climbed aboard the band wagon and fixed it so you have to fight for them too.

"You begin to see that while you are fighting for democracy, you are also striking a few inadvertent blows for one kind of dictatorship in Yugoslavia, another kind of dictatorship in Greece,

*and a disreputable little monarchy in Italy. While you are fighting
for liberty in France and Belgium, you see that you are fighting
to restore to several violent factions the privilege of trying to deprive their countrymen of the liberty to disagree with them. While
you are fighting for the United Nations, you see that you are
also fighting for re-alignments of power which must sooner or
later threaten all unity between nations. While you are fighting
for peace, you are fighting to nourish the greeds and passions that
might lead to another war.*

*"And more immediately, you see that while you are fighting
to drive the Germans out of France, you are also providing a new
set of customers for a few little clip joints whose owners' interest
in you is precisely the same as their interest in the Germans—
specifically, what color is your money? You see that while you
are fighting to take the hunger out of some Dutch baby's stomach
or the fear out of some old Belgian lady's eyes, you are also fighting
so that a few other Dutch and Belgian people can get rich and fat
off the profits of hunger and fear.*

*"When you see these things, you also see that the banners
which looked so new and vivid when you started out are frayed
and fading. And that's where the danger is. If you turn your
faces away from those banners before you find others to
replace them, you will pay for it in bitterness and despair for the
rest of your lives.*

*"That's why I think it's important that you think hard about
those home-made banners. You need them. Don't try to pattern
them after the store kind, Mike; that kind, as I said, are all right
away back here at the Elks' picnic, but maybe there's too much
sheen on them to take into a fox-hole or what your friend
Kennebec calls the swamp of Europe. Just look for a little modest
one, Mike, one that won't be too heavy to carry, and that will still
wear after it has ceased to glisten. Maybe your banner will only
be the conviction that, whether what you started out to do is*

turning out the way you hoped it would or not, it was still neces-
sary for you to start. Maybe it will be the conviction that,
whether the world ever reaches the place it's aiming for or not,
the little way that you helped to push it was in the right direction.
Maybe it will only be the belief that, absurd and savage as your
times have been, there never was another time in history
when, just by picking up a rifle, an ordinary man from a drug
store or a bakery or a mine could range himself against forces
far mightier than we ever dreamed could live outside God, and
have at least a chance of changing them.

"Look hard for that banner, Mike. Perhaps I haven't the
right to say it from my ivory tower, but I know you will look.
And I lost the right to pray long ago, but I still do pray, to my
own strangely obliging Gods, that you will find it."

Mike carefully folded the letter and put it in his tunic. He
was smiling, thinking of Pop's honest, pugnacious face twisting
and grimacing for the honest, earnest words. He stuck his head
above the brow of his slit trench and called down the dyke: "Hey,
Kennebec!"

Kennebec's narrow face peered out of the next trench through
the fine November drizzle.

"What?"

"Go to hell," Mike sang comfortably, "I just wanted to tell you
to go to hell."

CHAPTER
13

There were new elements in the battle of the Scheldt . . . the low, dreary polders, alternately snatched from the sea and reclaimed from the sea for three hundred years, and now half flooded and of no use either as land or sea, but only as battlefields. The swollen bridgeless canals, blocked by sunken barges, of no use now for commerce, but places of great utility and convenience for killing. The dykes, scarred and blasted and bulldozed, of no use now to protect the land against the floods, but fine for sifting the fertilizer of dead flesh out of the waves of living men who swam through the canals and ran through the polders.

There was a fourth new element in the battle of the Scheldt: the element of mathematics. According to the cornerstone of all military structure, the War Establishment, the strength of an infantry company was a hundred and twenty-seven soldiers of all ranks. The strength of a platoon was thirty-seven and of a section, ten. These figures were not arrived at by hazard; they were the product of much science and calculation, spread over many years. It was on the basis of these figures that a division was assigned its section of the front. On the basis of the same figures, the division made assignments to brigades, brigades to battalions, battalions to companies, companies to platoons, platoons to sections and finally, sections to individual men. It was on the basis of these figures that all field commanders, from major-generals to lance-corporals, had been taught whatever principles of tactics it was deemed advisable that they should know. It was on the basis of these figures that companies, platoons, sections and individual soldiers, had been taught the best and most economical methods of clearing a village or a house, of silencing a machine-gun post, or of winning a foothold on an enemy-held dyke.

In the battle of the Scheldt, the mathematics by which the infantry fought broke down. The fighting was steady and hard and the casualties rode upward on an orderly graph, not spectacularly but without interruption or relief. Reinforcements were needed every day and sometimes twice a day. The reinforcements did not arrive in sufficient numbers to maintain the system of equations under which a hundred and twenty-seven men equalled a company, thirty-seven men equalled a platoon and ten men equalled a section.

This had happened before, in the early days of the beachhead, and in the fight from Caen to Falaise. There had been resentment about it then, and impatience. Now, on the Scheldt, in the fifth month of the campaign, there was more than that. In the early days, when the mathematics of a hundred and twenty-seven men equals a company had shown the first signs of breaking down, the infantry had been told that the causes were inevitable but temporary, and would be corrected when there were better harbor facilities on the beaches and a few adjustments had been made in the army's administrative machinery. But now, in the fifth month, they saw that the causes went much further back, as far back as the good abundant country whose arms they carried on the battlefields. They saw that they were not getting enough reinforcements to maintain their vital equations because their country was not sending enough reinforcements overseas. The knowledge filled them with a slow-burning fury.

The Army did its best to maintain the reinforcement pools by converting artillerymen, service corps drivers and even cooks into front-line infantrymen. This did not work as badly as it might have. The Army continued to function as an Army, and it continued to beat the enemy wherever the enemy chose to stand and fight.

Nevertheless, the infantry missed its mathematics. Because a company did not equal a hundred and twenty-seven men, the infantry's job, much the hardest and most dangerous job of all, became still harder and still more dangerous. Sometimes ninety, eighty or even seventy or sixty men would have to attack an objective which the fundamentals of infantry fighting decreed should be attacked by more than a hundred. In planning the battles, the commanders made such allowances as it was possible for them to make. But there were still only so many men to do what had to be done, and so much time in which to do it.

At best, the irregularity with which trained infantry reinforcements flowed to the front meant that the men who were already there had shorter periods in reserve than they would have had otherwise. At worst it meant that the whole fine and intricate system of tactics was disrupted. For an infantry attack, whether it be by a section or by an Army, is not a brave rabble charging across a field with each man firing on every hostile movement. It is a gigantic, lethal football play, in which the right end has certain things to do, and the quarterback, the blocking half, the ball carrier and the inside and middle wings certain others, and if any one of them fails to fulfill his own assignment or is forced to fulfill the assignment of someone else, the result is to disorganize the whole play. In its most intimate and tragic terms, the shortage of reinforcements meant sometimes that a section would go into battle seven or eight men strong instead of ten strong, or a platoon with two sections instead of three, or a company with no platoon held in reserve. Thus, the failing mathematics came down through the lawful democratic channels to the man who carried the rifle, came across the desks at Ottawa, through Canadian Military Headquarters in London, through Army Headquarters at Tilburg or Grave in Holland, through corps and division and brigade, through the polders and across the canals and into the trenches to claim the reckoning from the Tullys and the Kennebecs and Nolans.

Canada was not sending enough reinforcements to its Army and because of this men died who would not otherwise have died.

* * * *

At last the long grey battle of the Scheldt ended. Mike's division went into rest at Ghent, its first rest since D-Day. The streets and bars of the old Belgian city were filled with tired soldiers bent on forgetting the war, but the air was filled with angry talk of reinforcements. It wasn't only the chronic malcontents who talked; some of the bitterest talk was from captains, majors, lieutenant-colonels and even brigadiers and generals. Many of the officers didn't care whether the men heard or not.

Mike listened to two subalterns from different regiments comparing notes one night over a series of cognacs and water.

The first said: "We were lucky for the last couple of weeks. I lost half my platoon at Breskins, but it wasn't anything like the Leopold Canal."

The second said: "My company was down to sixty-seven men when it came out. I had nineteen in my platoon, and half them gunners who never saw a PIAT or threw a grenade until three weeks ago."

The first subaltern said: "Well, they know about it back home, anyway. I got a bunch of clippings from my old man. The papers are raising hell. My old man says Quebec or no Quebec they'll have to send the Zombies over."

"Sure they will," the other said, "about the time I get the second pip to my crown."

"No," the first subaltern said stubbornly. "They'll send them. The country won't stand for anything else. Half the cabinet is ready to walk out already. They sent Ralston over here to find out the score and when he went back and told them they had to send the Zombies, they threw him out. But they can't ignore what he told them. Hell! He was the Minister. That was his job. It was one thing when the popping off was being done by a lot of ordinary soldiers. But they can't laugh off what the Minister of Defense says."

The other said: "Well, I still wish I was a Zombie. I'd take my chances."

"So do I," the first subaltern said. "But it wouldn't do any good. Word!" he exploded, "there's seventy thousand of them. It just doesn't make sense. I've got to use a lance-corporal for a sergeant and riflemen for corporals, and there's enough trained men for three whole divisions sitting at home and nobody with enough guts to say: 'To hell with Quebec! The party's over!' No sir, you'll see. They'll be here."

"They tell me the Zombies are not only wearing Canada badges now, but they've got battle patches up too," the other said. "Boy! What a way to fight a war! No shootin', no slit trenches, no Compo rations, see your wife once a month, eat bacon and eggs, Molson's or Black Horse in the canteen, just sit around three or four years as useless as tits on a boar and then line up for your old job when it's over. Probably get there ahead of the guys that did the fighting, too."

"Let's talk about something else," the first subaltern said. "I don't mind being a sucker, but there's no law that says I've got to keep reminding myself of it."

The anger of the Army fell into two shades. One shade was of a deep and even tone, a matured, settled and unvarying anger;

this was the Army's anger for the politicians whom the Army felt had sold it out in order to sustain themselves in office. The other shade was its anger against the Zombies; this was more uneven, more like a flame blown by a changing wind. For although nearly everyone despised the Zombies in some degree, the despisal of some was tempered by the reluctant envy which the victim of a confidence trick vouchsafes the man who has tricked him. "After all, why blame the Zombies?" embittered infantrymen sometimes asked. "If I'd known what it was going to be like I wouldn't be here either." But in their hearts they had no way of knowing whether they meant it or not. And in their hearts, whether they felt that they had been defrauded by someone else or had only defrauded themselves, the image of the Zombies still mocked and gloated over them like some baleful smirking shadow dancing on a grave.

On the afternoon of their last day in Ghent, Mike, Kennebec and Nolan carefully counted out their money. Thanks to a recent meeting between Nolan and a paymaster of the Wehrmacht, it was still a lot.

"Boy!" Kennebec said, with unusual but sincere enthusiasm. "We can still buy any two bars in town."

"How about that paymaster, Nolan?" Mike said. "You never did tell us the details."

"There really wasn't much to it," Nolan said. "He just came out of a dugout over near that place, that Nocke I guess it was, where so many of them got tired of it all in such a hurry. I don't exactly know what it was that attracted me to him at first, unless it was his briefcase. No, I guess it wasn't that either. He just seemed to look like a paymaster. Did it ever occur to you that all paymasters look the same, whatever army they're in? You know the look, that Goodness-gracious-see-all-these-rough-peasants-clam-oring-for-my-money look.

"Well," Nolan said, "I hustled this paymaster around behind

a bunker before the sergeant even spotted him. He didn't have a Luger or binoculars, and I never even batted an eye at his wrist watch. You know me: honest Nolan. Besides I had five watches by then. So I just dived into his briefcase without any fussing around and came out with the gelt. He started to holler bloody murder. In Deutsch though, so I was pretty sure I was gonna be all right. There wasn't an interpreter closer than Brigade. I just counted the money and stuffed it inside my tunic and gave him a neighborly pat on the shoulder. But he still kept hollering and I was just a little bit worried. You know how some of these new lootenants are—they've heard so much about how officers are supposed to be treated when they get captured that they almost believe it. I was half afraid this guy might nail some stray two-pipper and get the two-pipper to make me give him or his money back, or give it to the two-pipper, which would have been worse. He kept making writing signs with his hands and I finally got it. So I said: 'Oh, you want a receipt?' And he brightened up and said, 'Ja ja, receipt.' I said: 'Sure, Mac, I'll give you a receipt. In our army, we always give receipts. Heil Churchill!' So I borrowed his pen, took a piece of paper out of his briefcase and wrote on it, signed with a big flourish, and gave the paper back to him. I even gave him back his pen, but that was sheer absent-mindedness. He looked at the paper hard, trying to pretend he understood what it said. Then he nodded his head and grunted 'Gut!' and stuck the paper in his pocket. I marched him around to the other side of the bunker and handed him over to the sergeant and that was the last I heard of it."

"What did you write on the receipt?" Mike said.

"Oh that," Nolan said. "Well first of all I put the date. Then I wrote: 'To whom it may concern—This officer had three thousand guilders in his possession when he was taken prisoner by the undersigned.' I signed it Joseph Glutz, Captain. Then I put: 'P.S.: He hasn't got it any more'."

Kennebec said: "You know, Nolan, you're a lot smarter than I thought you were. I hasten to add that doesn't exactly entitle you to a diploma."

Nolan ignored it: "I figure if we try real hard, we ought to just manage to get rid of the rest of it tonight."

They ate supper in their billet, a large schoolhouse which the Wehrmacht had converted into a well-furnished barracks before its departure. Just as they finished their preparations to leave on the mission they had discussed during the afternoon, the mail clerk came in with a handful of letters. There were three for Mike.

"You guys go ahead," Mike said to Kennebec and Nolan. "I'll meet you in the pub around the corner in about twenty minutes."

He sat down on his bunk and inspected the postmarks on the letters and arranged them in the order of their dates. The first two were from Tina, written on pale blue air mail forms. He read each one twice, and then read the second a third time. Something in it puzzled him and he scrutinized it closely. Tina's letters were usually full of passion and uninhibited yearning, but this one was a gabble of trivia which filled every corner of the single page with small gossip and ended in a cramped line that might almost have been a sigh of relief: "Now I've gone and chattered so much that there's no room to say any more. Love, Tina."

He put the letter in his pocket. "Oh well," he shrugged, "I guess she's browned off too."

He had seen from the handwriting on the envelope that the third letter was from his brother Joe, and from the Salvation Army stationery that it was written from a training camp in Canada. He began to read the letter quickly and eagerly, but after he had finished the first three or four lines, his eyes continued to travel down the page only under the pressure of physical force. It seemed to require a wrench or tug to bring them from the end of one line to the beginning of the next. He frowned and before he was through reading, the frown melted and then hardened into an expression of disbelief and bewilderment.

He did not read this letter a second time. He sat on the edge of his bed for a while, holding it loosely between his fingers, and then he tore it into small pieces, allowing the pieces to drop in a white disarray on the floor. He raked the pieces close together with his foot and set them on fire with a match. He watched them burn and curl into brittle flakes of ash and when one piece fluttered away from the burning pile in the tiny draft created by the fire, he picked it up with his fingers and dropped it back into the centre of the flame.

The fire burned itself out. He scraped the ashes under his bed with the sole of his boot, pulled together the eye-fasteners at the neck of his tunic, took his khaki beret from his bed and walked out of the empty room.

When he reached the darkening street he turned away from the centre of the city and walked aimlessly down a succession of side streets and across a succession of unfamiliar canal bridges. At first he passed two or three groups of soldiers in every block, most of the groups noisy, some of them boisterous, all of them making the most of their last night out of the line. When this festive traffic thinned down to a trickle, he turned down still another side street and pushed open the door to a bar.

There were a few soldiers inside, each escorting a girl who took care to announce her respectability by giggling every time her escort proposed another drink. There were also several clog-shod Belgian working men sipping beer and the inevitable handful of bar girls hovering resentfully in the background and waiting for the anti-social alliance between the soldiers and the respectable girls to break down in mutual disillusionment and restore Commerce to her throne.

Two or three of the bar girls brightened and called, " 'Allo, Cheri," when they saw Mike. Mike grinned and said: "Later.

Attendez." He pushed his way to the dingy bar and said: "Cognac. Double."

He drank it straight in two long, raw mouthfuls and said "Encore." He drank the second in the same way and ordered a third, a fourth, a fifth, a sixth and a seventh. The liquor neither lifted nor depressed him, but had a queer filleting effect that he had never felt before. It seemed to dissolve the bones of his body and the sinew of his mind, so that as his body sprawled against the bar it became loose and sloppy though he could still feel the edge of the bar pressing into his chest, and as his mind sprawled around the room it became vague and hard to pin down to any thought though he could still feel a pain nagging somewhere near its base.

He heard a girl singing a French song that he thought he had heard somewhere before, and then one of the soldiers sang the verses of "Alouette," and everybody, even the beer-sipping workmen, joined in the choruses. Over his shoulder, he heard a fuzzy progression of squalls, caterwaulings and sniffs of Flemish virtue which betokened certain inevitable redeployments among the good girls, the bar girls and the soldiers. The room emptied and filled again. Mike drank some more cognac. An unattached soldier came and stood beside him at the bar and tried to make conversation with him. Mike meant his monosyllabic replies to be aloof, but they only sounded helpless.

"Word!" the other soldier said, "you're drunk, chum. You better get the word out of here."

Mike ordered another drink, but before he finished it, he pushed it away and said owlishly to the other soldier: "You're right." He drew himself up, stalked toward the door, and made it just in time to be enthusiastically ill in the dark street outside.

His head cleared quickly and he floundered through the twisting streets for home, striking a rough course by the shadowy pyramid of the cathedral spire framed in the starlit sky. An MP patrol guided him the last few blocks to his billet.

It was still early. The billet was still empty. He removed one shoe but then sat on the edge of his bed for a while chain smoking in the dark and trying to recall the exact words that had been written on the pile of ashes beneath the bed. He was sober now, but his mind still felt much as it had felt in the bar, remote and foreign and yet neither so remote nor so foreign that he could not feel its pain.

The door opened, silhouetting the figures of two soldiers against the dim light from the corridor outside. One of the men snapped on an electric light switch. Mike lifted his head resentfully and peered down the long room to see who the newcomers were. They were Kennebec and Nolan.

"Hey! Where you been?" Nolan called plaintively as they came toward him.

Mike said nothing.

"We waited three hours", Nolan said virtuously. "And all we drank was beer. We didn't want to get ahead of you."

"Then we went looking for you," Kennebec said. "I'll bet we were in every pub in town."

"Sure," Nolan said, "and the last place, we damn near wound up in the jug. We were sitting in a corner minding our own business and some guy from the Arty started to throw glasses. A bunch of Limey provosts jumped the whole joint. Word! I saw so many red hats I thought I had scarlet fever."

"What's wrong?" Kennebec said sharply. "You quit speaking?"

"I'll tell you what's wrong," Mike said dully. "Sit down."

The others looked at him more closely and Nolan said: "Word! I'm sorry. I didn't know it was anything."

"I wouldn't want anybody else to know," Mike said. "For a while I wasn't even going to tell you. But I've got to tell somebody. It's just this: my brother's a Zombie. My brother Joe that I've been telling you about. He's a Zombie."

For a moment neither Nolan nor Kennebec replied. Then

Nolan said, with a pallid attempt at humor: "Word! What's a little thing like that? My uncle was a horse thief."

"No," Mike said, "it's not a little thing."

Kennebec said: "How are you so sure? Just because he isn't over here yet doesn't mean he hasn't gone active. Maybe he's been categoried or he might have got stiffed in at some training camp on the permanent staff. How long's he been in the army?"

"Nearly two years," Mike said. "He's been a Zombie nearly two years and I never knew it. I guess my wife knew and my dad and mother must have known. Finally he told me himself. I got it in a letter today."

"Jesus!" Nolan said with deep sympathy. "What did he say?"

"Just the ordinary things that any Zombie would say. He's not ashamed of it, he said. He doesn't care who knows it. He didn't tell me sooner because he figured it would get me upset, but now he's decided it's better I heard it from him than from somebody else. And then he gave me his reasons. There's nothing new in them. They're the same reasons the Zombies had before we were even calling them Zombies. You know: if the government needs men, why doesn't it get them the right way? Why doesn't it draft them all the way to the front instead of sticking them in that phoney reserve army and then trying to persuade them to go the rest of the way by putting the boots to them?

"Joe's got it all down pat," Mike said. "I guess he even believes it. Some of it, anyway. No sir—Joe's not afraid to get shot at, he says, he's just as good a patriot as any flag-waving politician, he says, and if they need him over here, all they've got to do is send him—him and the other seventy thousand. Joe says if it's his war, all right, he'll fight it. But it's not his war any more than anybody else's, and as long as they're letting anybody sit it out that wants to, well he guesses he'll sit it out too.

"It'd make you cry, the things they've done to Joe," Mike said with fierce sarcasm. "Joe says he's been insulted by every broken-down parade-ground soldier between Halifax and Vancouver. Every doddering old newspaper editor and politician and chair-borne general without a life of his own to lose has been screaming that Joe's yellow because he won't lay *his* life on the line to make the world safe for them to keep on beating their breasts to a pulp. Joe says the government's getting so desperate about him that it's taking out paid advertisements in all the papers to call him a louse. It's disgraceful what they've done to Joe."

"Well," Kennebec said, "as far as that goes, it is. We saw a little bit of it back at Basic. You take a kid that's just married maybe, or only half dry behind the ears, or who's never been away from home and either doesn't understand what's going on in the world or understands it too well to want any part of it— you take a kid like that and start treating him the way Sumner and Forsee and Drayton and the other "R" Boys got treated when we were at Basic, and if he's got guts enough to ride it through the first few months and stay an "R" Boy, the chances are the Spanish Inquisition itself wouldn't make him change his mind."

"Sure," Nolan said consolingly. "It *is* about as stupid a way to raise an army as anybody ever thought of. I think seventy thousand Zombies is a lot less than they deserve to have on their hands. I'll bet if they tried to run the U.S. army that way, they'd have three or four million Zombies."

"But God damn it!" Mike cried savagely. "This is my brother Joe we're talking about! It's not some scared little rabbit that's still got one hand tied on to his mother's apron strings. It's not some superstitious Frenchman who's never been taught anything but raising kids and lifting his hat to the priest and farming his own smug little forty acres. It's not some smirking little angle-player who doesn't give a wording hoot about what anybody else does or says or thinks so long as he comes out all right. This is my brother Joe! The kid I grew up with. The kid I taught to swim and throw a curve and hit back when some bigger kid was trying to push his face in for him. This isn't just another Zombie we're talking about. Hell! When I read Joe's letter it was like going home and finding somebody in bed with your wife. Joe knows what the war's about. He knows it's got to be won, and he knows how badly we need reinforcements, but still he's back there hunched up in his nice comfortable funk-hole, with all the conveniences handy including the neat ready-made arguments that help him persuade himself he's really quite a fellow. No," Mike cried, "Joe's not ashamed of himself. He's probably ashamed of me. I guess he thinks I'm a sucker, like all the rest of the Zombies do."

Nolan said self-consciously: "Maybe we might as well go to bed."

Mike said, more quietly, like a patient adult reasoning with a child: "If Joe's wife was going to have a baby, or was sick, I could understand it. I could understand if he was just scared. Or if he was a conchie. I think I could even understand it better if he'd hit out for the woods like everybody used to say they would if there was another war. I'd rather he was an honest chicken-belly than what he is."

Kennebec put his hand on Mike's shoulder. "I guess there's nothing we can say that will do any good." He spoke with genuine sorrow for his friend. "There's no use pretending a Zombie is the same as all the guys we've seen go over the hill. But I don't think you should hate your brother. Maybe you've got a right to hate the people who made him what he is, but you shouldn't hate him any more for this than you hated him for getting his nose punched when he was a kid. He's just run into something a little too big for him, that's all."

Mike said slowly: "I don't think I could ever really hate Joe, no matter what happened. Just the same from now on, he can go to hell. He's just another stranger that I thought I knew because I knew the color of his hair and how he talked and what he liked to eat and read. But I never knew him at all. What's more I don't think I want to know him."

They went to bed.

CHAPTER
14

In February, Mike's division, along with the rest of the Canadian land forces in Western Europe and a swollen corps of the British Second Army, jumped off from the Nijmegen salient on the operation Veritable.

Veritable hung over their heads through all of December and January like a swarthy bird of prey. They were to have begun the attack just after Christmas, but the Runstedt counter-attack in the Ardennes ruled out all pretense of aggressiveness. They sat in the soggy evergreen forests between the Maas and Waal rivers for two months, looking toward the flooded flats of the Rhineland and the drowned weirs and thick bristling walds between, shielding their sodden trenches as best they could from the icy rains and sometimes from the fine wet snow and wondering when they would start to move again. Sometimes there were night patrols down across the weirs or out into the floods in rowboats, or to the dark fringes of the waiting pines. Once or twice there was a company attack on some mutilated farmhouse, set out in the middle of a bog and ringed by dead cattle and the wet, unburied corpses of men who had passed that way before.

All through the cold weeks of early winter, the preparations

went on behind them; the ammunition dumps piled up, the
Engineers hewed corduroy roads and railway spurs through the
forests and threw long sagging pontoon bridges across the swollen
rivers, and finally the troops that had been pulled away to stand
before Von Runstedt returned to their old positions. The forests
filled to bursting point with men and weapons and the air above
them was heavy with a leaden imminence. In the second week of
February, the front leaped to life with the sudden violence of a
charge of static electricity grown too large for containing. The
guns reached with hot, heavy fingers at the first outposts of the
enemy, the planes mashed the grey towns just behind into sour,
shapeless mounds, and the infantry stirred from their holes again
and shambled through the trembling forests.

Their progress varied according to the depth of the floods,
the density of the forests and the shrewd if fatalistic caprice of
the German troops in front of them. The Germans knew that they
had been left there to die in the defense of their last useful bridgehead west of the sacred Rhine. They died willingly, and so far as
their narrow terms of reference made it possible, intelligently.
Where they had to yield, they yielded, but where they had to stand
they stood. They gave up their mangled towns fairly easily, their
Kleves, Calcars and Gochs, but they fought for the forests tree by
tree. Of the last of these, the Hochwald, they made a narrow
filter, packed with breastworks and underground scurry trenches,
and strained out sections, platoons and companies from the stream
of their attackers until the thin slits between the trees were clogged
with dead. But at last the stream poured through to the banks
of the Rhine and the operation Veritable was over.

The attack's first preparatory lunges had carried them into
Germany. Now they were on enemy soil, fighting the enemy they
had learned to hate amid the rancid chaos that had once been his
home and under the wide and frightened eyes of the people who
had sent him into battle.

For a while it was good to look at the festering skeletons of the towns and know that these black and splintered bones had once belonged to an enemy and not a friend. The towns were never good to smell; when spring came their smell would be as foul and haunting as the dusty fossils of Normandy or the damp mildewing slag heaps of Holland, but it was better to know that the decaying shapes beneath them had once hunted with the carrion and accepted their tithe from the grey-green maggots that feasted on a dying continent.

Nevertheless, it was not so easy to exult from the perspective of the battlefields as from the just but deodorized and lofty levels of the pulpit, the press, the rostrum and the unbombed street corner four thousand miles away. As the refugees began to set their timid footsteps away from the wreckage, they did not look especially like Germans. They merely looked like drab, red-eyed women holding close to their forlorn bundles and their silent round-eyed children; like old men bending their backs to their rickety pushcarts and careful to tip their hats as the trucks splashed by; they merely looked like people come to trouble and great grief, and the depth of their trouble and grief was so boundless that it was not instinctive to remember its roots and whereofs. It was easier to look at the dead than at the living.

One day, marching through Kleve on their way back into the line, Mike's battalion passed a churchyard where a group of new refugees were being cross-examined before being sent back to the big relief camp at Bedburg. A weary little family group was coming through the gate, the grandmother and mother ahead and two little girls behind. The last of the little girls held her hands high above her head, and as she passed the first of the lounging M.P.'s at the gate, her small round face was white with terror. The M.P. looked at her, made as though to speak, and then shrugged and took another puff on his cigarette.

"That's non-fraternization for you!" Kennebec muttered angrily. "We can't even tell them we don't shoot babies."

Mike said: "I'll be right back," and loped out of line to hold a bar of issue chocolate across the stone fence toward the little girl. The child shrank away and lifted her arms higher.

"You sure fixed that!" Kennebec said when Mike came back.

Their section corporal fell out and walked a few steps beside Mike. "Listen, Tully," he said, "I know it's crazy the same as you do. But how about using a little common sense? Did you see the funny look that intelligence officer in the cage gave you? I'll bet if we hadn't been on the way up, he'd have turned you in."

"Tell it to Kennebec," Mike grunted sourly. "It was his wording idea in the first place."

On a few other occasions they defied the non-fraternization decrees to talk with refugees. They did so not because they felt any compulsion to show the Germans sympathy, but because they had a simple curiosity to know whether German civilians thought the same as German soldiers. These experiments were confusing and unrewarding. A few refugees defiantly proclaimed their loyalty to and faith in Hitler. A few others asserted, with much expressive sawing of hands across their throats and much crying of "Hitler, Kaput!" that they had never been privy to the errors of their countrymen in thought or deed. And still more admitted that they had been members or servants of the Nazi party and indicated blandly that this was the only way they had been able to qualify for employment. Mike and Kennebec agreed that the one certain thing about the Germans was that you couldn't believe any of them.

One day, after a short advance that started out as a full-scale battle and petered out in a sudden German withdrawal, Mike, Kennebec and Nolan went poking through an unnaturally whole German house in search of any pieces of property sufficiently small and detachable to qualify, under their somewhat arbitrary and highly unofficial definition, as souvenirs rather than as loot. They stood in the comfortable living room for a while, looking uneasily at a whole panorama of crucifixes and religious lithographs on the walls.

"It beats me!" Nolan said. "These places are all the same. They've got more pictures of Jesus lying around than any three preachers' houses back where I come from."

They continued to look at the pictures, and Nolan said: "I wonder if Christ belonged to the Nazi Party too."

"Sure," Kennebec said. "Probably the only way He could get a job."

The kitchen and basement of the house were filled with food, huge stone jars of preserved vegetables and fruit, cured meats, flour, and fresh eggs by the dozen.

"Word!" Nolan said. "You could feed a whole regiment in this place. From any houses I've been in, I'd say the Krauts have been eating better than anybody in Europe. Better than anybody in England too."

"How did we ever get the idea they were ready to starve to death?" Mike said disgustedly. "I'll bet they haven't missed a meal since nineteen-forty."

"I'll tell you how we got the idea," Kennebec said. "We got it from the same place we got all our ideas about the Krauts, from the same union of Babbitts who told us they wouldn't fight in the first place, and who have been telling us, every day since they started fighting, that they were sure to fold up next Tuesday noon at the very latest.

"In lots of ways I guess we're pretty smart," Kennebec said. "But boy! what suckers we are for a nice fat platitude. We get our teeth into a platitude, and by God! there's no power this side of the grave that will make us let it go; we gnaw it and worry it and let the gravy from it run down our chins, we scrunch it up under our noses and smell it, and put out our fingers to feel it, and we call the neighbors in to look at it, and get our newspapers to write editorials about it and our authors to write books about it and our preachers to preach sermons about it and our politicians to make speeches about it, and we generally manage to make such a hullaballoo and fooferaw about it that we forget to look at the God-damned thing and see what it's made of."

"You talk pretty, Kennebec," Nolan said. "It would sure be nice if you'd tell us what you're talking *about* now and then."

"Oil!" Kennebec snapped. "Oil! There's the fattest, juiciest platitude of the bunch for you. The Germans are out of oil. They couldn't start a war because they were out of oil and they couldn't possibly finish one because after they did start the war, they had even less oil than they had when they didn't have any at all."

"And morale!" Kennebec said angrily. "When was it that the poor stricken Wehrmacht last lay stricken under the relentless surge of your relentless flat feet, Nolan? Was it Wednesday or Saturday? Was it in Normandy or on the Scheldt or in that last patch of pines down the road? Or what are those familiar noises ahead? It couldn't be guns could it? No, it must be the guest speaker at today's luncheon of the Rotary Club clearing his throat. Or maybe it's some wording war correspondent's typewriter tapping out Chapter Thirty-Eight of that story proving the Germans were finished at Falaise. Sure, the Wehrmacht's through! Boy, I'd give a week's pay to sit in on one of those newspaper briefings at Army Group or SHAEF. I'll bet the carnage is awful. I'll bet every time one of those brass hats takes another breath he kills off a whole battalion of Jerries. I'll bet the boys at the back of the room can hardly see those shiny big maps for stiffs."

"I see what you mean," Nolan said more respectfully.

"This food you saw out in the kitchen," Kennebec said. "It told you the Germans made sure they ate all right even if the rest of Europe starved. But that wouldn't make any difference to the wording Babbitts. They know better. They know the Germans have been starving too. They've been telling themselves so for years. How could they be wrong?"

"The trouble with you Kennebec," Mike said, "is you have no respect for authority."

"Authority, word!" Kennebec cried. "It's not just the big shots that think that way. The worst one I know is a sixty-five-year-old aunt of mine who never even had a maid. And the next worst is an old school teacher I used to have who never raised his voice in his life. And the third worst is a girl who used to think she was going to marry me. They all say the same things. Just wait till we get the Krauts on the run, they say, and they'll fold like the rats they always were. Just wait'll we get 'em fighting in their own country. That's when they'll holler uncle! Well, the Yanks have been wallowing around their country since last September, but there's still a lot of shooting going on. And I'm still getting three letters a week saying: 'Don't worry. Hang in there. They can't possibly stick it out later than the day after tomorrow. They'll quit just like they did last time.' Of course they'll quit! But when they do, it won't be because they were yellow, but because they got cut up so badly it simply became a physical impossibility for them to fight any more. And then we'll all go home and spend the rest of our lives listening to our aunts and uncles and our old men saying: 'See, what did I tell you? I knew they'd fold. A bully always folds. A bully is always a coward'."

"Well," Mike said, "let's pretend you're right about all this. What does it mean? Why go into a fit about it?"

"Don't you see?" Kennebec said earnestly. "Don't you see that if the world keeps thinking in terms of phoney slogans and wall mottoes, it's only setting itself up for something worse than ever happened to it before? You think the worst our weakness for platitudes can do is help us bore each other stiff; I think the worst it can do is kill off a few million men every generation or so. I think one little six-word platitude that we coined in the last war had more to do with letting this one start than all the Hitlers and Mussolinis and Francos and Tojos put together. The War to End all Wars. It was a good ideal, so long as we remembered it was only an ideal. But we got mixed up and started using it as a fact, as something that was already done. And the plainer it became, or should have become, that the grand champion, blue ribbon, winner's bitch of all the platitudes was going to fail us, the tighter we hung on to it. In the end it not only robbed us of the power to stop the war but nearly robbed us of the power to win it.

"And right now," Kennebec said, "before this war is even over, you can see the platitudes growing up that might make it easy for the next one to start. You're getting mail from home, both you guys, and from the same kind of people that I'm getting mail from. And what do they say? Well, they say, Germany is certainly learning her lesson this time. Well, they say, this will certainly finish those terrible Fascists forever. Well, they say, one thing about those awful buzz-bombs and rockets, they'll certainly make it impossible for us ever to have another war. Well, they say, it's at least taught us to get along with Russia."

Nolan, who had disappeared in the middle of Kennebec's oration, came back through the doorway leading to the kitchen. He was wearing a shiny opera hat pulled low over his ears and his arms were full of provender.

"By the way, professor," Nolan said, "I have here a frying pan. I also have here twelve, one dozen, eggs, which appear to be in a reasonable state of health. Do you think it would unduly disturb the equilibrium of the universe if I were to place the eggs in the frying pan, cook them for a period of, say, two and one half minutes, and then distribute them among the members of our little study group for purposes of sustenance and pleasure?"

"Turn mine over," Kennebec said.

CHAPTER

15

Spring came to Europe like a street walker's smile, full of fraudulent allure, half-hidden tragedy and high promise at a cost. It was a spring of shattering contrasts. . . . Of fashion showings in Paris and grey hunger in Alsace. Of reopening sidewalk cafes jammed with soldiers in Brussels, and ambulance convoys moving slowly across the Rhine from the bridgehead at Remagen. Of spring seeding in the distant fields of Normandy and Dutch children stopping in their play to watch the robot bombs race down toward Antwerp. Of crocuses and budding tulips wringing life from between the dead, wet shell scars of the northern front. Of pine-wood air fouled by the fermenting carcases of the little German towns. Of blue skies filled with the silvered menace of bombers flying in tight formation. Of sleek men who had never lost their sleekness driving good cars on the roads of France and Belgium, and lean, pale women who would never lose their leanness lining up for bread. Of German soldiers dying wretchedly under the arm of the Moselle while the fathers and mothers who had dedicated them to that end shuffled woodenly into the refugee camps muttering wooden curses against the things they taught their sons to die for.

The spring was sombre with the threat of another great battle, but it was also bright with the promise of victory and peace. Even the infantry caught the timbre of the season; even the infantry was not afraid to hope. The soldiers talked more than ever of home, and they ceased to talk as though talking about home were vaguely funny, like talking about steaks on a ship-wrecked raft. And their dreams were no longer the meagre, hedging dreams of men who did not dare to believe. Their homes were not just symbols of something that they had lost and might never recover; they were places that existed, that had roofs of wood and walls of brick, and the smiling graceful wraiths who peopled them had blood and substance. Soon, perhaps before Christmas, many of the soldiers would be in their homes again, physically.

For the first time, Mike told himself how lucky he had been. One morning he made an inventory of his company from memory, and discovered that of all the men who had crossed the Channel in the June assault, only he, Kennebec and a signaller in company headquarters had escaped both death and injury. He was going mention it to Kennebec, but decided not to. Kennebec had probably noticed himself, and had his own reasons for not commenting.

He thought of his brother more often than he intended. Late in the fall, driven to action by criticism of its reinforcement policy and the approach of another election, the government drafted sixteen thousand Reserve Army infantrymen for overseas service. The bulk of the Zombies remained at home in non-combat roles, as before, and of the sixteen thousand re-conscripted for overseas duty, eight thousand went A.W.L. or deserted before they could be put on boats. Nevertheless, by early winter, enough of them had reached the overseas reinforcement depots to take up some of the slack in the fighting units. During the relative lull between the Scheldt and Veritable, casualties diminished, and the life-giving equation of a hundred and twenty-seven men equals an infantry company was partially restored.

Mike watched the new reinforcements come and go, and often wondered which of them were Zombies and which were not. He never really found out. For the reinforcements who came in February and afterwards were much the same as the reinforce- ments who came in June. They wore the same uniforms, the same insignia and the same expressions. In battle, or in moving about their trenches between salvos from the enemy guns and mortars, they often did things wrong, but when they did it was more likely to be the result of greenness than of cowardice. Often, for the first few days, they were braver than it was sensible to be. Often, there was no time to size them up at all before they were gone. Often the men they fought beside would not even learn their names until they were dead. The sergeant would be taking a roll call after an attack and he would say: "Jones!" There would be no answer and the sergeant would say "Jones!" again. Then he would say, with something like exasperation in his voice: "Does anybody know what happened to Jones?" Somebody else would say: "Was that the short guy with the sandy hair?" The sergeant would say: "Yes, I think that was Jones. It was either Jones or Smith. Come to think of it, it couldn't have been Smith because he went to company headquarters." The other man would say: "Jones got it over by that first little house. The one where the machine gun was. I seen him. He got it in the guts." The sergeant would make an entry on a paper and call the next name. Perhaps the man who had identified the blurred memory that went with the other name would whisper to the soldier standing beside him: "That Jones was all right. He shoulda kept his head down but he was all right. He walked right in." And this would be the full recorded impact of Jones on the ken of those who saw him die. In his battalion, only the padre and the adjutant would know whether Jones was married or single, what town in Canada he called home, and whether or not he paid formal homage to a God, and they would learn these things only from another piece of paper. Among the men he fought beside, there would be none to bear witness whether he sang baritone or tenor, whether the worn snapshots he carried in his pocket were of his wife or of his girl, whether his preference in the way of breakfasts was for bacon and eggs or for real pork sausages well grilled, whether he liked his music hot or sweet, or whether he deemed it more desirable, at the end of his service in the army, to work for wages or to open a business for himself. Least of all would it be known whether the stranger Jones was a volunteer or an unwilling conscript.

Shortly after it was announced that some of the Zombies had been drafted overseas, the platoon commander gathered Mike's platoon together and said: "You all know the Zombies are on the way over. We'll be getting some of them in this platoon sooner or later. From now on, I'm asking you to take every new reinforcement who comes up to this platoon exactly the same way the platoon took most of us when we came as reinforcements ourselves. Let's take every man at his face value. If he shows up with a rifle and looks like he's ready to use it, nobody has a right to start asking questions. God knows how badly we've needed reinforcements. Now it looks as though we'll have nearly all we can use. Let's not make it any tougher on them or on ourselves than it has to be."

Mike accepted the appeal as just and sensible. But he still felt ashamed and resentful when he thought of his brother, and he often wondered whether Joe was among the sixteen thousand Zombies who had been drafted.

Mike's division was in reserve for the assault crossing of the lower Rhine, but while the long, low-flying convoys of gliders and troop-carrying Dakotas were still thrumming across the river to unload their cargoes of airborne troops, the division began moving into the British Second Army's bridgehead north of Wesel. The river was ridiculously quiet after the noisy barrages of the night and early morning, and any special significance attached to the short run across by Buffalo was largely wasted on the infantry. Nolan did lift himself up to the side of their armored ferry to spit into the swift-running stream but Kennebec grunted: "Just a wide creek with a good press agent. They say this is the last one, but I'll lay twelve to five we're up to our ears in another one inside three days."

In spirit, at least, Kennebec's prophecy stood up. They fought hard to clear the river bank northwest to Emmerich and then cut back toward the sea. One day, just before dusk, they rolled down a narrow cobbled road and passed an army sign that read: "You are now entering Holland. You may fraternize. Do not loot."

"Get out the water wings," Kennebec said. "Here come the canals again."

*　　　*　　　*　　　*

They were fighting toward Zutphen when Mike met Hobey Vincent. Their battalion was in reserve and Mike was sitting in the sun behind a scarred farmhouse mending a pair of socks when the voice of his section corporal called his attention to Vincent's presence.

"Gentleman to see you, Tully."

Mike looked up to see a small, not quite middle-aged man dressed in an officer's forage cap, a black turtle-neck sweater, a pair of corduroy trousers tucked into the tops of his muddy full wellingtons, and a naval rating's fawn duffel coat at least a size and a half too large.

The man's eyes were large and jocund, his face was round and red, and at the moment was in a state of amiable perspiration. Mike clambered to his feet in haste and considerable confusion. Anyone who dressed in such unorthodox style must be a full general at least; more likely a field marshall.

"Don't get up," the man said. "Vincent. Hobey Vincent."

"How do you do sir," Mike stammered, not sure whether to

salute or offer his hand and compromising on a feeble indetermin-
ate wave.

"Never fails," the man chuckled. "Probably the pants. Once
had an English brigadier sirring me for a whole hour. Climax of
my whole career. Probably never happened to a lance-corporal
before in the entire history of the human race."

"Lance-corporal?" Mike said.

"Well, not now. War correspondent now. That's even lower.
Lance-corporal in the last one though. Paid."

"Oh," Mike said. "Well, you must be looking for somebody
else. I never did anything to get my name in the papers."

"You Tully? Michael Tully? Know Peter Martin?"

"Sure," Mike said. "He's my boss back in Toronto."

"Good friend of mine," the other said. "Asked me to look
you up. Said you were a good man. Asked your colonel. He said the
same."

Mike flushed. "Let's sit down," he said.

The war correspondent talked for an hour, in short aggressive
flurries that reminded Mike of a weatherbeaten prize-fighter he
had once seen punching a bag in a gymnasium and standing back
from it every now and then to see if the bag showed signs of
weakening. Mike liked him. At the end of Vincent's visit he was
talking back as freely as he talked with Kennebec or Nolan.

As he rose to go, Vincent said: "What d'you make of all this,
anyway?"

"You mean the army?"

"No. France. Belgium. Holland. Germany. The people. Europe."

"That's funny," Mike said. "I've been asking myself the same
question ever since I got here—before I got here, I guess, before
I even got into the army. And I still don't know. Oh, I know I've
got all of it I want. But you don't see enough of it from a spot
like this to really form any ideas that make sense. You see a few
Jerries over the next canal, or a few old ladies walking down a

road or a few hungry kids. You're mad at some people and sorry for others. When you get your forty-eight in Brussels you see a lot of whores and bartenders. Now and then you get near a radio or the Maple Leaf catches up with you and you find out roughly what's going on. But sometimes I think I'd have learned a lot more if I'd stayed home and read the papers."

"Know how you feel," Vincent said. "Same in my war."

Mike said: "I'm overdue for my leave. I guess I'll go to Paris. That'll be all right. For nine days I'll have a bed and some good food and I'll get some drinks, but still all I'll see is a few shows and honky-tonks that I could see in Montreal. And I'll still go home and have to depend on some orator or newspaper editor who probably wasn't here at all to tell me what it is that makes this part of the world go around or prevents it from going around or whatever it is that this part of the world keeps doing. I guess it doesn't make much difference anyway. You couldn't find out much under these conditions, starting from scratch."

"You're right there," Vincent said. "I been knocking around these places off and on since nineteen twenty-five. Haven't found out anything yet I didn't suspect when I was a lance-jack at the bottom of a hole nearly thirty years ago. Tell you what though. If you'd really like to look around come on with me. You've got a nine-day leave coming. I've got a jeep and driver. Aim to take a fast tour of as much of the front as I can before it breaks up for good. Russians and Yanks due to link up any day. Going down there. Want to see that Buchenwald place too. Might even make Paris for a day or two. We'll have to sleep in our bedrolls some of the time. But mostly we'll hit hotels or make the Krauts give us their feather beds. And the drinks are on my expense account."

"Do you really mean it?" Mike said. "What about my pass? I couldn't get a pass to go roaming all over the continent."

"You can be my spare driver," Vincent said. "Nobody'll look at your pass. Think you're a sucker not to settle for Paris, but if you'd like to come all you've got to do is get your pass made out to any place they'll give it to you for. Then get your orderly room to call me when you're leaving. I'll pick you up in Brussels. Here, I'll give you the phone exchange. Canadian press camp. Not far from here."

"It's a deal," Mike said impulsively. "And thanks a lot."

As he watched the little newspaperman waddle jauntily away, Mike thought of the words his wife's father had written him, back in another age: "There must be something over there, if you can only find it, that will help you to come back knowing that what you did was good and essential and that the good of it can never be altogether lost."

"Pop and I both ought to have our heads read," he announced to nobody in particular. "But they can't hang you for trying."

CHAPTER
16

The jeep skidded off the narrow, cobbled canal road and bounced across the open moor like a shying jackrabbit. The round fawn bundle hunched in the right-hand front seat floundered to life and Vincent's protesting voice rose above the rattling of the springs:

"Hubert! For God's sake! Remember my sciatica!"

The driver turned a grinning freckled face toward the back seat, winked solemny at Mike, and stretched his two hands above his head until they rested on the lurching vehicle's curtained top.

"Look!" he cried. "No hands!"

Vincent's round red face emerged from the fawn bundle like a ripe tomato bursting from the top of a paper bag.

"Hubert!" Vincent yelled plaintively. "Look. See that brown stuff? That's gravel. It's a road. A road, Hubert. What is your prejudice against roads, Hubert? Was your mother frightened by a road? Or is it true that the army discourages all jeep drivers from using roads as a matter of higher policy?"

The driver grabbed the wheel again, tugged the vehicle out of a staccato shimmy and allowed it to idle down until its bumping had slowed to the rhythm of an electric washing machine.

"That's better, Hubert," Vincent said. "Not good, but better." He turned his round face to Mike and said: "Mustn't mind Hubert. He never drove before."

The driver grinned again. "We sure have fun, Mr. Vincent, don't we?"

"Fun?" Vincent said. "Yes, I guess we do. I'll sure miss it. But when I miss it I'll know what to do. I'll go down to the Y.M.C.A. gymnasium and tie myself onto one of those electric horses. Upside down, under its belly. Then I'll hire a guy to hit me on the head with a monkey wrench every time the horse goes up. And I'll hire another guy to belt me in the small of the back with a lead pipe every time the horse goes down. And I'll think of you, Hubert, and this jeep, and all the fun we had together."

As the jeep dawdled across the moor, the few trees that had stood beside the last canal disappeared from sight. No other trees rose from the flat black ground to take their place. There were only a few weeds, still brown from winter, clinging to the roadside, and after a while the weeds thinned out and the moor became a black and tenantless bog, heavy with the smell of peat. In the far distance, a horse moved slowly across the bare line of the horizon; there was no other sign of life.

"Is this still Holland?" Mike shouted to Vincent.

"Germany. Might as well tell you where we're going. Going to see the bobby-sox girls."

"Bobby-sox girls?"

"From Warsaw. That's just my two-bit journalese coming out, but they're really pretty wonderful. Whole camp full of them. Fought the Germans all last winter. Fought their tanks with grenades. Hid from them in the sewers. Finally had to give up. This is where they've been ever since. Polish Armored Division overran the camp the other day. Guess it's the only all-woman prisoner of war camp in the world."

Now, far ahead, the black blob of a tower rose on spindly wooden legs from the waste, and as the jeep bounced on, Mike picked out a cluster of dark unpainted shacks lying beneath the tower, and later a tall wire fence around the shacks. The jeep shook itself around another turn and he saw people moving behind the wire. The evidence of habitation in so desolate and barren a place made him catch his breath.

Hubert stamped on his brake pedal and the jeep screeched to a stop in front of a sentry hut standing before a thin opening in the barbed wire. A girl stepped out of the hut and saluted, slapping a small grimy hand across the butt of a Mauser rifle with sufficient force to produce a loud Guardsmanlike thud. She was unlike any girl Mike had ever seen before. He would have guessed her age to be thirteen. Her freckled face was thin and drawn and her eyes had the unnatural, disturbing wisdom that he had seen in the eyes of so many other children on the way from Normandy; yet there was a hint of humor in them too, a solemn jocosity that might have whispered: "None of this has really happened; it's only pretending." The girl's dress was a flamboyant medley of the uniforms of many nations. On her head she wore the rough-textured wedge cap of the Army of France, a shirt of Royal Air Force blue protruded beneath a jacket of American G.I. serge, and her British battle dress trousers were tucked into the tops of a pair of German jack boots.

"You wished, sir?" the girl said to Vincent.

"If you please, madam," Vincent said gallantly, "we would like to see Sergeant Major Wanda Maczek."

"You will come in?" The girl waved them through the gate and left them standing at the edge of a square of asphalt, underneath a flag pole surmounted by the green and red flag of Poland. The square was ringed with the dingy wooden huts they had seen from the moor, and into, out of, and between the huts there swarmed the disorderly traffic of some garish and preposterous bazaar. There were perhaps a thousand women in the square, no two dressed alike, and almost all dressed, like the girl at the gate, in the quartermasters' odds and ends of half the world. But now and then, as though to lend emphasis to the riotous caricature of military elegance, a woman walked past in the same clothing she must have been wearing when she dropped her cooking and needlework nearly a year before and stepped straight from her kitchen or drawing room into the battlefield of Warsaw. As Mike watched, two girls strolled by in battle dress, their belts ringed with hand grenades, and behind them, with a pail of peeled potatoes, came a grey-haired woman in a black silk dress that reached almost to her bare feet. A little later, a tall and soignée blonde sauntered across the square in jodhpurs, short riding boots, and an expensive looking tweed jacket. In one hand she carried a long cigarette holder and in the other a baby's bottle. A farm wagon drove out the gate, piled with garbage. Two dejected German peasants sat at the top of the garbage, gazing dispiritedly into the muzzle of a submachine gun held carelessly under the arm of a girl no older than the freckled sentry in the guard hut. At the far end of the square, a small group of women were doing rifle drill and another group, dressed in gym suits that had the unmistakeable glaze of brand-newness, were doing P.T.

"Here comes Wanda," Vincent whispered. "She's class. Her old man was a count."

Mike had barely had time to sort out his reactions. But when he saw the girl who stopped in front of Vincent and saluted, he knew what it was about this fantastic colony that was more fantastic than anything else—more fantastic than how it had arrived there, or its being there, in this bleak desert, or the busy self-sufficiency with which it appeared to be looking after itself. The most unbelievable thing was that they were all so good-looking and clean.

The girl who stood before them now so clearly invited the comparison that he almost blurted it out in words: Hedy Lamarr travelling incognito. Her face was of such white and perfect symmetry that it almost missed being beautiful, and the large black horn-rimmed glasses which framed it only added to its symmetry. The girl was engulfed, rather than clad, in a British Army cap, a G.I. tunic, a grey tweed skirt and a pair of British Army shoes, and yet she was as poised as any woman Mike had ever seen. She ought to be walking across a campus with a few books under her arm, he told himself, or dancing at the Royal York; and what was more she could get away with it just the way she was now.

The girl's voice was cool but friendly. She spoke carefully, though not especially slowly, and her accent, such as it was, lay not in her pronunciation, but in a tone of perpetual query.

"Ah," she said, "Mr. Vincent. You promised that you would come back and you have come back."

Vincent's hands groped beneath his duffel coat and he held a bundle of newspapers toward the girl. "They're old and they're English," he said. "But perhaps you could pull off some translations on your typewriter."

The girl said earnestly: "You are so kind. You could not have brought anything that would be half so welcome."

"This is my friend, Mr. Tully," Vincent said.

The girl smiled and said: "Would you like to see our home?"

They walked across the square, the girl a pace ahead. She talked over her shoulder as she led them into one of the huts.

"You see we are a little crowded," she said as she ushered them through a musty aisle lined on each side with wooden bunks three tiers deep. "In the winter it made for warmth. We had very few blankets. Some had one and some had none at all."

They passed through a dark kitchen in which four or five women were peeling vegetables. "We have wonderful food now since the liberation," the girl said. "The British Army gave us all we need and then, of course, we requisition more from the

German farmers. When the Germans were here we were hungry but we did not starve. We had some unpleasantness, but when the Germans surrendered the camp, we found it necessary to shoot only one of them."

They passed a long low building at the back of the kitchen. Mike and Vincent involuntarily turned their heads away from an odor as strong and sudden as a physical assault. The girl said casually: "Our latrines. They are better than they were, but they are still not pleasant."

They walked around another building and saw two girls sitting in the sun, one carefully inspecting the other's hair. "I am afraid we have lice too," their guide said. Abruptly she lost her composure and blushed. "And I am afraid we have lost some of our modesty too."

Vincent said quickly: "We must be going."

The girl led them to the gate and when she stopped to say good-bye Mike said: "Have they told you when you'll be leaving?"

"Perhaps in a week or so. There is another prison camp across the moor, only three miles from here I think. It is cleaner than this. I believe we are to be allowed to move there soon."

"I guess you won't be there long," Mike said. "You ought to be able to go home soon after that."

"Home?" the girl said. She looked inquiringly at Vincent. "I thought everybody knew," she said. "So long as those Russians are in Poland, going home is out of the question."

"But where will you go?" Mike asked, almost anxiously.

"England perhaps. America. But not Poland. Not until those Russians are gone. And that will be a long time."

Vincent put out his hand and said: "Well, good-bye again sergeant-major."

"Thank you for coming," the girl said.

They bumped across the moor in silence until they had almost reached the road beside the canal again. Mike leaned forward in the wind that cut through the speeding jeep and shouted: "Hobey?"

Vincent cautiously eased his face out of the folds of his duffel coat and said: "Yes?"

"What about that business of *those* Russians? I can understand them not liking the idea of having anybody else carrying guns around their country. But when she talked about the Germans, it was *the* Germans. She didn't even seem to be particularly mad at them. But when she said anything about the Russians it was *those* Russians."

"Thought you'd notice it," Vincent said. "With most of the Poles it's always *those* Russians. We got a whole division of them fighting in our army. They say *those* Russians too. Fight damn well against the Germans though. There are three things they hate: the Russians, the Germans and the Jews. And they hate the Russians worst. After Yalta the Poles up here had to be pulled right out of the line."

Mike said: "I guess there's a lot to be said for them."

"A hell of a lot," Vincent said. "But when it's all said you still can't get past that one thing: the Poles hate the Russians. Always have, for more centuries than it makes sense for one country to have to hate another. I'm not talking about that fine, pretty girl back there either. She comes from a class that hates the Russians in any language or dialect from Saint James Street in Montreal to the Faubourg St. Germain in Paris. I'm talking about several million other Poles."

"What's the answer?" Mike asked him.

Vincent shrugged. "When a little nation undertakes to hate a big nation, there's only one answer. And whether its hating is justified or not hasn't got much to do with it. The Russians know how the Poles feel and from there on nothing else has any bearing on what goes on in that part of the world. All the silk hats and striped pants will go right on talking themselves black in the face about ethnology and self-determination and democracy and the Curzon line. And nothing they say will have any more effect than a baby crying for the moon. Joe will go right ahead and do whatever he thinks he ought to do to push that mass of venom away from his doorstep."

"Do you figure he'll be right?" Mike asked.

Vincent frowned. "Probably not," he said. "But when a thing gets that inevitable, old Doctor Vincent refuses to worry whether it's right or not. Whatever's going to happen to Poland is as inevitable as the French Revolution or the American War of Independence. And that's where the Doctor bows his stately head to Kismet."

The jeep shied around a right-angled curve and Vincent clutched wildly at the dashboard.

"Hubert!" he cried reproachfully. "My sciatica!"

*   *   *   *

From the plains of Northern Germany, it took them two days' leisurely driving to reach the concentration camp at Buchenwald. For Mike's benefit, Vincent plotted their route to take them through the Ruhr. As they bounced through the blackened ulcers that had once been cities and saw the weary people who had lived there ferreting through the rubble like insects invading a scrofulous corpse, Mike felt a strong tug of pity, and the fact that pity was as irrational here as anywhere else in Germany would not put it down. He almost cried to Vincent: "Why do we have to pretend this is good? We had to do it, but do we have to gloat about it?" Nevertheless when a woman standing with a broom in her hand before the gangrenous skelton of a house tried to wave, he stared right past her, as he had been taught to do.

He was grateful when they left the Ruhr behind and cut across the green bulging downs of Westphalia. The villages they passed through now were as tranquil and unscarred as his own Saskatchewan village on a Sunday morning. Most of their shops were

shuttered and their streets were nearly empty, but from the sheds
at the back of their timber-and-plaster, Grimm's-Fairy-Tales
houses there came the fruitful living smells of fodder and new
manure, and the fields between the villages drenched the roads
with clover scent. They often passed peasants in old two-wheeled
carts riding behind black and white milk cows.

Once, as they crossed a wide valley, the only dwellings in sight
were two mediaeval castles glowering down from the surrounding
hills. Vincent waved across the spacious acres and said: "Living
space! Too bad they didn't think of looking for it here."

They stopped before the gates of Buchenwald late on a sunny
afternoon. The camp was smaller than Mike had expected.
Except that it was set in a quarry and surrounded by the chalky
ashes of the newly bombed prison factories, it did not look much
different from the weathered settlement that housed the girl
guerillas from Warsaw.

The main gate was patterned after the entrance to a hunting
lodge, with a log gate-house on each side and a square brown
archway above. While Vincent handed their passes to an
American M.P., Mike tried to decipher an inscription cut into
the archway in Gothic lettering.

Vincent studied it for a moment. " 'To each man his desserts',"
he said, "or words to that effect."

As they went through the entrance, a man in the uniform of a
prisoner shuffled up to Vincent and stood in front of him with
the air of a friendly but too-much-disciplined dog waiting to be
noticed. The man was desperately thin. His gray unhealthy skin
clung so closely to his bone that the hollows about his eyes and
in his cheeks had the dead finality of sores that had eaten themselves dry. The wastage of his body was so complete that it called
forth the unclean vision of self-devourment, the vision of hunger
feasting on itself through shrivelled, rotting gums. Against his
fleshless arms and legs, his wrists and ankles had the bloated

appearance of cankers on young saplings and his light-blue and black cotton uniform flapped above them like the costume of some gaunt and bloodless Harlequin.

Vincent smiled at the man and held out a cigarette. The man reached for the cigarette quickly, but he did not accept the offered light. A row of yellow insecure teeth smiled back in an expression somewhere between apology and craft and he carefully put the cigarette away in a pocket inside his tunic.

"You would like a guide?" he asked. His accent was thick and heavily ingratiating, but there was no hesitation over the words.

"If you would be so kind," Vincent said. The prisoner led them eagerly across an empty stretch of concrete and Vincent said: "Do you feel like telling us about yourself?"

"There is nothing to tell," the man said with a shrug that was meant to be casual and worldly, but only seemed abject. "I am a Flemish schoolteacher. I was in the Resistance. I was captured and brought here."

They walked a little further and their guide said in a tone of wheedling apology: "It is too bad you had not come a week ago. There was much more then to see."

He escorted them into a narrow yard surrounded on three sides by a wooden fence and on the fourth by the wall of a one-storey concrete building. Stacked against one side of the fence, like misshapen sticks of poplar cordwood, a small pile of corpses glinted whitely in the sunlight. A few were partly covered with prison rags, but most were naked. The bodies had not yet begun to swell and most of them were so thin that it was difficult to believe that they had ever served as bodies at all, or that the departure of life from them was a thing to be remarked upon.

Mike and Vincent turned away together and the guide said anxiously: "There were many more a week ago. The pile was higher than the fence every morning."

Vincent said gently: "Could we go somewhere else please?" But the guide threw him a look of nervous pleading and ran across the yard and squatted down beside the corpses, inspecting them intently.

"Look sirs!" he cried eagerly. "Here is one with marks of torture."

Neither of the other men approached closer and at length the guide shuffled back to them, shaking his head and murmuring regretfully: "You should have come a week ago."

He ran in front of them and opened a door leading to the cement building. They followed him inside, into a low room of concrete with a row of cold vault-like furnaces at one side. The guide hastily threw open the door of one of the furnaces and ran to the edge of the room and came back holding a long shovel-like blade by its long iron handle. The instrument was almost too heavy for him. He staggered weakly with it, but by levering the handle against his forearms he raised it up and thrust it into the empty oven, clanging it back and forth across the steel rollers inside.

"This is how they put the bodies in," he cried, panting with exertion and excitement. "I saw them. Once they made me help."

"Look!" Mike said. He pointed to a framed poster on the wall near the entrance to the room, a German verse superimposed on the painting of a man's face which looked out serenely from behind a wall of red and orange flame.

"God!" Vincent whispered. "God!"

They looked at the poster in silence and then Vincent said: "I think I can translate it. Roughly, anyway."

He read, making every syllable a separate sigh of wonder:

"I do not wish the cold wet earth for my bones,

"I do not wish the cold slavering worms for my flesh,

"I wish the fire,

"The good warm friendly fire."

"God!" Vincent said again. And then he wrenched himself away from the poster and said sardonically: "Edgar Guest".

The guide led them deeper into the camp and they went into a tiled laboratory. "Here they did their experiments," the guide said. "And here is our most famous thing of all. This is the lamp shade that was made for the wife of the commandant from the skin of a prisoner." They looked inside a glass case at a hollow parchment-like cylinder, bound with wire and flowered with red and blue tattooing.

"Here they used to fill the prisoners with the germs of terrible diseases and watch them die." the guide said. "They performed strange operations. Most of the men who came in here did not come out alive and those who did come out alive were often not men any more."

Vincent was absorbed in the study of another piece of literature above the door, a framed wall motto, smaller than the poster in the crematorium and without decoration. "It's something about the boons of science," he said. "My paraphrase is: 'It is a far far better thing to be a dead guinea pig than a live rabbit'."

The guide opened the door for them and said with a hopeful smile: "You will see the hospital now, sirs?"

Vincent glanced enquiringly at Mike and said: "No thank you. Our time is running short."

The guide said persuasively: "You will see the wooden bunks where the sick were crowded together on bare boards, six in a box less than two metres wide. And the trough into which the dead were kicked after they had been killed by a needle."

"I'm afraid we must go," Vincent said gently.

The guide's wasted face screwed up into a fibreless grimace, as though he were going to cry.

"You should see the hospital," he said desperately.

Vincent led the way back to the gate, through a thin stream

of insubstantial sallow figures shuffling across the square to get their supper. He pressed some money and a package of cigarettes into the guide's hand, and the guide threw a furtive, cunning glance at the men shuffling past toward the kitchens and quickly stuffed the cigarettes out of sight inside his tunic.

"Thank you, sir," he said. And then he added sadly: "It is too bad you had not come a week ago. There was much more to see."

As the jeep jolted them away from the camp, Mike was chilled and depressed in a measure he had never experienced before. For a while the source of the feeling eluded him. It was not the little pile of dead, for he had learned too well to look unmoved at dead friends to be much moved by the sight of dead strangers. Nor could it be the evidence of the long writhing anguish in which these strangers had died; he had heard too many screams on too many battlefields to believe that death was often painless. It couldn't even be the whining, morbid little daub of sludge that had replaced the spirit of the man who left them at the gate. On the aching roads to the refugee camps, in the mounds of ruin beside the roads, and once or twice in the haggard ranks of his own platoon, he had seen the souls of other men shrunk to rubble. There was some greater horror about the place that overrode all of these familiar horrors. A sudden tempest of Gothic type whirled into his straining mind. . . . "To each man his desserts." . . . "The fire, the good warm friendly fire." . . . "It is better to be a guinea pig." . . .

That was it. The signs!

He leaned forward and shouted into Vincent's ear: "God damn them, they believed in it! They might have been trying to sell Coca Cola or a new kind of liver pills."

They spent the night in a hotel in Weimar. Vincent was awake early, looking up a public relations officer of the First American Army who was quartered in another wing. When he came back, he announced amiably: "Scooped Vincent scores again! The Yanks and Russians linked up yesterday."

Hubert said self-righteously: "See, Mr. Vincent? If you'd let me drive the way I want to, you wouldn't always be turning up late."

"Late?" Vincent said. "Who's late, Hubert? I filed my story yesterday. Or was it the day before? Whatever it is, Hubert, it will work out all right. If it gets there a few days late, the office will blame it on transmission and the censors. They're very well trained back there. I've been beat by everybody but Horace Greeley on this assignment and they still think I'm just unlucky."

Vincent spread a 1938 Michelin's Auto Guide on the hood of the jeep, studied it for a moment and said:

"There's the place, Torgau. We turn off the Autobahn this side of Leipzig. We should get there in three hours, Hubert, but let's try and take five."

Rolling up the winding hill leading out of Weimar to the East, Hubert and the jeep went simultaneously into a paroxysm of sheer giddiness when a dark Fraulein dressed as though she were trying out for a sweater girl rolled her eyes and beckoned toward a cool lawn under an arch of oak trees.

"Lady!" Hubert squealed as he yanked the jeep back to the road. "My sciatica!"

They received many other salutes as they drove on toward the east. Children stopped their play to wave at them, men raised their hats, and girls and women smiled. One girl held out a bundle of early spring roses and three boys riding west on bicycles lifted their hands in the V sign.

"Liberation!" Vincent snorted.

"What's the deal, anyway?" Mike asked in genuine bewilderment. "It wasn't like this in our part of Germany."

"Liberation," Vincent repeated. "They've been yelling boo at themselves so long they finally got to believe it. They figure if we're here it means the Russians won't come this far."

When they turned off the Autobahn, they began passing long convoys of refugees who were unlike any refugees they had ever seen before. The homeless of France, Belgium, Holland and the German Rhineland had seldom seemed to be in a hurry; if they were going away from their homes time had lost its meaning, and if they were going toward their homes, the fear of what they might find when they arrived made every step a separate decision, to be taken only after the weighing of many separate unnamed dreads. And the homeless they had seen before were also without property. They carried their bundles on their backs or in tiny pushcarts, or at the best lashed to bicycles or bouncing forlornly about the light farm wagons they had "requisitioned" from the German countryside.

But the refugees they saw now were the incarnation of property and haste. They travelled in substantial family caravans: farm wagons piled high with household goods, tables, chairs, sofas, beds, stoves, mingled in heroic disarray with lesser objects, pots and pans, hampers of food and occasionally a few live chickens or a squalling pig. Some of the wagons were drawn by two horses and some by four, and at the rear of many a cow or two sobbed and sweated at the end of a straining halter-rope. Most of the wagons were driven by grimly impatient men of middle age, who walked on the gravel roadside to ease the burdens of their panting horses. Usually a woman walked behind the wagon, and often, a little further behind, a child or two alternately walked and ran to keep up.

Every line and lineament of these caravans spoke of hurry, the disorder of the inanimate things speaking no less loudly than the anxious concentration of the animate.

In many of them, the faces of the men and women had the unpigmented tightness of terror, and their terror had been communicated to the children and the animals, so that when the children fell behind they cast frightened glances over their shoulders to the serene sunlit fields in the distance, and when the horses came to an incline in the road they rolled their eyes in dumb dismay and flailed their feet at the giving gravel without waiting to be whipped.

The jeep slowed to a crawl and Vincent leaned across to shout to one of the men: "Ausgebomft?"

Without looking up from the wet flanks of his horses, the man shouted back: "Nein!"

"Just what that P.R.O. told me," Vincent said. "Nothing's happened to them. Nobody's shot at them, or turned them out. I don't suppose more than half of them ever saw a Russian. Look at 'em though. Scared blind. Remind you of the pictures you used to see of people haring across the steppes with the wolves behind. Throw out another Gauleiter, Meinherr, Joe is breathing down your neck! That's what propoganda will do."

And a little later Vincent said more thoughtfully: "The Germans had five years to get it across with the rest of Western Europe. If this is a sample it was a pretty good job. I wonder if it will stick in the other countries too?"

Mike said: "Do you really wonder? Or have you made your guess already?"

"Only to this extent," Vincent said. "My guess is that wherever Russia is concerned, the rest of Europe is frozen up in its thinking just the way these people are frozen up. How it will come out when the thaw sets in, I have no idea. But right now, I don't believe that where Russia is concerned there is any large body of speculation or inquiry anywhere in the world that you could call real thought. As nearly as I can make out, the world is divided right down the middle into people who believe Uncle Joe gets the party line piped in straight from hell and people who believe he gets it in a vision every morning with the personal compliments of Jesus Christ. And the opinions of each group, if opinions is the word, are as fixed and rigid as the beliefs of a third-generation Holy Roller. The Russians do something friendly or something suspicious, either in their own country or maybe in the Balkans, and there aren't three non-Russians in a thousand who will sit down and try to figure out what it means. Say the act is friendly on the surface: out of every thousand people, five hundred will say, 'See, I knew it all along, if we give 'em their heads they'll show us the way to the millenium in spite of ourselves,' and the other five hundred will say, 'What did I tell you, you can't trust the bastards, they're a bog of deceit and guile.' And if the act is suspicious on the surface, five hundred people will say, 'Good for them, they're sick of being outsmarted and sabotaged by the rest of us,' and the other five hundred will say, 'See, what can you expect of the God-damn barbarians?' "

"And which five hundred is right?" Mike asked.

"Neither!" Vincent shouted. "The simplest fact I know about the world, the only fact I know for sure, is that every nation that ever existed has, at some time in its history, done some fine and generous things and also some dangerous and predatory things. There never was a nation that dealt exclusively in one kind of thing or the other. But here, by Jesus! we've got half the world insisting that Russia operates exclusively for the good of humanity and the other half insisting she operates exclusively for the ends of the Devil. And neither half has any more flexibility and balance to its views than those peasants out there on the road, running their legs off because Goebbels told them Russia means the same thing as rape and murder."

"Sometimes," Mike said, "I think this whole damn continent is crazy."

"No," Vincent said. "No crazier than the rest of us. Over here they just get more and better chances to prove it. Considering our geographical handicaps, we hold our end up all right."

"Well," Mike said, "I'll still take our corner. Anybody that wants my share of Europe can step right up any time."

"Me too," the driver Hubert cut in enthusiastically. "The only place I ever felt at home over here was in a cat house in Brussels and even there they rolled me for a month's pay."

Vincent regarded the two soldiers seriously. "What do your pals think about it?"

Mike said, "The same." Hubert nodded and added, "Only more so."

"That's what I thought," Vincent said slowly. "And any G.I.'s I've talked to have got an even bigger scunner on it than you fellows."

Vincent reflected and added: "It's a lot like it was in my war. Only this time it's more aggravated. While the isolationists stayed home talking themselves into becoming internationalists, all the good internationalists were over here becoming isolationists."

There was no more talk until they came to the edge of a small and undistinguished town which Vincent announced must be their destination. The town was almost deserted and they found their way to the river by stages. They stopped for a few minutes in the main street to watch three or four stalwart Slavic-looking women with handkerchiefs tied around their heads going through the leisurely process of looting a row of unoccupied shops. The women were late and knew it, but they went through one broken plate-glass window after another to inspect each of the shops with patient conscientious thoroughness. From one window one of them emerged with a large, shiny accordion, and another held aloft a bedroom chamber of flowered porcelain. They smiled to the men in the jeep. Their smiles were both proud and rueful and said plainly: "These articles are of little use, but they belong to us. They are possessions, and possessions, no matter how foolish, are good in themselves."

The jeep crossed a canal and drove along a high stone wall.

It turned down an opening in the wall and brought them to the bank of the river.

A broken bridge, sagging out of sight among the splinters of its girders, made the river look wider than it was, and a small flat-bottomed boat struggling from the far bank with a few American soldiers exaggerated the speed of its muddy current. And as they took in the rest of the scene, everything else seemed overdrawn and sharpened, as in a symbolic painting. On the near bank, a group of Russian slave workers and liberated prisoners of war had hoisted the red flag of their country from the limb of a tree and were sitting near the tree preparing to eat a lunch of American Army K rations. Coming down a winding trail toward the far bank, like bright butterflies flitting above a black serpent, they saw the flags of Belgium, France and Holland clinging to the edges of a straggling procession of refugees bound for the west.

There were not many soldiers in sight, perhaps two dozen American officers and enlisted men on the near bank and another dozen or so on the far bank mingled among the murky grey-brown uniforms of thirty or forty Russians. As they watched, a swarthy man dressed in swarthy rags went to the edge of the stream and waved across to the Russian soldiers. "Tovarich!" he cried in a voice full of hoarse good will, and also faintly edged with the consciousness of absurdity, as though he were making a beautiful joke. "Tovarich!" He held up a bottle of cognac, took a long drink from its neck and cried the word again. A bearded soldier rose among the Russians on the other side of the river, held a bottle to his lips and then, in exactly the same tone the other man had used, called "Tovarich!" back.

Vincent introduced himself to an American major and asked if they could go across on the ferry. The major looked doubtful but said: "All right. Only there's a sentry on the road over there about two hundred yards back from the river. He's guarding their command post. He's not letting anybody past anyway, but I'd just as soon you didn't try."

"How you been getting along?" Vincent asked.

"Wonderful," the major said. "Yesterday it was like a wording clambake. I've still got a few G.I.'s over there that I ought to think about getting back, but hell! they haven't had so much fun since the first night they saw Piccadilly Circus. You just hate to blow the whistle on them."

Mike and Vincent stepped aboard the boat and balanced themselves against its yawing sides while it made the short choppy run to the other side. An officer was waiting to greet them, a dark amiable man whose age appeared to be about the same as Vincent's. There were so many medals on his chest it was like a coat of mail. When he smiled, he showed a row of silver false teeth and his brown eyes crinkled up in his brown face like little stones of amber. "Suvorov," he said, extending his hand. "Not general. Captain."

"Vincent. Not anything much. War correspondent. This is Tully. Private."

The Russian peered in candid bewilderment at Vincent's exotic costume, but after he had studied Mike for a moment he said confidently: "English?"

"Canadian," Vincent said.

"Ah," the Russian said. "First I see." He led them across the grass to where three or four other officers, all equally amiable and equally bemedalled, were sunning themselves.

He waved them to seats around a white table-cloth spread with big chunks of greasy meat, loaves of black bread, cardboard packages of German army cheese and tin water bottles streaked with red wine. Before the introductions were over, two of the water bottles were pressed on each of them. The wine was sweet, but not so sweet that it wasn't wet. Mike drank gratefully and after he had returned the first canteen to its owner, he was pleased to see that the second was still waving invitingly under his nose. He took a long pull from that, and when he handed it back it was almost immediately replaced by a small glass of colorless liquid.

"Vodka!" Suvorov said, raising a glass of his own.

One of the other Russians said: "Churchill!" and Mike taking his lead from Vincent, repeated, "Churchill," and drained his glass. "They can't kid me," he whispered to Vincent when he caught his breath again. "No matter how they spell it, it's still potato whisky." The glasses were filled again and Vincent said quickly: "Stalin." In rapid succession they toasted Truman and Roosevelt, and then after a decent pause to mark the end of the formalities, someone whom the proposer identified as Donna Dobbin.

"Donna Dobbin," Suvorov explained patiently. "Sings in pictures. Very liked in Russia."

Suvorov reached on the ground behind him and produced a bayonet with which he improvised a few ferocious sandwiches of meat and bread from the supplies on the cloth. They ate and drank without speaking for what seemed a long time. The food was as good as the drink, and the silence was good too; it was like an amalgam or compendium of the many good things around them—the green cool grass on which they sat, the cool rushing river nearby, the sunlight, the absence of shellfire or powder smells in the spring air, the homeless from the East and West turning their faces across the river toward their homes, the soldiers from Russia and America arrived together at the end of their long journey and now with nowhere else to go. Mike accepted a long hollow-stemmed cigarette from Suvorov and began to look around him.

There were several other groups of soldiers sitting in the grass nearby, usually three or four American enlisted men to a group and twice that many Russians. Some of them were eating and drinking. Some were trying to talk, saying one word at a time and then repeating it loudly and slowly, striving for understanding through volume and reiteration. One Russian was playing

on an accordion and singing a melancholy accompaniment. An
American pfc was teaching several Russians to roll dice and apparently losing money at it, but each time one of the Russians
made another pass, the American cried "Da da" in a pleased
voice and pushed out another handful of German occupation
marks. Two or three pairs of soldiers had exchanged weapons
and were taking the weapons apart to see what made them work.

Unaccountably, Mike was surprised to see that the Russian
soldiers were as various and unpatterned as any other soldiers.
Their grey-brown uniforms were scruffy with wear and dirt, and
the similarity between them was by no means exact; there was a
considerable latitude as to cut and color, and where one man
might wear a blouse and ankle shoes, another might wear a
sweater, tunic and jackboots, each apparently governed by nothing
but his individual preference and his standing with the quarter-
master. It was no different in Mike's own platoon, or any other
unit whose function was fighting the enemy at close quarters.
Several of the Russians carried German pistols or elaborate SS
daggers, but they all had competent-looking submachine guns of
Russian make.

The Russians were not quite so large as the Americans around
them, but their bodies looked sure and hard; some of them
wore fresh wound dressings on their heads or arms without ap-
pearing much less healthy than the rest. Their ages, Mike guessed,
might run all the way from sixteen or seventeen to forty. Many
of them wore beards, but one boy, who had fallen asleep, seemed
scarcely to have begun to find his growth. His round face, relaxed
in the sun, reminded Mike of his brother Joe when Joe was not
quite into his adolescence. The memory of his brother splashed
like cold water at the warm fringes of his mood, and he put it
quickly away from him.

There was very little about the faces of the Russian soldiers
that invited generalities, except one thing perhaps, a thing that

Mike had grown accustomed to in the faces of his comrades and which was in his own face also—a thing so familiar and yet elusive that he had never tried to catalogue it. A painter, coming on it suddenly and not having seen it before, might have captured a little of it without finding a name for it. Their look had a tentativeness and caution to it, as though its bearers had found themselves on the verge of some great, wise and painful discovery and, daring go no further, had ruled that all further thought and emotion be kept within safe and specified boundaries. Within these boundaries, their faces showed a little of all the wisdom, pain, excitement, humor, gentleness and violence that man has ever known, but not so much showed of any single thing that it could be said the look was one look or another. Mike only thought they had the look of infantrymen who had been in the line a long time, which was a shorter way of saying the same thing. He decided the war had probably seemed pretty much the same to them as it seemed to him—that, whatever depth of zeal and conviction they had brought to it to start, it must have begun soon to seem like nothing more than the endless stacking up of days, the walking through barrages, the burying of friends, the yearning for far-off bounties, the rushing over hills and dykes and rivers and always finding another hill or dyke or river on the other side.

Suvorov was addressing him and Vincent jointly.

"Mae Murray," he said, showing his silver teeth in a companionable smile. "What happens with Mae Murray?"

Vincent looked puzzled.

"Also in pictures," Suvorov explained. "Also very liked in Russia."

"Oh!" Vincent said. "Mae Murray."

"Da da," Suvorov said eagerly. "What happens with?"

Vincent shrugged. "Sorry," he said. "Don't know."

"Don't know?" Suvorov said incredulously. "Don't know what happens with Mae Murray?"

Vincent shrugged again. Suvorov explained the conversation to the other officers and they all began to exclaim unbelievingly. But Suvorov hastily silenced them, flashed Vincent an understanding smile and firmly steered the talk away from dangerous state secrets. He pointed to a lieutenant seated next to Vincent and said: "Was at Stalingrad." Vincent murmured respectfully. Suvorov pointed to another officer and said: "Also at Stalingrad."

"You too, Captain?" Vincent asked.

"Also," Suvorov said. "Myself also at Stalingrad."

They drank another toast. Suvorov waved toward the Russian N.C.O.s and privates in the grass nearby. "All from Stalingrad," he said.

Suvorov turned to Mike. "And you?" he asked.

"From Alamein," Mike said.

Suvorov glanced at him with heightened respect, then pointed to him dramatically and made an announcement to the other Russians. They all broke into clucks of tribute and began pouring drinks from their flasks. In the confusion, Vincent whispered to Mike: "What the hell did you tell them that for?"

Mike looked at him solemnly and whispered, a little thickly: "It's what they expect. They're pretty sure I'm lying just like I'm pretty sure they're lying. They just couldn't all have come from Stalingrad. If they've been fighting, and I guess they have, it's quite a trick to come a hundred miles. It's just as reasonable for every soldier in the British Empire to come from Alamein as for every soldier in the whole Russian army to come from Stalingrad. Besides, a little bull never hurt anybody."

Vincent said, also a little thickly: "By God you're right." And when Suvorov shoved a glass of vodka at him, Vincent pointed to himself and said: "Also from Alamein."

Another hour passed lazily. Mike stretched out in the grass and was on the point of going to sleep when an indignant voice, raised not far away, brought him back to consciousness. "Of all the wordin' crust!" the voice cried, and then it subsided into a murmur of other voices, in all of which there was a note halfway between protest and incomprehension.

Mike sat up. He saw that the other soldiers, both American and Russian, were rising from their places in the grass, the Russians shuffling uncomfortably away from the river and the Americans brushing the loose grass away from their uniforms and exchanging uncertain frowns with one another. He became aware that Vincent was getting to his feet too. He scrambled erect himself just in time to see Suvorov, standing stiffly to attention, salute an officer who hadn't been there when he closed his eyes. The newcomer was tall and respendently dressed, and his expression was as severe as the nod with which he acknowledged Suvorov's salute.

"Colonel Kavalov," Suvorov said anxiously, inclining his head toward Vincent.

The colonel nodded as brusquely as before. "I am sorry, gentlemen," he said coldly. "You are without authorization on territory occupied by the Red Army. I must ask you to return to the other side of the river."

He spoke a few words in Russian to Suvorov and the other officers. All but Suvorov, without glancing at Vincent or Mike, began hastily gathering up the remains of their lunch. Suvorov hesitated, quickly shook hands, and then hurried away.

Vincent and Mike walked the few paces to the river bank and stood there waiting for the flat-bottomed boat to return from the other side. The American soldiers began to drift down and stand beside them, muttering among themselves in sore, querulous voices and turning their heads every now and then to glare at the Russians dispersing back up the bank toward the road.

"What's the trouble, chum?" Mike asked a pfc he thought he recognized as the soldier who had been shooting dice.

"No trouble," the pfc growled. "We was just sittin' around

like we been doin' for the last two days when all of a sudden this long bastard of a colonel comes along, looks at us like we was somethin' out of a sewer drain and says: 'I must ask you to return to the other side of the river at once.' Well that's all right; maybe they was wantin' the grounds for a football game for all we knew. But you know how it is, a guy don't mind bein' pushed around only he don't like people doin' it just for the exercise. So one of the guys ast this colonel if we'd done anythin' we shouldn't a done. Word! He ast him respectful enough—he even said sir. But this colonel just looked down his wordin' nose again and said: 'There is nothing to discuss.' And then he said somethin' to them Russian G.I.'s in their Hunyak language and they all turned their backs on us and blew like he'd told them we was SS men in disguise."

"Great boys!" a corporal said bitterly. "I just finished giving my fountain pen to one of those sonsabitches, but suppose he even knew me after that colonel spoke his piece? Word he did!"

Another soldier fingered a German Luger, glared at a Russian sentry standing not far away, and said loudly: "I bet I could plug that worder standin' on my head."

And another said: "Who the hell do they think they are? Come all the way from Stallingrad, did they? Well, by Christ! I come all the way from Topeka, Kansas. And if it was to help out bastards like that I'm surer than ever I shoulda stayed there."

A sergeant broke in hastily: "All right, all right. Let's forget it."

The ferry had to make two trips to get them all back to the other bank. When the second load had been disembarked, the major they had met earlier came up to Vincent and said: "The boys tell me our friends over there cooled out pretty fast."

Vincent said: "That's an understatement. But I don't think there's much to worry about, Major. It certainly wasn't anything to do with your boys. I don't think it even had much to do with the other people. My guess is it was Army. Just plain Army. Army is the same in any war or any language, and you can't escape it."

"That's my hunch too," the major said. "But I think I'd better ride over and ask just in case there's something that ought to be smoothed out."

They watched the ferry creep back across the stream carrying the major and its two-man crew. By the time it arrived at the low shoulder of clay it had been using for a jetty, most of the Russians had melted out of sight. But half a dozen privates and N.C.O.'s came to the river's edge to meet it, and before the boat's prow touched shore, two of them stepped into the water, grasped the boat by its sides, and gave the boat a quick wrench which twisted it back into the current. The boat rocked and righted itself, and made as though to nose into the shore again, but then about-turned as the major waved to the coxswain.

The major's face was paper white when he stepped to land again. He walked quickly away from the other soldiers and stood alone for a minute, fumbling with a cigarette. A G.I. walked to the water's edge and savagely kicked a few loose pebbles into the current. Several others gathered around him. Their narrowed smouldering eyes glared across the stream and their voices strewed it with oaths and the jagged driftwood of sentences too angry to be completed.

The major ground out his cigarette, strode up to the other soldiers and barked: "That's enough! Keep your shirts on! I want every man who isn't on duty off this river-bank in one minute."

He came over to Vincent and said, in an even, earnest tone, as though it were himself he sought to persuade: "It's just one of those things, I guess. When I got over there there was nobody around but a few Russian G.I.'s. They had their orders and acted on them." But after he had lighted another cigarette he said: "I hope they don't think Uncle Sam sent us all this way just to take that kind of stuff."

They stood looking at the river. In a few minutes two small

parties of Russian soldiers moved slowly across the grass on the other side, toward the water's edge. Each party carried a heavy machine gun. With a slow deliberateness that could easily have been taken for ostentation, the soldiers planted their guns in the ground, fixed their feed belts in place, turned the muzzles of the guns to face the river and then sat down behind them.

Later, when they had pulled the jeep over to the side of the Autobahn near Leipzig to eat their cold supper, Vincent said reflectively: "You know that was the perfect newspaper story. And only a perfect idiot would write it."

He didn't wait for an answer. "No," he said, "the trouble is people would think it was just a fancy allegory that somebody dreamed up on them."

He plucked a chunk of bully beef from the end of his clasp-knife with an expert forcep-like stab of his bared teeth.

"As long as they were left alone they got along like three in a bed," he said. "And then, whambo! somebody away back in the beyond, maybe a thousand miles away, maybe all the way back at Moscow, gets some kind of a bright idea. And in two seconds flat the whole thing is the father of all cafuffles. I wonder how many wars do get started that way, if we really knew it: with the little people of the world sitting around in the grass and warming themselves in the sunshine, and then looking up to find that a few brass hats of various stations and vocations have started to feel their oats again and fixed it so that the little people have either got to pack up and go home or start throwing punches at each other? I wonder if the brass hats realize how much it can cost people like us when people like them do a pompous or thoughtless thing?"

Vincent wrapped his duffel coat around him and waddled back to the parked jeep. "Let's go, Hubert," he said. "And do spare the horses."

CHAPTER

17

They spent a couple of days in Brussels and Vincent delivered Mike back to his battalion on a late-April afternoon. The country was as cold and flat as ever, but from Antwerp north they were on familiar convoy routes, and seeing the signs "Maple Leaf Up" and "Diamond Up" again was almost like coming across a row of hot-dog stands or billboards. The back areas still stirred busily, but their tempo had softened and relaxed a little. The supply convoys seemed shorter and made less haste. Near Almelo they saw a column of 5.5 guns moving back from the front and further on some engineers were playing softball in a field. The faces they saw bore little sign of strain—everything seemed to have gathered itself for some final easement, like the beginning of a sigh.

Mike felt a tumultuous little gust of excitement. But it ended soon. Shortly after they picked up his battalion's tactical signs on the roadside, they passed a field full of twenty-five pounders standing ready for action with their crews around them, and just before they reached battalion headquarters they heard the moody throat-clearing of a ranging mortar burst less than a mile ahead. Mike blew on his fingers, chilled and stiffened from the long jeep ride, but his breath had no warmth to give them.

He said good-bye to Vincent and Hubert, checked in at the orderly-room and walked through a field to where they told him he would find his company. Kennebec had saved bedroll space in a dry barn and helped him carry his kit there.

"What goes on?" Mike said. "I thought it would be all over by now. Down around the Elbe it is."

"At that it looks pretty good," Kennebec said. "There hasn't been a thing since you left. Dog Company had one fairly rough night going over a canal, but there hasn't been anything like a real show. We've been hearing all kinds of talk about surrender and for once I think you can believe some of it. And for once the plumbers back at Div have quit shoving us into battles just so the staff officers can keep in practise."

Mike started to open some mail, but Kennebec interrupted him.

"There's somebody waiting to see you." He said it with a hint of reluctance and Mike looked up quickly.

"Not Joe?"

"He got in this morning with a new draft," Kennebec said. After a moment he stammered: "Nobody knows he's—I mean they know he's your brother, but nobody knows anything else."

"Where is he?" Mike said.

*   *   *   *

He found Joe sitting alone on the edge of a pile of mangels near another barn. His brother was cleaning a rifle and didn't see him approach. Mike stood looking at him for a while before he spoke. Joe looked well. He should have stopped growing three years ago, but he was much huskier than when Mike had seen him last. His face was unchanged though; in spite of its deep spring windburn, it was delicate and sensitive, still a little like a girl's. But his close-cropped hair was thick and wiry, as virile as his body.

"Hello Joe," Mike said.

Joe started to smile and get to his feet, but his eyes rested full on Mike's face for an instant and something he saw there made him change his mind. He neither smiled nor rose, but moved over and said diffidently: "Want to sit down?"

"Sure."

Each waited for the other to speak again and a full minute dragged by without a word. Finally Joe said:

"I'm sorry. I shouldn't have done it. I asked them at the reinforcement unit if they'd send me here. I told them why, but I shouldn't have done it. I'm sorry."

"No," Mike said. "I'm glad you came here, Joe. It just takes a while to get used to it."

"You know," Joe said, "there's nothing for you to worry about really. Nobody around here knows what I am. They can guess, but they won't know. Nobody knows your brother's a Zombie. And for your sake, I'll try not to faint if I hear a truck tire blow out."

Mike blurted impulsively: "For God's sake, Joe! Let's cut it out! Maybe some things have happened that you can't forget and there are some I won't be able to forget for a while either. But let's quit acting this way anyway."

"All right, Mike," Joe said with sudden eagerness. He looked Mike full in the face again. His look was of gratitude, companionableness and trust. It was the look Mike knew better than any other, the look of his little brother. He put his hand on Joe's shoulder and withdrew it in embarrassment.

In that brief instant it seemed as though it was going to be all right again. They lighted cigarettes and lay back against the mangels, looking at the sky. Mike told himself it was not an important thing that stood between them, but when he tried to think of what he would say to Joe next, he realized that it was important. There was nothing he could say that would not bring them back, sooner or later, to the very thing they were trying to avoid. It was like trying to find your way across a desert in which there was only one landmark. If you met someone and wanted to tell him where you had been or where you were going, you couldn't do it without reference to the landmark. In whatever direction you pointed you would always have to fix your bearings by the same unmoving feature.

Mike saw that they would have to talk it out. And as though he saw it too, Joe began to speak.

"Mike?"

"Uh huh."

"Mike, I know it's no use trying to persuade you what I did was right. But God, Mike, they did ask us to take some things no man should have to take. Oh, I know the obvious answer to that: do what they want you to. Go active. Quit being a Zombie."

Mike looked away.

"But what if you don't see it that way?" Joe said earnestly. "What if you see it different? You aren't sure there's anything in the world that's got a stronger call on you than your wife or your girl. And maybe you're not sold on the idea that the best way to look after your wife or your girl is to come over here and help capture a few towns that you can't even pronounce. Or maybe you *are* sold on coming over, only you don't think it's right that you should come while some of the guys that were drafted the same day you were stay home."

Mike said: "I know."

Joe said: "Oh, they told us we were needed. But on the same day some brass hat who was never shot at in his life had us out behind the barracks or locked up in a drill hall telling us how badly reinforcements were needed, there was nearly always some politician standing up in the House of Commons and telling the country they were getting as many reinforcements over here as they could ever use."

Mike said: "Yes Joe, I understand everything you say. And I'm not arguing now, I'm just saying how it looks from over here. No matter how hard I try, I can't understand how anybody that was in the army anyway could refuse to come over here and fight. If they'd said you could get discharged from the army and go back to doing something else, I could understand a person wanting his discharge. But it's pretty hard to understand just sitting there and doing nothing while all this—"

Joe looked at him hard. "Mike," he interrupted. "Do you by any chance think a man is yellow if he's a Zombie?"

"No, Joe. But some of them must be."

Joe said: "I'm no different than the others. Let's quit sparring, Mike."

"That's a good idea. Let's quit sparring. Joe, I think you made a mistake, a hell of a mistake. And I'm as sure as we're sitting here that you'll see your mistake some day, and you won't find it very easy to carry around with you."

"You still don't get it, Mike," Joe said hopelessly.

"Yes I do. I know how you figured it. But I say you're wrong. As wrong as you could be."

"There's no use talking," Joe said. "You don't get it."

"I do get it, Joe, I just want to tell you I think you're wrong."

Joe said: "But Mike, you haven't seen all the workings of it. You've been away. I don't think you've got the right to sit in judgment on other people."

"Right?" Mike said. "Right? I don't know about that, Joe. Maybe I have got the right. Maybe I've earned it. I paid my money at the gate."

Joe threw his rifle to the ground. "By God!" he cried, the words gushing forth in a hoarse tumult, "so you're a hero too. This whole wording continent is full of heroes. Sneering cheated heroes, sold down the river by a gang of politicians who'll give you a nice white cross, give you a nice fat pension, give you a nice new wooden leg, but wouldn't give you the one thing you really needed when you needed it because that might have cost them votes. Well, that's one edge I'll always have on you and the other heroes, Mike. I'm a Zombie. They made me come. Oh, they tried to smooth it over, because they were still worried more about their votes than about you and me. Even after I was on the boat they were still trying to get me to 'volunteer.' But I didn't volunteer. I'm still a Zombie, Mike!" he cried. "Go ahead, Mike, let me have it: say it, Mike! You bought that bag of confetti and I didn't—so that makes you a hero and it makes me yellow. Say it! You're right. You've got a right to say it. You paid your way in."

Mike stumbled to his feet. "You little bastard," he swore. "I ought to punch your face in." He lurched away on legs weak and rubbery with sick fury.

He didn't see Joe again until the next morning. He deliberately made himself late for breakfast, and when he sat down outside the cookhouse with his mess tins, his brother was nowhere in sight.

While he was scraping the greasy remains of an army sausage into the swill pail before the cook-house door, a lance-corporal came over and said: "Make it snappy, Tully. Mr. Robertson wants to see the platoon over behind the barn."

The men were sitting around the barnyard in a loose semi-circle when he plopped himself down between Kennebec and Nolan on a shallow pile of straw. Out of the corner of his eye, he saw Joe sprawled over a wheelbarrow several places away, absorbed in a letter.

Their platoon commander strode briskly around the barn and smiled a suspiciously hearty good morning. "Ohoh," Kennebec whispered. "It looks like those plumbers at Div have decided to start playing soldiers again."

"Men, we've got a little job this morning," the lieutenant said in a tone of forced cheeriness that was the natural adjunct to his smile. "It seems those paratroops up ahead still aren't reading the papers. They still don't know the war is over."

The lieutenant waited hopefully for the snicker the same pleasantry had been bringing ever since Falaise. Then he continued: "As you know, they're already in the bag. They're not an organized force any more and there's no way they can get out without swimming. They're just an assortment of odds and sods, a few marines, some paratroopers, maybe a company or two of the Wehrmacht and perhaps a few SS. But the other day down below Apeldoorn a pack of their people tried to fight their way out of another pocket and they got right into Fifth Div headquarters before they were stopped."

"What stopped 'em then?" Kennebec whispered. "A written order in triplicate from the general?"

"Well," the lieutenant said, "there's been a lot of movement in the last twenty-four hours up ahead here. We can't make out for sure whether they're thickening up or pulling out. Div and brigade are a little worried about it."

"We better go right back there and hold their hands," Kennebec whispered.

"So there's going to be a patrol," the lieutenant said. "And it looks as though we're elected. Six men will be enough," he added hastily. "And it's a straight recce job. The patrol isn't to fight. Just go up and find out where they've moved their FDLs if they've moved them. Sergeant Barnes has the details. He'll go himself."

A thick-set soldier with a band of khaki cotton cloth fastened around each arm where his NCO's stripes would have shown scrambled to his feet and faced the platoon. He said brightly: "Any volunteers?"

A jeering chorus answered him. "Sure, sarge, let me go." . . . "I had my hand up first, Sergeant." . . .

The sergeant let the venerable joke exhaust itself and then said: "Corporal Olonski's section—their turn. That right, Pete?"

"Uh huh." The corporal made his answer sound bored.

"Well, have your five men ready in half an hour. We shouldn't be gone more than five, six hours at the most but they better take a few rations in case we get stuck awhile."

"I only got four men," the corporal said indifferently. "Zelznyk and Murphy are on forty-eights and Smitty's in England. McIntyre's got a bum foot. And I was two short anyway."

"Hell!" the sergeant said. "Well, I guess we gotta draw lots then for the other one. This job winds up a full roster and the way the war is goin' it wouldn't be fair to start at the top again."

Joe Tully sat up on his wheelbarrow, yawned and said: "I'll go, sergeant."

The Sergeant looked surprised and the other men turned toward Joe and regarded him as though he were some barely identifiable curio.

"Do you mean it?" the sergeant said.

"Sure," Joe said. "I'll go. There's no law against it is there?"

"No," the sergeant said. "No law at all." For a moment it seemed that he was about to say something else. He mumbled "Thanks," and turned away.

As the platoon dispersed, Mike hurried to Joe's side and put his hand on his arm. Joe tried to shake away, but Mike dug in roughly with his fingers.

"Joe!" he said sharply.

Joe answered him flatly. "Why don't you go to hell?"

"Joe!" Mike said. "You don't have to prove anything to me."

"Who said anything about you?"

"You were excited yesterday," Mike said earnestly. "So was I. I still won't apologize and I'm not asking you to, but Christ, Joe, look after yourself."

"According to you, that's the best thing I do," Joe said. He wrenched his hand free of Mike's fingers and walked rapidly across the barnyard.

Mike sat on top of a wooden farm cart outside his billet and watched the patrol move off. Some of the ground over which it would pass was cut off from his view by a thin row of evergreens running parallel to a gravel road, and after the trees broke, some more of the ground was hidden at the bottom of a three-sided box of farmland. The box was bounded on the right by the elevated road, in front by a low dyke and at the back by another dyke. The first dyke was perhaps half a mile away and the second about the same distance further on. They were not canal dykes, but polder dykes, bulging grass-covered ribs of earth flung across the sparse and precious land to protect it in time of flood.

There would be no water between the dykes now, except perhaps a little lying at the bottom of the drainage ditch below the road. But the land inside the box would be fallow. It would be drenched and dead and its clay would be heavy and clinging. There would be shell-divots in it, most of them left by twenty-five pounders or German Eighty-Eights and not deep enough to afford cover to a man. The patrol would have to work its way across the box by crawling along the drainage ditch beside the road. If there happened to be a second ditch not too far from the first, the patrol might split up. Mike knew this much without thinking of it, out of his knowledge of the character of patrols and polders.

The reconnaissance would have been easier to make at night, but even by daylight it was not an unfair or particularly difficult job. Their own battalion's forward defense lines were anchored on the first of the two dykes, so that all the way across the box-like polder they would be covered by their own heavy machine guns. The first crisis was likely to occur when they approached the second dyke. If the Germans were still there, they were almost certain to detect the patrol. But the patrol would still be under its own machine guns and unless it was unlucky enough to get cut up in the first few seconds, it didn't figure to have much trouble pulling out. When and if the Germans started shooting, the patrol's job would be done, except for the detail of getting back. On the whole, Mike decided, it would be a good sign if he heard shooting inside the first two hours. But if there was shooting and it began after two hours, it wouldn't be so good. The patrol would be across the second dyke by then and entirely on its own.

At first the six men stayed on the road, walking at the edges of the gravel, instinctively hugging close to the line of trees at the roadside. It gave Mike a tiny stab of pride to see that Joe walked as the others did, with his free arm hanging slack, his other arm lolling snugly in the little hammock formed by his rifle sling and the butt of the rifle, his head tilted forward with the hint of a droop to it, his helmet set well back so that it rested on his head at the exact centre of balance, and his feet gliding like slow pendulums, never more than an inch or two above the ground. His body did not rise or fall between steps, his arm did not swing, nor did his knees bend appreciably. The gait was the antithesis of marching; it was the soldier's gait as distinct from the military gait, the gait of men who had grown miserly of their energy, not through present weariness but through the knowledge of weariness to come. Most men never learned to walk like that until they had stumbled back from a battle half dead with exhaustion, cursing every betraying braggart muscle and swearing they'd never so much as wiggle a finger again unless they could find a reason for it.

A few hundred yards down the road, the patrol turned off through the evergreens. It was lost behind the trees for a while and when it came into view again it was smudged and contracted by the distance. It merged briefly into a dark huddle at the foot of the dyke and then, one by one, six small segments broke away from the huddle, crawled slowly up the dyke and rolled out of sight across its crest.

Mike dropped off the farm cart and stood uncertainly in the barnyard. He looked at his watch—nine-thirty. He thought of writing letters, but he didn't want to write to his father and mother while things were as they were between him and Joe. And writing Tina had almost become a torture. Her letters, since early winter, had been feverish gabbles of small talk, invariably terminated with the single robot-like endearment, "Love". Each time he wrote her now, he had to struggle with the impulse to ask her if something was wrong, and each time, he admitted that he didn't dare.

He talked for a while with Kennebec and Nolan, exchanging guesses mostly on the date of surrender. Kennebec had decided it couldn't last more than a month. "And when they start calling for volunteers for the Pacific, the Zombies can move over and make room for one more," Kennebec said. Mike bit his lip. Kennebec flushed and started to stammer some kind of apology.

"It's all right," Mike said.

He lined up at the cookhouse for lunch, but dumped his food into the swill barrel untouched. He cleaned his rifle and sorted out and repacked his kit. At one o'clock he set himself a task of abstinence: he wouldn't look at his watch again until one thirty. When he was sure the time was up he counted slowly to five hundred. Then he stared for what seemed a long time at the buckle on the strap of the watch before he turned it over and looked at the dial. The hands were at one twenty-five exactly.

At two o'clock he told himself that it was probably over. The patrol had reached the German lines undetected and was now on its way back. Even Barnes, cautious as he was, wouldn't take more than five hours on this kind of job, just going one way. But suppose the enemy had pulled back after all? It might take half a day to find them. Mike's optimism won the brief tug o'war from his forebodings and he ruled arbitrarily that if he still heard no shooting by two-thirty, it would mean there wasn't going to be any.

He walked across the road to the big red-brick farmhouse

that his company headquarters was sharing with batallion headquarters, and sat down outside with his back against the low stone
stoop. If any reports came back from the patrol, they would
probably be relayed here by runner from the FDLs, or, if they
had a set near the FDLs, by wireless.

It was two-thirteen. He unfastened the strap on his wrist
watch and began to idle with the stem. And as he did so the
sound he had been waiting for came hammering faintly through
the pale air like a far but monstrous echo of the winding of his
watch. First there was a quick multiplicity of small ratchety
cog-wheel noises, running so close together they could not be
counted, and then a rattle, lower and steadier in tone and a little
louder, with a pause after each separate note. This was the sound
of a German MG 42 opening fire and being answered by a Bren.
It was one of the sounds of history, as much a herald to the destiny
of men as the crunch of oarlocks in Caesar's galleys or the rushing
hoof-beats of Mongol horses on the steppes of Asia.

To Mike, the sound was as familiar and unhistoric as the
clattering of mess tins, and after the first instinctive moment of
tensing, his body relaxed under it as under the fingers of a masseur.
His shoulders slacked against the stoop beside the farmhouse, he
cocked his head easily on one side, with unhurried steady fingers
he extracted a cigarette from the package in his pocket and
lighted it, and his mind divided itself between watching the smoke
curl away from the cigarette and listening for a repetition of the
sound. There was no need for excitement now. Whatever was
to happen was already in the process of happening, or in the
process of being ordained. Now it was irrevocable, and therefore
better.

The sound repeated itself several times, with variations of
tempo and overlappings. This in itself was good. The fact that
the Bren, the patrol's key weapon, had fired back so quickly and
continued to fire made it unlikely that the patrol had fallen into

an ambush. It was probably working its way back now under cover of the Bren, concerned only with kicking up enough dust around the Forty Two and whatever else might be firing on it to discourage a real fight.

At the end of half an hour the distant hammering ended. This too was as it should be. The patrol had disengaged itself.

But twenty minutes later the faint slurping and brracking began again and in the new context it had the clammy ring of doom. For an instant every nerve and tendon in Mike became distended and frozen. Then all his fibre dissolved and left his body a flaccid pulp of dread. The dread was stronger than he had ever felt before, so strong that it reached like a claw into his belly and dragged forth a trickle of colorless slime which he coughed helplessly across the breast of his uniform. It was several minutes before he was capable of ordered thought, and then his thoughts were irrational and harshly withholding. They would not tell him that this was the sort of thing that happened on nearly every patrol; they only told him that the patrol was in trouble, that it had tried to disengage itself and had not been able to.

Through the open window of the farmhouse he was suddenly aware of the thin urgent astral wheedling of a human voice trying to make itself understood over a field wireless set. "Abel-Charley Abel-Charley," the voice whined in the ghostly tone of some down-at-heels divinity begging for a cup of coffee. "Abel-Charley Abel-Charley, can you hear me, can you hear me?"

Mike stood up and walked away from the window, not quite willing to hear what might follow. He heard a full-fleshed voice answer the wireless, heard some further fourth-dimensional wheedling in response, and then, almost at once, heard his battalion's colonel shouting through the window: "Runner!"

A rifleman ran around the edge of the farmhouse.

"Get the Foo!" the colonel ordered.

The rifleman loped away and in a moment a captain wearing

the shoulder badges of an artillery regiment hurried across the farmyard and presented himself to the colonel.

"We've got a patrol out," the colonel said briskly. "About nine hundred yards beyond the second dyke. Their runner got back to the FDLs to report the rest of the patrol is pinned down. They're in too close quarters to use H.E., but what can you do with smoke?"

"Just a minute, sir," the artilleryman said. He stepped away from the wall of the house, turned his face into the slight breeze, then wet his finger and held it up until it had begun to dry.

"It looks pretty good, sir. What there is is almost straight this way. It's not very strong, but if we dropped a good chunk of stuff three or four hundred yards ahead of the patrol, some of it ought to drift back on them."

"Good," the colonel said. "Come on in and I'll give you the map reference."

The smoke stonk came in less time than it would have taken Mike to walk back to his billet across the road. It had a puny, unfinished ring to it, hardly more than a tuning-up of the regiment of twenty-five-pounders dispersed two miles further back in the trees and polders, and the low-charged smoke shells bursting on the ground ahead sent back no sound to match the initial yammering at the gun breeches. But after the guns coughed out, there was only one more short exchange of stuttered epithets between the distant machine guns, and for a long time everything was quiet. In the farmyard a few chattering hens and a lowing orphaned calf reclaimed the floor, and a water lorry growling up to the battalion cookhouse in low gear made the only sound that challenged them.

At first the smoke could not be seen from the farmyard, but as the breeze pumped a thin stream of life into it, it stirred and ghosted back and upwards above the trees, expanding on the horizon like morning fog. The colonel and the artillery officer came out and looked at it. They listened to the silence and the artillery officer said: "They must be on their way out already, sir."

Mike sat down against the stoop again, removed his watch, put it in the palm of his right hand and absorbed himself in the study of its second hand. He was surprised to discover that the hand did not advance a full second at a time, but progressed from one notch to the next in three separate bounds. He was also surprised to discover that if he held the watch perfectly still and fixed his eyes on the tip of the minute hand he could see it moving.

At last he heard the wireless set snivelling for attention again. Still afraid to listen, he walked away from the window, but when the wireless set had subsided once more to a self-abnegating dumbness, he heard the colonel's voice calling through the farm-house to someone in another room that the patrol had reached the FDLs.

"How did they make out?" the other person called back.

"They lost one man," the colonel said. Mike was grateful that he hadn't said only one man. Even if the one man wasn't Joe, it was good to have the kind of officers who knew there was no such thing as only one man.

The news itself seemed neither good nor bad to him. The only feeling it induced was a terrible impatience to know more. He hurried to the road and stood at its edge, looking to the break in the trees where he knew the five men who had got out would soon be reappearing.

Almost at once their dark smudges began toiling up the bank from the polder to the roadside and coasting slowly down the road at the peculiar unstriding gait of the infantry, like anchored parts on an assembly line. When the fifth and last man had taken his place in the file, Mike turned his eyes to the figure in front, waiting for its outlines to sharpen and become identifiable. By walking along the road to meet the patrol he could have found out sooner. He stayed where he was, nevertheless, his body rooted by the same essential though unexplained discipline that had taken charge of his mind after its one sick seizure of dread nearly two hours before. He would know soon enough.

The figures on the road changed in color first, their blackness turning to a dull brown and then to khaki. Their legs and shoulders came into focus, their width and stature and the various other elements that set them apart as individuals. Finally their weapons could be distinguished. The first man carried a Sten gun and the second held a Bren by its muzzle balancing the butt across his shoulder like a tramp carrying a bundle on the end of a stick. Neither of these could be Joe. The other three men carried rifles, but one of them was too short to be Joe, and another was much too tall. The last man in the file might have been Joe; he kept lurching out of sight behind the fourth man and it was not until he was less than a quarter of a mile away that Mike recognized him as Burdett, another newcomer to the platoon.

Mike remained standing on the edge of the road until the patrol passed him and turned off into the farmyard to report in. The faces of all of them were grave and a little surprised, and when they saw the farmyard again, their eyes played around all its corners, retrieving the memory of each separate detail and re-assimilating the place into the phenomenon of their being alive. The sergeant was the only one who spoke to Mike. "Sorry, Tully," he said.

"It can't be helped," Mike said. The words seemed banal but they were the only words to say.

Mike walked back across the road to his billet. When he saw Kennebec and Nolan there, he knew that they had watched the patrol come in too. Kennebec spoke to him, but Mike made no answer and after that everyone in the platoon accepted his unspoken wish for privacy.

He betrayed no other feeling, perhaps because his feeling had not yet identified itself even to him. The feeling was there, but it had not yet taken shape. It was like the men of the patrol when they first came into sight on the road; it hammered insistently for recognition from the centres of his consciousness, but the demand for recognition was still premature. And this was only natural. For eleven months almost, his mind had been conditioning itself to meet the constant shock of death and now, out of habit and training his tough, cross-grained defenses repelled emotion.

He had not been able to eat lunch while Joe was engulfed in the frowning mystery of the polders, but now, when Joe was dead, he ate his supper hungrily. After he had finished, his company commander, a youthful major, came to see him. The major saw that sympathy would not be welcome yet and came to the point at once.

"We've moved a standing patrol out to the place where that recce party got bumped this afternoon," the major said. "It's clear up there now. We're sending out a burial party."

"Thanks, sir," Mike said. "I'd like to go."

"The padre will go with you," the major said.

"I'd rather he didn't, sir," Mike said.

"All right," the major said. "How about Sergeant Barnes? He knows the place."

"That would be fine sir," Mike said.

Barnes carried a short-handled spade across his shoulder as he led Mike down the road. For the first half-mile Barnes said nothing, but after they had swung off the road and gone across the fat springy rib of the first dyke into the muddy box beyond, he began to explain what had happened, using the matter-of-fact tone of a guide conducting an impromptu tour of some ancient and not very exciting battlefield.

They walked along the grass at the top of a drainage ditch, avoiding the heavy clay as best they could, and Barnes said: "I thought we might have had some trouble here, but we didn't have no trouble at all. There was a couple of S mines in one place in the ditch but whoever put them there must of thought he was plantin' wordin' rhubarb. There was nobody at all on that second dyke. We could of walked across this field just like we're doin' now."

They crossed the second dyke and went down into another polder much like the one they had just left. Barnes waved to a third dyke straight ahead and said, "That's where we bumped the bastards. It took us two wordin' hours to get across this patch and even then they seen us. I figure they must of seen us when we was about forty yards out. But some God damn fool of a Jerry pulled back his rifle bolt and it warned us. I figured with the ditch we could still get up to the dyke or at least to the edge of it and get an idea how many of them was there."

Near the edge of the dyke, the drainage ditch they were following ran at right angles to another ditch which paralleled the base of the dyke. The two ditches made a T.

The sergeant stopped beside the second ditch. Directly below them, the sodden grass of the ditch was strewn with brass bullet jackets. "We got in here easy enough," the sergeant said. "Right here is where Olonski was with the Bren. The rest of us was spread out on the left, all but the kid. He was over there on the right, just below where the dyke takes that little bulge. Burdett stayed back in the first ditch. He was getaway man.

"Well," the sergeant said, "I wasn't sure whether we ought to try to go any further or not. I started to edge up the dyke and that's when this Forty Two let go his first burst. He was over there on the right too, just above where the kid was. He fired wild. I don't figure he even seen me. Olonski give him a burst right back, firin' wild too. I got back into the ditch. I figured we was entitled to leave if we could get out. But when this bastard let go with the Forty Two again I seen it was dead on the place where the two ditches met, so that meant we couldn't go that way.

"It didn't look bad," the sergeant said. "There was a few other bastards up there lettin' go with Schmeissers and Mausers, but there didn't seem to be many of them and as long as they stayed where they was they couldn't mortar us. I knew Burdett wouldn't have no trouble gettin' back anyway, and I was pretty sure when he told them we was pinned down they'd lay on some smoke.

"Olonski and this wordin' Forty Two kept bangin' back and forth for maybe twenty, twenty-five minutes. Then I give Olonski the sign to pipe down because I thought he must be runnin' short of ammunition. The Forty Two piped down too. I never seen what the kid was doin' until he had worked down the ditch, almost to where the dyke makes that bulge. I guess he had spotted the Forty-Two and was goin' to take a crack at it himself.

"I don't mean he got panicky," the sergeant said hastily. "He wasn't tryin' to be no glory boy neither. I guess he just couldn't see how we was goin' to get out unless somethin' was done about the Forty-Two. And all of a sudden he up out of the ditch with a grenade and the Forty-Two let him have it. It happened as quick as that. I don't think he even had time to throw the grenade. The kid stumbled ahead out of sight around the bulge in the dyke. Olonski let go another fast burst and tried to work down the ditch to where the kid had been but he couldn't get his gun up on the edge of the ditch because the Forty-Two had the drop. So we just stayed where we were till the smoke come and then we got out. The Jerries must of been gettin' out at the same time. I guess they thought it was an attack."

The sergeant walked down through the ditch and turned away along the foot of the dyke. When he came to the place where the dyke bent slightly back on itself, he said: "The kid should be right here."

A rifle lay on the ground outside the ditch, but the body was almost thirty feet away, nearly to the top of the dyke, pitched headlong up the slope with its face almost touching the shallow sand-bagged rampart of a slit trench.

"Holy Jesus!" the sergeant cried. "He God damn near made it! He came all that way after he was hit! The son of a bitch was pumpin' it into him all the time and he come all that way!"

Mike took his eyes away from the body and looked mutely at the sergeant. The sergeant lowered the shovel from his shoulder. "I'll go and start," he said.

Mike knelt beside his brother's body and tugged it over until it lay on its back. One arm was crunched up underneath its chest, the wrist doubled back beneath the weight of the body, and Mike eased the arm clear as carefully as though care still mattered. The sun had sunk low, but the slope of the dyke tilted the dead boy's face straight into the slanting light, so that its chlorine pallor still seemed to have life in it and around the eyes and mouth the small lines setting into protest against death were diffused and softened. The face was unmarked. Its eyes were closed. There was no violence in the face, only the hint of surprise and avowal that what had happened here was not right.

Mike looked at the still body, at the mash of blood and khaki cloth across its chest, and at the one shoulder almost wholly chewed away by machine gun bullets, and began to make the preparations he had made on other bodies. He unfastened the collar of the tunic and the top button of the collarless shirt beneath, and fumbled inside until he brought forth two fibre identification discs attached to a double-looped necklace of sweat-soiled white twine. The discs were sticky with blood. Mike detached his army knife from a hasp at his waist, snipped the lower disc away from its private loop and tucked the other one back inside the boy's tunic. He studied the punched lettering on the disc he had removed:

B1999876

TULLY JD

CDN

UC, and as though resenting any such glib and niggardly condensation of the facts pertinent to a human life, he began hurrying through the boy's pockets in search of the boy's credentials as a member of mankind.

He made a little pile on the ground of the things he found: two keys on a key ring, a soggy ball of paper money, some Belgian, some Dutch and some German, a few coins, a pearl-handled penknife, a red pen and pencil set, a comb, a few letters, and a bill fold filled with photographs.

On the envelope of one letter he recognized the handwriting of his father, and on another the writing of his mother. The others were addressed in the thin careful hand of a schoolgirl. The photographs were of various ages and states of wear, some clean and glossy and some cracked and lustreless with years of carrying. Most of the new ones were of a small, smiling girl, pert and nice-looking, with good clean eyes and a good figure. One was of their father and mother. Another, somewhat older, was of Mike standing alone before a white house, in a baseball uniform. And another, the oldest of all, so old that it had the deadened pliancy of heavy newsprint, was of two boys standing before the same house, barefooted, with bamboo fishing poles across their shoulders and cotton bathing suits wrapped around their wrists. Mike remembered this one well; it was taken on Joe's sixth birthday, the first day Joe had been allowed to go all the way to the river in his bare feet, the day Joe caught his first pike, the day they built a fire on the river bank and heated a can of beans in it for their lunch.

Mike put the pictures down. He closed his eyes and turned his face into the sinking sun, holding it high so that it felt what little warmth the sun still had to give.

I never asked about his wife. The words swelled in his heart like a mute invocation. *I never gave him a chance to tell me about his wife. I never gave either of us a chance. He was home last summer too, and I never asked about that either. I never asked him how the fish were biting. I never asked him if the water at the dam was high enough for swimming or if the Saskatoons ripened early or late. I never asked if you could still hear the coyotes in the wolf willows at the bottom of the valley. I never asked him if he saw the prairie grass and mustard weed and crocus on the hills. We never talked about anything that mattered. All we talked about was something that had nothing to do with us at all, that was foisted on us by strangers because they were afraid to handle it themselves. And now it's too late. It's too late to do anything but lay him in his grave.*

This was the only prayer Mike said for the boy lying on the ground beside him. He scooped the pictures, the letter and the other articles into the deep pocket on the thigh of his battledress. He put his hand on the boy's cheek and let it rest there for a moment; under the tightening skin, the firming flesh was like a rounded cheese under cool gauze.

He rose and walked down the dyke to where the sergeant was at work on the grave. He reached for the handle of the shovel and said: "I'll dig now, Sarge. I'll finish it."

CHAPTER

18

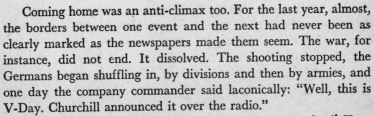

Coming home was an anti-climax too. For the last year, almost, the borders between one event and the next had never been as clearly marked as the newspapers made them seem. The war, for instance, did not end. It dissolved. The shooting stopped, the Germans began shuffling in, by divisions and then by armies, and one day the company commander said laconically: "Well, this is V-Day. Churchill announced it over the radio."

Nobody was very excited. "I thought it was yesterday," Kennebec said. "I thought it was going to be tomorrow," Nolan said.

The repatriation machinery, backing and filling with the desperate complacency of army red tape at its worst, assigned part of Mike's platoon by error to the army of occupation, and by the time the mistake was straightened out, it took just under ten months all told to get Mike from Holland to Halifax. In the meantime, the futilities and lacks of their existence compounded themselves to make a mockery of the past and a parody of the future; they soaked in their fed-upness until it became a form of seasoning. During the long wait, the weaker parts of Europe fumbled unsurely to repair the shredded fabric of their society, while Big Three and Big Five power politics squared off for the indoor Donnybrook called "the peace." What little the soldiers could see of the spectacle left them feeling more chilled and defrauded than ever. And under unnatural strains, even the bonds of sympathy between the soldiers and Europe's little people weakened and began to pull apart. Burgomasters and brigadiers, bargees and batmen competed and conspired in the black market, and the greedy scramble for the offal of a decayed economy proceeded with no more dressing-up or apology than a fixed wheel at a two-bit carnival. The friendly little towns they had fought to liberate seemed to be saying to the soldiers: "You are no longer welcome here. Send us your food and clothing as you sent us your dead before. But get out yourselves; there is no room for you." Their compassion for the hungry and the homeless began to turn to cynicism and distrust. They began to act like arrogant pawnbrokers. The soldiers were tired too.

When they pulled away from the Channel coast, Kennebec looked back over the stern of their ship and said: "Well, there goes Europe. And for my dough, they can give it back to Attila or the Saracens." And when they sailed out of Liverpool for home, Nolan said: "They can have that too. You take your gallant little England—give me the fat old sloppy wordin' old U.S.A." Mike had no wish to argue with either.

And as for coming home, he had known for a long time that that wouldn't be at all as he used to picture it either. He knew Tina wouldn't be at the station. He knew their life together was ended. In the same breath he cursed himself for not making her come out and tell him why, and sardonically congratulated himself for helping her to maintain the fiction that nothing was changed. It was like Tina to delay hurting him until it could no longer be avoided. It didn't make any difference anyway, it was all the same.

Troop trains had ceased to be a novelty in Toronto long ago. There was not much confusion at the station. He said good-bye to Kennebec and Nolan and they made vague plans about seeing each other again. Then a small, talkative civilian wearing rimless glasses grabbed his kit bag and said that he would drive him to wherever he was going.

The man talked ceaselessly as the car wedged its way north through the morning traffic of Yonge Street. . . .

"Well, sir, I guess Germany's pretty much a mess. They got what they asked for all right. I guess they won't forget for a while. . . . The Germans always fold when things stop going their way. I figure it's because they're natural bullies and a bully just can't take it." . . .

When they turned east and began to wind through Rosedale, the man was talking about the atom bomb. "Greatest thing that ever happened," he said. "Nobody will dare start another war now." . . .

"I guess not," Mike said politely.

The place looked the same. The flowers hadn't begun to blossom, but the trees were in bud and the grass was green and fresh. Before he thought of it, Mike started to let himself in with the key he had been carrying attached to his army knife for nearly five years. He stopped and rang.

Tina said: "Hello, Mike."

He left his kit in the vestibule and followed her into the living room. It was the same too, except that the chesterfield had been covered with some kind of flowered chintz and there was a new radio. He sat down on the edge of a green Queen Anne chair, the one that had cost them thirty-two dollars and seventy-five cents on credit through an organization called, of all things, the Home Lovers Club.

"Mike," Tina said timidly. "I haven't done this very well." Her face was strained, really strained, not faking anything, but pale and tightened. It was still a beautiful face. In spite of himself his eyes played up and down the length of her body, her beautiful show-girl's body, austere in a tweed suit and only more desirable because of its austerity.

"It's all right," Mike said. "I knew a long time ago."

"I should have told you," she said. "But for a long time I thought I could beat it. But I can't. It's too tough to beat. It's so tough that even if it's going to cost me Joe, I still can't beat it."

"Who is he?" Mike said.

"His name is Bruce Devlin," Tina said. "Do you want me to tell you about him?"

"No," Mike said, "it doesn't matter. I guess he must be all right."

Tina said: "Mike, I won't try to explain. But I did do my best for a long while. I told myself how rotten it was to do this. But I guess there's something missing in me, because a voice kept whispering: 'It's not so rotten as you think. It can't be helped. He went away when he didn't have to, and now you're going away when you don't have to. He tried to fight going away for a while, and you tried to fight it for a while too, but it just didn't work for either of you'."

"You know, that's right," Mike said.

"This must sound rotten too," she said. "But if they'd made you go, I'd have stuck with you whatever happened. I know that's silly. Like a woman. Oh, I was proud of you, Mike, when you went. But I was hurt too, and lonely. You know that awful thing I said about the man down the street going in the early days of the war, the thing that made us have that fight. I was ashamed and sorry afterwards, but I still believed a little bit of it. I think every woman believes a little bit of it. It's ridiculous and childish to feel that way, but I envied all the girls whose husbands waited to be drafted. I told myself that you were better than their men because you went before they made you go. But there was some mean, bitch streak in me all the time, asking me if you weren't putting me second to something foreign and far away, that belonged to your foreign, far-away man's world."

"In a way that was closer to the truth than anything," Mike said. "Not quite the truth but not so far away from it. Whatever it was that made me go, it wasn't all patriotism and nobility. It was a lot of things, all mixed up together. I'm not sorry for any of them. I'm still glad I went, if only so I can tell myself I was there. But you're right, Tina—I can't be sure I did the best thing for all of us, for you and me and the baby, any more than you can."

"Oh, Mike," Tina said, in a little voice, "I didn't mean to put it that way."

"Try and forget it, Tina," he said gently. "It's really not your business, or mine. It's just part of the same business that happened between me and my brother Joe, the day before he was killed. If we'd had sense enough to see that Joe being a Zombie was none of my business, and not much of his, it would have been a lot easier for both of us. Maybe Joe would even still be alive. As long as we had two kinds of army, some people had to belong to one kind and some to the other. If there'd only been one kind, perhaps I wouldn't even have been in it. But having two kinds meant they had to have volunteers and well—I volunteered. Whichever Army you decided to belong to, or even if you decided not to belong to either, there had to be a struggle, and you had to hurt somebody who wouldn't have been hurt if there'd been only one. Maybe the only person you hurt was yourself, but as long as we ran the army the way we did, there had to be some kind of hurt."

Tina walked over and put her hand on his arm. "Thanks, Mike," she said.

In a moment she said: "Joe's over at Mary's. I hope you'll let me see him sometimes."

"As much as you like. He'll have to decide who he wants to live with," he said. "I'd like to take him out home for a while if he'll go. I won't have my discharge for a month or so, but I can get away tonight."

"He'll be ready, Mike," Tina said. "He's thrilled about you. He's a wonderful little boy."

"I wonder if Mary could bring him down to the station," he said. "I'd like to see Pop, but not just now. I don't feel much like talking, I guess."

As he walked away from the house, she watched him through the window, but he didn't turn his head.

CHAPTER

19

The remnant of a late Chinook was blowing in from the west, tidying the hills of the tiny drifts of old snow that hid beneath the boulders, and turning the ice in the shaded ravines to lissom, contralto brooks. The warm wind dried the prairie grass and pompadoured it back on the scalps of the hills, baring the new green roots beneath the brown scurf of winter-kill. The trees in the ravines had not yet begun to leaf, but the furry silver buds of the poplars shone in the sunlight and the wind carried the clean wet smell of rising sap from the dwarfed maples and cherry bushes. A nesting meadow lark flopped across the narrow, two-rutted trail, simulating grave infirmities. A gopher sat immobile, before its burrow, like a brown root, and a small green garter snake sauntered primly into a thick bed of early weeds.

When the soldier and the boy cleared the top of the long hill that sloped into the river, they stopped walking and looked for a while, the soldier remembering each thing he had seen before and the boy remembering each thing he had been told about.

"Is the flood over?" the boy asked.

"Just about," the soldier said. They began walking again.

"Some years, the whole valley would be covered. You could just see the tops of the trees. In the spring we'd go down to the edge of it and watch the last of the ice go out. One year the ice ripped the swing bridge away and they had to build another one. The ice and water were so high sometimes that you couldn't even see where the dam was supposed to be."

"Tell me about the rest," the boy said.

"Well," the soldier said, "swimming was always one of the best parts. It's still too early to go swimming. We always used to go in for the first time on the Twenty-Fourth of May. That was a school holiday. The water was nearly always cold and still dropping. We'd go in below the dam then. Afterwards, when the water got right down, it was only the little kids that swam below the dam, but in May below the dam was best even for the big kids. You could dive right in off the timbers. The current was very fast and choppy, like a big rapids. We'd try to swim into it and get up on the dam, but it was nearly always too strong. We'd fight into it till we tired out and then we'd let it carry us away downstream till we could grab a clump of willow shoots and haul ourselves back on the bank."

"Then," the soldier said, "when the water went down a little more, we'd fish in the dam with our hands. We'd put on our bathing suits and climb in among the rocks and pull the suckers out just like picking berries. The suckers were slow and fat but as long as the water stayed cold they were good enough for eating. Afterwards, we'd fish for pike with worms and spinners. There weren't many pike, but you could always get a few."

"What about the mud turtles?" the boy asked.

"They didn't come till still later, in the hot weather," the soldier said. "In June or July. There were clams too, buried in the mud above the dam. We'd dive for them and dig them out of the mud. They weren't good for eating, but it was fun diving for them. And sometimes we'd go down into the shallow fast water, where the rocks are, and catch crabs. You couldn't eat them either, but you had to be fast to catch them. We used to catch the turtles sunning themselves on the rocks. They were smart. They nearly always looked to be asleep, but if you weren't careful they'd just slide off into the water and swim away before you could get to them. None of the white people ate the turtles, but the Chinamen in the restaurant used to make soup out of them for themselves. They used to give us fifteen cents for big ones and a dime for little ones."

The fascination on the boy's round face changed abruptly to suspicion, as though he heard a sudden warning.

"I still want to go back to Mum," the boy said.

"Sure," the soldier said. "We've decided that already. That's what's best. You're going back."

"Tomorrow?"

"Tomorrow," the soldier said.

The soldier turned his lean face away, but not so quickly that the boy did not see the lines of hurt and loneliness in it. The boy said, with mature kindliness: "I hope I'll be able to see you sometimes."

"Me too," the soldier said. "We'll fix it somehow."

They had reached the bed of the valley now, and they stopped there while the soldier hunted among the black bare cherry bushes for the kind of branch that would make a sling-shot handle. While he was cutting through the branch with his knife a jack-rabbit ghosted past, its coat still more white than brown after the winter.

They found the path again and it led them out at the river's edge, beside the wooden ramp lofting up to the suspension bridge. The bridge had weathered to the color of slate and the deep sag of its rusty cables barely kept its drooping belly clear of the swollen water below. They walked across the bridge carefully, listening to the water rush beneath their feet and to the roaring of the dam upstream.

When the boy saw the dam through its mask of naked maple trees, he cried out in excitement and ran ahead of the soldier, not stopping until he stood on the high bank immediately above the dam, and could look straight down into its virile turbulence of foam and wet black rooks gleaming in the sun. The soldier hurried after him and at first neither he nor the boy saw the fisherman sitting close to them on the bank. The fisherman arose with some difficulty, holding an artificial leg at right angles to the rest of him until he had levered his body high enough to let him set the leg back under him on the ground.

"Hello, young Mike Tully," he said, pushing a cloth cap back across his face so that he could see more clearly. His face was gnarled and weathered and a growth of stubble glinted on it like iron filings. It was, however, a tranquil face, not unduly aged and such ageing as it had appeared to have been arranged with care and restraint.

"Charley!" the soldier said warmly.

"I heard you were back," the fisherman said. "And this is your boy. Looks a lot like young Joe did at that age."

The fisherman saw the boy looking enviously at his yellow bamboo pole. "Try it for a while," he invited. The boy took the pole eagerly and sat down on the bank. The two men sat on a log a piece back from the river. The soldier lighted a cigarette and the fisherman began filling a pipe. Neither of them seemed in a hurry to talk. For a while they watched the boy getting the feel of the fishing line in the swift water. The fisherman made a short covert study of the soldier's face, trying to decide what degree of permanence there was among the wispy filigrees of unease etched around the corners of its eyes. At length the fisherman said: "Well, how do you figure it turned out?"

The soldier thought. "About like yours, I guess."

"That's bad," the fisherman said. "I thought it would be anyway a little better."

The soldier said: "Hell, I guess it's crazy for a guy like me to think he can work out the answers for himself. But we heard so much about us being an army of enlightened individuals doing our own thinking that I guess a lot of us believed it. And if you were in that frame of mind, you could see a lot, even scrambling in and out of holes. I was lucky enough to have a friend who knew a lot of odds and ends about what went on over there, or thought he knew, and I met a newspaper guy who took me around with him for a while. And for the last year nearly, we had enough time, God knows, to read the papers. I don't claim to understand it, but I did work at trying."

The fisherman waited for him to go on.

"This friend of mine used to say that whole continent was a wording swamp," the soldier said. "And Jesus! how right he turned out to be. For five years they were slaves, scurrying up alleys, counting the years till they'd be free again. And then the minute they're free, what do they do? Everybody grabs a Sten gun and wants to start hounding his neighbors up alleys. Not in the name of justice. Not even always in the name of vengeance. Just for power; grab power, quick, before the guy next door grabs it. If he's got the power and you haven't, he's a collaborator, a traitor. And if you've got the power and he hasn't, he's a Communist, a bomb-thrower. Greece wasn't the only place where it happened that way. It happened in Belgium for a while, only without quite so much racket, and if it hadn't been for DeGaulle I guess it would have happened in France. And God knows what it must be like in those other countries, Italy, Yugoslavia and the Balkans."

"It hasn't been much to cheer about," the fisherman conceded. "But don't you think a lot of it would have been avoided if they'd had a chance to hold elections?"

"I don't know," the soldier said, "I got the impression elections were at the bottom of a lot of the trouble. Everybody was trying to rig them, and not just the people that had a right to vote either."

The soldier went on earnestly: "It doesn't sound reasonable that a whole continent could be torn apart like that without learning something out of it; but honest, Charley, I don't think those people learned one God-damned thing that matters. Oh, they learned the value of big armies and the cost of losing a war, and I guess now they're learning how important it is to be able to make atom bombs. They learned war is awful, if they didn't know it already. But as far as I could see, yes and as far as smarter men then me could see, they didn't learn the one simple little truth that counts. They didn't learn that, somehow or other, they've got to start getting along—getting along in their own countries, whatever their politics are, and getting along with the countries next door, whatever their differences with the other countries are. Even the Germans didn't learn it, and look at the pasting they took. Oh, they want peace, they all want peace, even the Germans. But they don't seem to realize that if they don't quit trying to push each other around, they just can't have peace.

"And that's only the weak nations," the soldier said, "the ones that haven't got much left or never had much to start with. Maybe the people that live in countries like that have got some excuse for going on the muscle for power inside their own countries or power for their countries in the world. But look at the big countries. They're worse. What's San Francisco boil down to—a guarantee that there won't be any more wars unless some country that's strong enough to start a war decides it wants one. That's not even as good as the League of Nations. Why can't the big shots get it into their heads that countries are only men multiplied a few million times? What makes them so sure that a man who is willing to sacrifice his life for peace wouldn't be

willing to sacrifice just a little bit of the soveriegnty of his government or the dignity of his diplomats to get the same thing?"

"It seems to me those other sacrifices you speak of were tried
out not very many years ago," the fisherman said. "At a place
called Munich."

"No," the soldier said. "I didn't say one nation ought to make
all the concessions. Unless they'll all play it the same way, it's
hopeless, and we've just got to keep using the blackjack. But that
doesn't defeat my argument. It strengthens it. My argument is
only that the whole business is a mess."

"Your enthusiasm for human nature is about as limited as mine
was when I came back," the fisherman said drily.

"No," the soldier said, "I haven't got one of those straight-
place-and-show scunners against people. You couldn't help feeling
sorry for the people over there, even after they were through
milking our paybooks and heaving bricks at us for looking at their
girls. If there's any people I figure I've got a right to have a
scunner on, it's the people right here who let them get away with
that deal on conscription. But you can't come out of that other
place and really be sore at Canada. All you can be is glad you're
back and hopeful that you'll never have to go away again."

"That's about the way it hit us," the fisherman said. "We had
a few causes for being mad too, but we forgot them quick enough."

The soldier said: "This newspaper guy I met said something
the same. He said that while all the good isolationists were staying
home learning to be internationalists, the good internationalists
were over in Europe learning to be isolationists. That's pretty true.
It's even truer of the Yanks than of us."

"Well," the fisherman said, "I never thought I'd turn out to
be a Rotarian. But it doesn't look as bad to me as it does to you.
Not quite, anyway."

"You know," the soldier said, "my wife's fath—the kid's
grandfather there—used to write me a lot and we had a corny

phrase that covered what we're talking about now. The old man
called it 'Home-made banners.' He said it was important for a
fellow to try to find something over there that he could get his
teeth into when he got feeling like this, something that would make
him feel that what he had done wasn't wasted and never would
be wasted, no matter what happened afterwards. I don't want you
to get the idea that I'm feeling sorry for myself, Charley. It's going
to be a lot different for me than it was, but I'm still going to have
a pretty good life. I've got no worries about a job, and I've got
my health and in spite of all the balls I may be talking now, I
don't think I've got any complexes. But I do wish to hell there
was something I could fasten on to, something short and clear
and tough enough to stand wear, like a—well, to be corny again—
like a saying on a banner."

The fisherman's eyes were grave with concern. "It's important
as hell," he said. "There's nothing more important. After the last
war a lot of us went looking for the same thing. A few of us found
it. Some of us didn't and spent the rest of our lives . . . fishing
for fish that we knew weren't there."

He stood up. "But our war wasn't wasted," he said, "any more
than yours will be. Ours had to be fought and won, whatever came
afterwards. It's the same with yours. No matter what comes out
of it, even if the worst things you have a right to fear come out of
it, your war checked something that was worse than war, and
gave us a chance—slender maybe, but still a chance—to beat it.
Because your war was fought, millions of people who would have
had no chance to be free have got their chance, slim as it looks
to be. And your war strengthened a vision that my war tore out
of aeons of darkness, the vision that peace could come true, that
it wasn't just something you read about in the Bible and certain
other pious works, along with the tale of the Garden of Eden, but
something practical men could strive for. Wherever it goes from
here, they can never take that away from you."

The soldier looked doubtful. As he opened his mouth to speak, the boy on the bank called to him. The boy had put aside the fishing pole and was standing above the dam, throwing pebbles into the tall foam below its spillway.

"Dad!" the boy called fretfully, "they won't splash."

The soldier walked over to him and pointed to a small eddy at the edge of the spillway. "Throw one there," he said.

The boy tossed another pebble and in the quieter water this one produced a satisfying clunk and dipped widening target rings in the eddy around its white bullseye. But the design was engulfed almost at once in the movement of the water and the boy's smile changed to a frown of disappointment.

"It's gone," he said.

The fisherman had limped up to stand beside them. He said quickly, "No, Joe, it isn't gone."

The boy glanced at him questioningly.

"You can't see it now," the fisherman said. "But it isn't gone and it never will be. You made the water splash and when you did that you changed the shape of the water over there where the stone fell. In that place the shape of the water is the same now as it was before you threw the stone. But because you changed the shape of it there for an instant, some of the water going downstream went to a different place than it would have gone, and other water came in from somewhere else to fill the space that the first water left. In that way you have affected the whole current. Eventually a cupful of water, or perhaps only a few drops, will end up touching the bank at a time and place where the bank would not have been touched by water. A few grains of soil will be washed into the river. Some day the whole shape of the river at that point will be changed. Maybe the whole bank will drop away and leave the river wider, or maybe the water will creep into the bank and make a willow grow out of a thirsty shoot. It may take ten years or a thousand years, but what you have put there will leave some kind of a mark forever."

The boy looked puzzled, but the soldier grinned. "That's a little corny too, Charley," he said. "But it's a better attempt than I ever made. And it was good of you to try."

The two men said good-bye and the soldier and the boy walked away, down the river bank in the direction from which they had come. They crossed the suspension bridge again and began to climb the hill, the boy holding the soldier's hand.

The boy stole several glances at the soldier's face and saw that the soldier's thoughts were far away. The man's eyes roamed across the yellow hills and their interlacing ravines, but they were focused on neither the hills nor the ravines; they seemed to look not into space but into time, and whatever they saw soothed and quieted them a little. His lean face smoothed by degrees into a relaxed, what-the-hell expression, an expression of acceptance.

As they came to the top of the hill and saw the village lying ahead the boy said: "Apple pie for supper."

The man smiled. "Apple pie!" he said and shook his head appreciatively. He swung the boy's hand shoulder high in sheer good spirits. "Boy!" he said, "I sure go for apple pie."